ALL
ABOUT
EVA

Also by Deidre Berry

The Next Best Thing

Published by Kensington Publishing Corp.

ALL ABOUT EVA

Deidre Berry

KENSINGTON PUBLISHING CORP.
www.kensingtonbooks.com

DAFINA BOOKS are published by

Kensington Publishing Corp.
119 West 40th Street
New York, NY 10018

All Kensington titles, imprints and distributed lines are available at special quantity discounts for bulk purchases for sales promotion, premiums, fund-raising, educational or institutional use.

Special book excerpts or customized printings can also be created to fit specific needs. For details, write or phone the office of the Kensington Special Sales Manager: Kensington Publishing Corp., 119 West 40th Street, New York, NY 10018. Attn. Special Sales Department. Phone: 1-800-221-2647.

Dafina and the Dafina logo Reg. U.S. Pat. & TM Off.

ISBN-13: 978-0-7582-3834-4
ISBN-10: 0-7582-3834-7

First Printing: April 2010
10 9 8 7 6 5 4 3 2 1

Printed in the United States of America

To Richard, as always

No one should come to New York to live unless they are
willing to be lucky.

—E. B. White

ALL
ABOUT
EVA

Prelude to a Scandal

When the scandal first broke, it was front page news in every major newspaper across the country, including the *New York Times*:

> Donovan Dorsey, the Wall Street wizard who had amassed a staggering fortune by the time he was thirty years old, now stands accused of padding his personal bank accounts with upwards of $150 million dollars, which he allegedly stole from longtime clients who trusted him implicitly. . . .

I sure as hell didn't see it coming. No one did, except for the guilty party, of course. But what's really unfair about the whole situation is that I have automatically been made guilty by association.

Whatever happened to "innocent until proven guilty"? Apparently, it's null and void when you've been convicted in the court of public opinion, which I have. Unjustly, I might add; which is why on this day, I take the stand in my own defense.

Now, to fully understand how and why I found myself in such a predicament, you would have to know the whole story, starting with the day I tucked my life savings securely into my bra ($827.16) and bought a one-way bus ticket to New York City.

It was four years ago. I was twenty-two years old and fresh out of college when I got off a Greyhound bus at the Port Authority Bus Terminal on West Forty-second Street.

Up to that point, it was the single most thrilling moment of my life.

You have to understand that as a little girl, I spent hours upon hours staring out of my bedroom window, letting my imagination take me off to glamorous, faraway places with names that sounded like magic. Greece, Japan, and Tahiti were oceans and light years away from the housing projects where I dwelled, but New York City was a little closer to home, and was the place that I visited most often in my head.

I had never visited the city in real life, but of all the places in the world, the Big Apple spoke to me the most, and seemed to be seductively calling my name, with promises of a wonderful and exciting life.

Of course, I had heard all of the sentiments that were associated with "The City That Never Sleeps," but the one that intrigued me the most was, "If you can make it there, you can make it anywhere."

It seemed like a direct challenge to me, and I was the kind of person who never backed down from a challenge.

The bus ride was more than 700 miles, and seemed like it took *forever*. But once I finally arrived, I knew that I would never leave. On that very first day, I stood in Times Square among all the honking, concrete, and commotion, with my neck craning upward. I took in the bustling activity, bright lights, and skyscrapers, and thought: *This is exactly why I've come here!*

The pulse, vibrancy, and energy that New York has is something you just can't get in small-town USA, or anywhere else in the world for that matter. If it's true that every town in the world has its own personality and intensity level, then NYC's swagger was on a hundred-thousand trillion. We were a perfect match.

I had been in town all of seven minutes, but I felt as if I owned the place and whatever I wanted to make happen, I could.

If I had had a hat, I would have thrown it in the air à la Mary Tyler Moore. Damn right, I was going to make it. I had to, simply because there just weren't any other options.

For better or worse, I was now one of many transplants who had come from far and wide to try their hand at making it in the greatest metropolis of them all. There were roughly eight million stories in the naked city, and as I would later learn, some of those stories were more remarkable than others, yet all of them were unique in their own way.

I have come to witness that some of those stories have happy endings, while others end abruptly in a cruel twist of fate.

Some are able to reach soaring heights, and many more fail to even make it off the ground.

There are those who meet with triumph and infamy, while others meet with scandal of such proportions that they are sent running back to their hometowns with their tails tucked between their legs.

Yeah, everyone has a story. Here's mine.

The truth, the whole truth, and nothing but the truth. So help me God. . . .

Who Wants to Date a Millionaire?

It started like most things do in this town: at a party. To be more precise, it was one of those mixers that *Gotham Magazine* throws every other week to celebrate the fabulous and accomplished. That particular soiree was in honor of the city's fifty most eligible bachelors. Kyle, who does double duty as my gay husband and oldest and dearest friend, invited me to the event, which I quite frankly could not have cared less about attending.

"Come on, Eva, it'll be fun!" Kyle had said. "And I need you there as my wing-woman, because you know more than likely that half of those so-called eligible bachelors are on the down low."

"Believe it or not, some of us have to actually *work* for a living," I'd said. At the time, I was beauty editor at *Flirt,* a glossy women's magazine, and was on a tight deadline to edit several articles from in-house writers, and make sure that they were ready in time for the next issue. "Besides, why are you on the prowl for a man? What happened to Jonathan?"

"Chile, I had to cut that loose, 'cause ain't nothing worse than closeted trade!" Kyle had said. "And what about you? You look like you could definitely use some pickle in your love life."

He knew me so well. It was sickening sometimes.

It had been a while since anyone had floated my boat. Reason being, I had just gotten a huge promotion at work and was so focused on showing and proving that I rarely had the extra time or energy to give to mixing and mingling.

But, persistent bugger that he is, Kyle wouldn't take no for an answer, so that evening after work, the two of us arrived at the Grand in midtown, where along with the fifty-dollar price of admission, we received catalogs that had alphabetical listings of each of the fifty eligible bachelors, including their headshots and business profiles.

"Eva, girl, we both are gonna find a man up in here, up in here!" Kyle said excitedly.

I surveyed the scene, which was typical of what could be expected at those sort of things: Each one of the fifty bachelors were respectively holding court for a flock of shameless and desperate women who were all vying to be the chosen one. I wasn't impressed. I can't stand those types of parties where there's nothing but a bunch of egomaniacs taking full advantage of the fact that the ratio of single men to single women is 1 to 80 in New York City.

That means you take eighty single women, put them all in one room, and there is only *one* eligible man available, with "eligible" meaning that he is *breathing.*

Yeah, 1 to 80. Daunting statistics, right? And that is without taking into account the man's personality, looks, education, sexual preferences, personal hygiene, financial status, mental health, and credit rating.

If you want to figure all those things into the equation, then the statistic goes from 1 to 80 to around 1 in a million.

Since we can't all be lesbians, what usually happens is that discernment goes out the window, giving rise to the phenomenon known as "interfacial dating."

You've seen them—they're everywhere. A gorgeous woman

with a less than attractive man, and she's trying to pass him off like he's Boris Kodjoe instead of the Elephant Man.

"Eva," she says, "meet my new boyfriend John. Isn't he handsome?"

"Umm, what's wrong with his head?"

"Oh, that's just a little swelling. It'll go down. . . . He's *eligible,* you know."

Yeah, believe me, I know!

Daniel was the last "eligible" guy I dated. We met at a cocktail party in Chelsea and got along fine for a few months until it started to dawn on me that he was a compulsive and habitual liar. One day he was 007, and the next day he was the Crocodile Hunter. Daniel claimed to be an international operative for the CIA and had all these fantastic, swashbuckling tales of being on safari in Botswana and being attacked by a pack of rabid hyenas.

And Dexter, the one before Daniel? Oh, he was *real* "eligible." He also had the distinction of being the brokest real estate agent I had ever met. Every time I turned around he was always hitting me up for money and expecting me to pay for everything whenever we went out. Then the break-ins started. At the time, I lived in Fort Greene in what I thought was a safe neighborhood.

I had never had any problems before, but within three months of meeting Dexter, my apartment had been burglarized on four separate occasions. Now, I may not be a member of Mensa, but I put two and two together very well. "It's your own fault," Kyle had told me. "This is New York City, girl. You can't just be picking up strangers all willy-nilly. I thought I taught you better than that!"

So yeah, the vibe that night at the *Gotham* party was all wrong. Ten minutes into it, like Wanda from *In Living Color,* I was *ret-ta-go.*

"About face!" I said to Kyle, looking for the nearest trash can to throw my catalog into.

"Uhn-uh, I paid too much money to get up in here and I'm not leaving until I find out which one of these guys isn't playing it straight."

"There you go again, searching for the gay needles in the haystack," I said. "Believe it or not, Kyle, every other man you see is *not* gay."

"Humph! Honey, you don't know what I know. . . ." Kyle said as he gazed around the room, sizing up the other men with his queer eye.

I sighed. Since Kyle was my ride, and he was hell-bent on staying, I figured I might as well look around too. It didn't take long before my eyes settled on one of the few black bachelors in attendance.

He had virile good looks that reminded me of a young Harry Belafonte, even down to the tall, slender build. Unlike some of the other bachelors in the room, he did not appear to be trying too hard to be suave and cool. Instead, there was an expensive gentleman vibe about him, which he exuded effortlessly. In other words, the man had swagger for days!

Kyle spotted the guy at the same time I did.

"Hottie at six o'clock!" Kyle said, frantically flipping through his catalog in search of the man's photo and profile. Once Kyle found what he was looking for, we both inhaled sharply at the same time. In the picture as in real life, the man was insanely handsome and meticulously well groomed.

"What's his name?" I asked.

"Donovan J. Dorsey . . ." Kyle said dreamily. "It says here that he graduated magna cum laude from Morehouse, and received a business degree from Columbia—come on, let's go make his acquaintance." Kyle grabbed my hand and led the way through the crowd of women that surrounded Donovan J. Dorsey. As it turned out, Donovan Dorsey was straight as Indian hair. Kyle was disappointed when Donovan failed to set off his gaydar, but was gracious enough to introduce me and Donovan without missing a beat.

I had never believed in love at first sight before meeting Donovan. Lust, certainly. However, when Donovan and I shook hands, sparks flew, and there was a current of chemistry between us that was so strong, it felt like I had been struck by a lightning bolt.

A few nights later we had our first date at Da Silvano, an intimate Italian restaurant in the West Village, where we shared a bottle of crisp pink wine and a four-course dinner for two that started with a hot antipasto and ended with tiramisu.

Over candlelight, we filled each other in on our life stories and plans for the future. He told me how rough he'd had it growing up in Queens with just his younger sister and hardworking single mother. And I told him about being abandoned by both parents and then raised by my God-fearing maternal grandmother, Juanita Cantrell, who I affectionately called Mama Nita.

We were so relaxed with each other that our conversation flowed as easily as if it were our one hundredth date instead of our first. We were on the same page when it came to ideals and sensibilities, which is why I was completely open and vulnerable with Donovan as I gave him all the details of how I put myself through college and, soon after graduation, packed up and moved to NYC, where I moved in with Kyle and subsequently landed the job as beauty editor at *Flirt*.

"And here you are." He smiled, reaching across the table to caress my hand. "Lucky me."

Donovan and I were so fascinated with each other that three hours had passed before either of us realized it. And even then, we only noticed the time because the server had delivered the check without being asked for it, which was another way of saying, *"Come on, I'm working for tips here! Go get a room already, so I can seat another party!"*

After that first date, we went out almost every night.

Seven years my senior, Donovan was the worldliest man I had ever met. He lived an extraordinary lifestyle and was a connoisseur of all things luxurious. As I would come to find out, he

especially had an insatiable taste for fine art, and we began fre-
quenting auctions together, where more often than not, he
walked away the highest bidder.

For me, Donovan's discriminating tastes were a huge part
of his charm. It is also what made me feel so privileged just to be
around him. Here was this man who expected and demanded
the best of everything; he could have any woman in the world,
but yet he chose me.

Prior to meeting me, Donovan had been a notorious play-
boy. I mean, after all, he was one of the city's most eligible bachelors, so my sudden appearance in his life did not automatically
stop other women from coming at him. But as our relationship
deepened, all of the other women fell to the wayside, one by one,
and before either of us knew it, I was the last woman standing.

And just like that—*finger snap*—I entered into a platinum-
dipped VIP lifestyle that took me to hot spots around the
world, including Dubai and St. Tropez, and most of the faraway
places I had fantasized about when I was a little girl. Nothing I
wanted was off-limits, and when *Flirt* folded overnight without a word of warning, Donovan insisted that it was the perfect time for me to give up the lease on my Fort Greene
apartment and move in with him. And the real kicker was that
as far as he was concerned, I didn't have to work.

Wait a minute, *WHAT!!?*

I don't care how much of a feminist you are, I don't believe
that there are too many women out there who don't want to
hear those words, or who would turn a man down when he
said them. Consciously or subconsciously, aren't we all searching for a man who has the ways and the means to swoop in
and save us? Whether you call him a sugar daddy, a sponsor, a
knight in shining armor, your husband, or Captain Save a Ho,
it is all one in the same.

For me, the very thought of being taken care of was in itself a page out of a fairy tale, but at the same time, I was anything but a lazy woman. Ever since I was fourteen years old, I

had always kept some type of employment, no matter how menial the labor or how small the pay.

I wasn't 100 percent comfortable with the thought of being dependent on Donovan for financial security, so I took up freelancing, even though the jobs were few and far between.

In the meantime, I found other ways to fill my days, like workouts with a personal trainer, lunch dates with the girls, beauty maintenance appointments, committee meetings, and galas for some foundation or another.

Oh, and shopping.

For the first time in my life, price tags became a nonissue, and I began shopping so hard that it became a sport for me.

It was a wonderful life. One I could get used to, and most certainly did.

Allabouteva.org (It's So Official!)

The city was New York. The month was October, and the day was so damn special that it should have been a national holiday—at least as far as I was concerned.

"Happy birthday to me. Happy birthday to me. Happy birthday, dear Eva, happy birthday to me!"

I lay in the massive sleigh bed covered with luxurious linen sheets, and stretched, a big ole smile on my face. However, that smile quickly turned into a scowl when I remembered that I was now the big two five.

"Damn, I'm getting old. . . ." I grumbled as I sat up in bed and stretched some more.

It was time to add another candle to the birthday cake, and what did I have to show for it?

Oh, just a sprawling 5,200-square-foot, nine-room penthouse apartment on Central Park West and Seventy-seventh Street that was in a word *exquisite.*

It had been two years since Donovan had swept me off my feet and brought me to Funderburk Towers, a sleek, futuristic-looking glass structure that was so high up in the sky that we had a full, unobstructed view of Central Park, and on a clear day I could see the White House. Well, okay, that's a wee bit of an exaggeration, but one I'm sure Sarah Palin would totally understand, seeing how she can see Russia from her backyard in Alaska and all. The point is, it was one helluva view! One that both literally and figuratively gave the feeling of being on top of the world.

Located on the fifty-fourth floor of one of the most exclusive co-ops in the city, the penthouse had a terraced master bedroom suite, complete with a dressing room and two walk-in closets; a library; formal dining room; private movie theater; eat-in kitchen; and private elevator.

Not bad for a little black girl from the South Side of Chicago, where infants were born with plastic spoons in their mouths instead of silver, if in fact you were given any spoon at all, and where despite the fact that my grandmother worked like a rented mule every day of her life, the household seldom had two of anything.

There wasn't a day that went by that I didn't count my blessings and recognize the fact that I was one lucky girl.

It was a little after eleven AM and I felt refreshed and energized despite the fact that I hadn't made it home from a night of partying until well after the sun had come up.

Getting in at that time of the day wasn't all that unusual for me, which is why I guess more than a few people liked to throw the term "party girl" my way.

I hated that, because it couldn't have been further from the truth.

Yes, I had been known to shut down a club or two in my day. And yes, I could be seen shaking my thang at least three nights a week until the wee hours. *However,* this is New York we're talking about, not Idaho. What was I supposed to do instead? Take up needlepoint and gardening?

Truthfully speaking, I was practically a homebody compared to most of the people in my social circle who went out every single night of the week.

When I first hooked up with Donovan, he introduced me to his friends and colleagues, who in turn introduced me to their wives and girlfriends, which is how I met and became best friends with Zoë Everett. She happened to have been dating one of Donovan's colleagues at the time, and we hit it off immediately, even though we had vastly different backgrounds.

Now, if you want to see the true definition of a party girl, then you need look no further than Zoë. She was out on the scene 7 days a week, 365 days a year, and was only at home long enough to shit, shave, and bathe. After changing clothes, she was right back out on the scene again, drifting from one club or social function to the next.

The Energizer Bunny couldn't even compete with Zoë, and I can't say for sure how she was able to carry on like that, although I have heard the rumors. I'm not one to gossip, but let's just say that Red Bull and methamphetamines aren't exactly sleep inducers. Okay? In fact, it was Zoë who just the evening before had insisted on treating me to an all-expenses-paid night out on the town in honor of my birthday.

She had arrived in front of the Funderburk in a rented hot-pink Hummer limousine, filled with ten of our mutual friends. Among them had been Sandra Morgan, whose claim to fame was being Kanye's ex.

Sadie Cohen, daughter of the legendary rocker Ben.

Giselle Joyner, season 12 winner of *Who Wants to Be a Supermodel?*

And Pilar Daniels, the telecommunications heiress slash wannabe fashion designer.

Last, and certainly least, there was Bianca Benson, incorrigible instigator slash incorrigible bitch. She and Zoë had grown up together and their mothers were close, lifelong friends, which is why I guess Bianca was so protective and possessive of Zoë that she came off as if she were her lover or something. My nickname for Bianca was Skeletor. She was all cheekbones and forehead, and had these crazy overarched eyebrows along with a really strong Arnold Schwarzenegger jawline.

Very rarely do I meet someone who I dislike on the spot,

but Bianca was this grumpy, humorless thing who was always glaring suspiciously at anyone who even dared breathe in Zoë's direction.

I'm not entirely sure what that was all about, but again, there were rumors.

Despite Zoë's best efforts, Bianca and I never hit it off. From day one, our personalities clashed like floral and plaid, so consequently we both steered clear of each other, preferring to hang out only with Zoë whenever the other was not around.

No, there would never be any love lost between Bianca and me, and why Zoë had thought that it was appropriate or even necessary to bring Bianca along on my special night out was beyond me.

Surprisingly, though, everyone had been on their best behavior that night and the infighting was kept to a minimum as we had kicked my birthday celebration off at the fabulous and insanely expensive Crustacean Palace restaurant.

Our party of twelve had descended upon the restaurant and ordered just about every item on the menu, except for the ostrich fillet and the spicy buffalo meat, which we unanimously decided were just *wrong*.

We'd had sake with our appetizers, white wine with the entrees, and champagne with dessert. By the time it was all said and done, the tab had come to $9,168, including tax and tip.

Not that it had mattered, because Zoë was paying, and to her that was just chump change, really, because she had it like that. The bill could have been quadruple that amount and she still would have nonchalantly passed the waiter her Platinum AmEx card, without even bothering to examine the bill for possible errors or overcharges.

Zoë had money to burn.

"It ain't trickin', if you got it!" was one of Zoë's favorite catchphrases, and that was really easy for her to say, seeing as how she was the sole heir to the Everett & Everett Hair Care empire that had been a staple in the African-American community for close to fifty years and was estimated to be worth well over a billion dollars.

I, for one, was a loyal customer and couldn't go one day without their active hold hair spritz and jojoba oil moisturizing hair lotion, which was capable of working wonders on even the kinkiest head of hair.

Zoë's parents were doting, but clueless. Thinking that their daughter was just trying to "find" herself, they fully supported her rock 'n' roll lifestyle with an ample monthly allowance and credit cards with no limits. In exchange, Zoë was the face of Everett Hair Care products, and her only duties were the occasional photo shoot for packaging and advertising purposes. Not a bad deal. One that often made me wonder how nice it must be to have parents who actually gave a damn about your welfare and well-being.

Since both of my parents were deadbeats, I *so* could not relate.

After having stuffed ourselves with Chinese food, we all climbed back into the limo, where the girls showered me with an assortment of fantastic and interesting gifts, including Valentino sunglasses, a very on-trend Betsey Johnson cocktail ring, a set of sterling silver bangles, a gift certificate to Bliss Spa, and a state-of-the-art personal pleasure tool.

We stopped in at Hyde Lounge, an uber-exclusive, two-level dance club that was notorious for their discriminatory admission practices. It was simple: Either you had the right look or you didn't.

If you were hot and you looked like money, you were allowed in. If not, you waited in line only to be told when you finally got to the front that "There's no party going on here tonight," which was a blatant lie and a double insult. Fortunately, I didn't know what that was like. I had never been turned away from any club, and that night was no different. Even though there was a long line of would-be partygoers waiting to get inside Hyde, Zoë and I led our group right to the front of the line where Frank, the beefy doorman, greeted us with warm hugs.

"Well, if it ain't Eva and Zoë," said Frank, flashing a winning smile. "Double trouble!"

"Hey, honey bunch, how is it in there?" I asked.

"Bananas!" Frank said, incredulous. "You ladies go and have a good time!"

Without even asking any of us for ID, Frank stepped aside and allowed our posse to pass beyond the red velvet rope, where the young and oh-so-sexy crowd were partying like it was 1999.

Once inside, we went up to the VIP section located on the upper level, where we danced and drank even more champagne until we all unanimously agreed that it was time to move on to the next club.

It was around seven AM when the hot-pink Hummer had finally dropped me back off in front of my building. The double Grey Goose martinis I had been sipping all night had me hot and bothered, and I couldn't wait to get upstairs to the apartment where I intended to pounce on Donovan like a lioness in heat.

I started stripping my clothes off the second I walked inside the apartment, but when I reached the bedroom, I was dismayed to find that Donovan had already left for work at the plush suite of offices he kept in the Lipchitz building, down in the heart of the financial district.

He had obviously left in a hurry because he hadn't taken the time to make up the bed, which he was a stickler for, and the massive fifty-inch plasma TV was still on and tuned to CNBC, where the news anchor was talking about the mortgage crisis and predicting another dismal day on Wall Street. I sighed, and turned the television off.

I needed some sexual healing, and even though Zoë had

given me that fancy vibrator as a gag gift, the fact that it would actually be put to good use was no laughing matter.

You see, the downside to being with a guy in finance is that his sex drive often fluctuates right along with the stock market. The peaks and valleys were astounding!

One day he was up, so to speak, and the next day he would be so far down that even Cialis couldn't help turn the situation around. It was a complete wear-out, and that was the way it had been for the past few months.

Donovan blamed his erectile dysfunction on the fact that he was preoccupied with some kind of crisis looming on the horizon that had the potential to destroy the economy as we knew it, and he even went so far as to admit that for the first time in his illustrious career, he was having a crisis of confidence. Along with the world economy, the stock market was also sliding further and further into the toilet with each passing day, and he was suddenly unsure of which sticks to buy and sell, and which ones to hold.

I didn't know how serious to take his Doomsday prediction. All I knew was that if Donovan had a problem, then I had a problem, and my problem was that I hadn't had sex on a regular basis in months.

It had gotten to the point where I had trained myself to be happy with getting it once a week, but there were times when Donovan couldn't even deliver on that. It was so frustrating, there were times when I wanted to scream, "Why the hell can't you get it up, and keep it up, you limp dick motherfucker!" But I took the opposite, softer approach and came to understand how the Dow average falling more than 500 points in one day could make a moneyman flaccid.

I didn't like it, but I *understood*.

After all, Donovan had a lot on his shoulders. At age thirty-four, he was his own man, serving as the founder, CEO, and chairman of Dorsey Capital Management LP, the second-largest African-American–owned investment bank in the United

States, which boasted an impressive roster of uber-wealthy clients, from professional athletes, to entertainers, to music industry moguls. I, on the other hand, double-majored in English and print journalism, and knew very little about the technical aspects of the financial sector.

While Donovan rambled incessantly about home prices falling 11 percent in the third quarter, a credit crunch, and something about the S&P index, I would be examining my nails to make sure that my polish wasn't chipped and thinking about how Marc Jacobs and Tom Ford could possibly top last season's collections.

Now, before you get it all wrong, let's be clear. I was not some vapid, self-centered moron who cared only about consumption and excess. I cared about what was going on in the country. However, my attitude was economy, shmeconomy! Why preoccupy your mind and stress yourself out over stuff you can't do anything about, anyway? Don't worry, be happy!

Hell, let experts like Alan Greenspan and Suze Orman figure it all out.

After lounging lazily for several minutes, I decided to quit all the griping about being one year closer to thirty and to make this birthday the best birthday ever. I sprang out of bed and threw open the curtains to see what the weather was like. The sky was blue and clear, sunny and gorgeous.

Yep, from the looks of it, it was gonna be a great day!

The bugle horn on my cell phone sounded, signaling that I had just received a text message. I grabbed the phone off the nightstand and saw that the iPhone was *jumping*. Eleven missed calls and seventeen text messages, the last of which was from my old friend Tameka, the soon-to-be ex-wife of New York Jets player, Jamal Harvey: Hey young lady, happy birthday! Whatever you do today, do it in a BIG way . . . xoxo Meka

It had been almost a month since Tameka and I had hung out and spent girl time together, but even if she had been in the mood for socializing, she still would have most likely declined an invitation to the previous night's blowout extravaganza because she was not a big fan of Zoë and the socialite set in general.

I smiled, thinking that it was so sweet and thoughtful of Tameka to remember my birthday, especially since she was in the midst of a divorce that was getting to be so nasty that she'd decided to remove herself from the social scene until after the dust had settled.

I didn't blame her. Jamal's womanizing ways were legendary, and there were way too many rumors that she would have had to clear up. Tameka was one of my besties, and I missed hanging out with her, but you have to respect a girl's right to save face.

I was just about to check my e-mail when the phone rang and Donovan's face popped up on the screen. I grinned and giggled because I couldn't help it. The contact photo that I had for him was the picture I had taken of him shirtless on the beach in Costa Rica; plus, I was so smitten with Donovan that I smiled whenever I saw him, thought about him, or even heard his name.

"Good morning, Boo-Boo Kitty," I cooed into the phone as if he were three years old instead of thirty-four. "How's it going?"

"It's going. . . ." He sighed in a way that let me know that he was not having a good day at the office. "But listen, I called to say happy birthday, and to tell you to be dressed and ready to hit the town tonight at seven sharp."

A burst of excitement shot through me, causing me to do a happy dance. Donovan wasn't like most men who *maybe* bought you a greeting card and then *maybe,* if you were lucky, took you out for dinner and a movie. My man knew how to do birthdays right!

"Why, do you have something big planned for me?" I asked hopefully, with fingers crossed.

"No, sorry to disappoint you, babe"—he sounded distracted and I could hear him shuffling papers in the background— "since it's a weekday, though, I was thinking we should do it low-key this year. I have to come right back to the office bright and early tomorrow morning, so I went ahead and made reservations at your favorite restaurant."

"And what's my favorite restaurant, Donovan?"

"Le Cirque, of course."

Cue the buzzer sound. . . . *Ennnnntttttt! Wrong!*

You see, that's why it's good to give your man a pop quiz every once in a while, just to see how well he really knows you.

As awesome as Le Cirque is, it was actually *his* favorite restaurant, not mine. I much preferred Daniel over Le Cirque any day of the week. Not that Donovan would notice, due to his overconfident but slightly endearing habit of assuming that everything he loved, I automatically loved also.

Donovan couldn't talk long, but before he hung up, he instructed me to go into the kitchen where I would find my birthday present.

I did another happy dance as I wrapped myself in a silk Chinese robe before heading to the kitchen. I had to cover myself first, because as much as I would love to walk around the house half-naked, Donovan employed a household staff of six, and the thing about hired help was that on any given day, you rarely had the place to yourself.

I opened the bedroom door and padded barefoot through the spacious apartment, wondering if I really smelled food cooking or if I was hallucinating. It was Tuesday, and Hazel, our personal chef, was off on Tuesdays.

"Happy birthday, Ms. Eva!" Hazel greeted me when I entered the kitchen. She had put together a veritable feast. There was enough spicy-sweet bacon, scrambled eggs, and fresh fruit to feed several people. A pitcher of freshly squeezed orange juice stood on the table, and she'd even gone to the trouble of getting my favorite caramel pecan pastries from The Royale Pastry Shop down on Seventy-second Street.

"Hazel!" I said, reaching out to hug the older, diminutive woman who was from Honduras. She was so sweet and nurturing, she reminded me of my maternal grandmother back home in the Midwest. "What are you doing here? You're supposed to be off today."

Hazel gave me a dismissive wave of the hand. "And miss your birthday? No way! Besides, Mr. Donovan pay me extra!"

We both laughed. Hazel had a wicked sense of humor, and often made me laugh, even though I couldn't understand half the things she said in her adorable Spanglish accent.

"Extra? Whooo! What are you gonna do with all those monies, girl?"

"Send back home like all the rest. . . ." she said, then looked me over and shook her head. "You too skinny! Go sit down while I make you plate."

I didn't have the heart to tell Hazel that I wasn't all that hungry. I had plans to meet Zoë for lunch later that afternoon, but everything smelled so divine, and Hazel was such an excellent cook, that I obeyed her orders and sat down and ate.

When I finished my meal, Hazel immediately cleared the dirty dishes from in front of me, and it was then that I remembered just why I had come into the kitchen in the first place.

"Look next to the flowers," Hazel said, reading my mind.

"And just how do you know that I'm supposed to look for something in here?"

"Mr. Donovan tells me everything," she said with a wink.

I dashed over to the stone countertop where hidden ever so slightly behind a fresh bouquet of flowers was a square, black lacquer box that I knew from experience could only contain one thing—jewelry!

I flipped the box open and what was inside literally took my breath away. It was a white diamond necklace set in 22-

karat gold, which I estimated to be around 6 carats. It was by far the most magnificent piece of jewelry that Donovan had given me to date. "Oh, baby!" I said as if he were actually there in the room with me. "You are so good to me!"

Hazel stopped cleaning long enough to look over my shoulder and examine the gift for herself. "Si." She nodded her approval. "Mr. Donovan love you muy muy mucho."

"And I love him, too," I said. "Very, very, much!"

And I did.

Contrary to what Donovan's mother or any other detractors might have thought about me possibly having ulterior motives, I honestly and truly loved that man with every fiber of my being. Sure, he was worth an insane amount of money, but even if he wasn't, I would still love and cherish him just the same if he were slinging packages down at UPS.

The next step for us would be marriage. We were forever.

Social.Net

Heads turned as I breezed through the lobby of the Bryant Park Hotel, my four-inch snakeskin Louboutin heels clicking coquettishly across the espresso-colored floor with each step I took.

All eyes were on me because I was serving them grown woman self-assuredness. I had the vamp appeal of a sex kitten in my frilly, black Tuleh blouse and a short olive miniskirt that showed off my long, graceful legs.

I carried my Giorgio Armani python bag in one hand and my cell phone in the other, which kept buzzing incessantly with even more birthday wishes.

Destination: Koi Restaurant.

Zoë was waiting for me near the entrance, giving the most sparkle ever in a colorful Indian tunic, super-skinny jeans (size 4), and silver metallic sandals, also size 4. A panama hat was perched on top of her lovely flowing tresses that the adoring public had no idea was actually a 30-inch Indian Remy Body Wave in Jet Black. Or, to put it in nontechnical language: it was a weave.

I know because we both got our tracks sewn in at the same salon, and by the same person, none other than Helene Lamar, weave-ologist to the stars and anyone else who could afford her overinflated prices.

"That is so haute, I'm *dying!*" was the first thing Zoë said to me after exchanging double kisses.

"You like?" I asked, sweeping my 26-inch Hawaiian silky, caramel-colored hair to one side, so that Zoë could get a better view of the flawless multicarat sparkler that was causing her to practically foam at the mouth.

"Like, are you kidding me? I covet!" That was the ultimate stamp of approval coming from Zoë. She rarely dished out compliments, due to the fact that she considered herself the only person in the world with any real taste.

To her credit, Zoë was a fashion maven in the truest sense of the word, and was the only person I knew who kept a mental inventory of all of her friends' wardrobes and accessories, and could quickly point out whenever someone was wearing something new. Zoë was really quite remarkable in that way, like a savant. Unfortunately, though, it was the only marketable skill that she had developed so far in her twenty-six years—well, that, and giving head to just about any guy in the club who asked.

Lunch was fun.

We were seated at our usual banquet near the back and had a sumptuous lunch of seafood miso soup and warm baby spinach salad, with a side dish of spilt tea. Gossip, that is.

"So did you guys keep the party going after you dropped me off, or what?" I asked.

"Well, yes, and no. . . . We stopped by Isaac's after-after party . . ."

"Oh, yeah? Was it a good look?"

"You know Isaac. He always gives good party, and it was actually quite splashy until Sierra Jones showed up."

"Oh, yeah, that reminds me!" I said. "Chantal told me that she saw Sierra at Bianca's the other night, fresh out of rehab, and *still* getting her Amy Winehouse on."

"Tragic, but true," Zoë said. "You should have seen her drunk ass doing handstands in the middle of the floor, while wearing a dress with no panties on."

I laughed, struggling to keep from choking on my soup. "She got it from you!" I said. "Isn't that your signature move when you've had a little too much to drink?"

"It depends on the time and the place, but at least when I do it, you can rest assured that I've had my kitty-kat waxed. Eva, I'm telling you, Sierra looked like she was starting to dread down there!"

"Eww . . . okay, stop! Enough! I don't wanna ruin my appetite thinking about that shit."

"Well, she is from Jersey." Zoë shrugged, "What more can you expect?"

"But please, tell me, what was that Pilar was wearing? It looked like something straight out of my grandmamma's closet."

"O . . . M . . . Effen . . . G!" Zoë was incredulous. "I couldn't believe that girl actually came out of the house in that old, *late-ass* purple dress, looking like *Barney*. She's lucky she jumped in the limo before I had the chance to tell the driver to take off and leave her ass."

"Like really, polyester? Eccentric may be the new black, but Pilar is wearing me out with these insane fashion choices of hers."

"That, and if I see Giselle in those run-over YSL knockoffs one more time . . . I'm gonna cut her."

"*Girl!* Not if I get to her first!" I said.

"And what about Sandra?" Zoë asked. "Could her blouse have been cut any lower?"

"Right? It's like, girlfriend, we all know you have tig ole bitties, but damn! I don't need to see your big, shiny boobs every time we go out."

"She obviously didn't get the memo that everyone isn't as obsessed with her breasts as she is," Zoë said. "Maybe I should resend."

I took out my iPhone and made a voice memo to myself: "Don't forget to put Sandra on the Christmas list for an assortment of turtleneck sweaters—cashmere, of course!"

We laughed. "But seriously," I said. "I had a ball last night. What about you?"

"Good times! But it would have been even better if Kelly's personal hygiene issue wasn't so distracting."

"Oh, I know. She had the limo all funked up, smelling like *two* cans of sardines!"

"I know, right? So, two seconds before we walked into Revival, I pulled her aside and told her that Massengill was her friend and that she didn't have to be afraid of it."

"Ouch! So that's why she was all teary-eyed and kind of shut down toward the end of the night," I said. "I tried to ask her what was wrong, but she just said she didn't want to talk about it."

Zoë shrugged. "The truth hurts."

"Well, you could have used a bit more tact, but she definitely needed to know," I said. "Lord knows I can't stand to smell another woman's personal business."

"See? I did us all a favor—oh! It's official. . . . My new nickname for her is *Smelly-ass Kelly*." Zoë fanned her hand in front of her nose.

Zoë gave everyone nicknames. "TUF" was what she had bestowed on me shortly after we had met, short for "The Ultimate Flyygirl," which I really didn't mind because it summed me up perfectly.

Still, Zoë being so venomous toward Kelly made me pause, because they were first cousins. If Zoë could talk so viciously about family, I couldn't help but wonder what kinds of things she said about me when I wasn't in the room.

"A dog that will bring a bone will carry one!" is what Grandma Nita always warned me about gossiping friends. Not that I wasn't guilty of it too, but Zoë took it to a whole 'nother level, which led me to the thought that Grandma Nita would be sorely disappointed if she were to ever meet Zoë Everett, who belched like a pig at the table and used her manicured forefingers to pick food from between her teeth.

My grandmother was a great admirer of Zoë's grandfather, Howard Everett, who had started his hair care company back in 1959 with little more than a few dollars and a dream. As his business and his fortune grew, the excess fruits of Howard's labor could be seen in almost every issue of *Ebony* magazine.

There was the April 1972 issue where his wife, Claudine, showed off her fox fur coat, the newly purchased mansion in Westchester, and the brand-new Rolls Royce that was driven by a white chauffeur. And there was the July 1982 issue that documented the birth of Zoë herself. Of course I wasn't old enough to remember that particular issue, but the Everetts and their rise to success were a source of pride for Grandma Nita and those of her generation.

If she only knew that behind closed doors Howard Everett had been a raging alcoholic who terrorized his wife and children. Zoë's grandmother, Claudine, had almost a dozen failed suicide attempts under her belt, and Zoë, the one who stood to inherit it all, was a gorgeous girl, but her good looks were made null and void by the fact that she wore a perpetual scowl on her face that made her look as though she was always smelling something foul, which very well could have been her own funky attitude.

Why be friends with such an awful person? The answer to that was, Zoë was spoiled rotten, but she wasn't all bad. Not once since I had known her had she ever directed her dark, evil side toward me, or said or did anything that could be construed as snarky or disrespectful. Other people? Oh, all the time! There are different levels of friendship, and admittedly, Zoë was not the sort to call up at three in the morning seeking advice or to share your innermost feelings with, but she was a ball of fun who knew how to party, and was exceedingly generous to those she considered her friends.

But just as most sociopaths have redeeming qualities, like a magnetic personality or great listening skill, Zoë's saving grace was that she could be thoughtful and kind whenever the mood struck her.

For dessert, there was spiced apple and cranberry crisp for me and molten chocolate cake for Zoë. Just as we were about to dig in, Zoë slid a gift-wrapped box across the table, and said, "I hope you like it. . . ."

I opened the box to find a stainless steel Movado bangle watch with a diamond bezel and mother-of-pearl dial. At a retail cost of around three-thousand dollars, it wasn't a terribly expensive watch, but as is always the case with Zoë, it was the thought that counted most.

"Thank you, mi amour. It's gorgeous!" I said, reaching over to give her a hug.

"You're welcome, doll. Anything for you," Zoë said, and then lifted her wineglass in a toast. "To my sista from another mista, who I love more than cooked food. Happy birthday, Eva. Love ya to pieces, girl!"

"And I love ya back," I said as we clinked our glasses together.

Right at that moment, I received a text message from Donovan, and I read it aloud: "Change of plans: We're having dinner at the Rainbow Room tonight instead of Le Cirque. Formal attire is required, but of course you know that. Also, pack a suitcase or overnight bag, because you never know where we might end up. Love, Donovan."

"Awww," I cooed. "Donovan is the sweetest!"

Zoë rolled her eyes and puckered her lips at the mention of Donovan's name. Unfortunately, she was the type who couldn't keep a man, and she found it hard to be happy for those of us who could.

"Yes, we all know how sweet Donovan is," Zoë said with a

trace of envy in her voice. "So, what are you wearing to the party tonight?"

I gave Zoë the side eye. "What party?"

"Never mind, forget I said anything," she said lamely, helping herself to a forkful of my dessert. "Umm, so good! I should've ordered this instead of that cake."

Zoë was trying to play something off but failing miserably. She was a terrible liar. Mainly because she got a kick out of telling the truth, no matter how brutal or painful it was for someone else to hear.

"Come on, Zoë, spill it. What party are you talking about?"

And without any more prodding than that, Zoë pulled a fancy party invitation out of her red Hermes bag and slid it in front of me. The invite was to an exclusive surprise birthday bash at the illustrious Rainbow Room high atop Rockefeller Center.

The party was set for eight that night. The host? Donovan Dorsey. The guest of honor? None other than Ms. Eva Cantrell.

Champagne Wishes

Later that evening, Kyle and I were in my bedroom where he was helping me get dressed for my "surprise" birthday extravaganza. Music from my iPod filled the room, and I felt mellow and lifted from a precelebration glass of Bollinger Rosé champagne.

I had already packed a suitcase and an overnight bag like Donovan had instructed me to, and was anxious to see how the rest of the night would unfold.

"I can't believe that heifer!" Kyle said, while helping secure the straps on the Valentino pumps that I was wearing for the evening. "I'm telling you. I've met some messy bitches in my life, but that Zoë Everett is the messiest of them all! I mean, it's a surprise party, bitch! *Hello!*"

"Calm down, love, it was just a little slip of the tongue, and it is certainly not worth you stroking out over it."

"Uh-uh, 'just a little slip,' my ass." Kyle wagged a finger in my face. "Zoë actually went so far as to show you the damn invitation—I mean, who *does* that? I got my invitation weeks ago, but I still managed to keep my big mouth shut!"

"And Lawd *knows* that couldn't have been easy!" I joked.

"Never mind all that. I'm telling you, Eva, that girl is pure evil."

"Well, it's not like the party is *ruined*. I just have to pretend that I don't know what's going on."

"And doesn't that defeat the purpose of what Donovan was trying to do for you? Damn! Look, you can make excuses for that girl if you want to, but you know she ain't right."

"Yeah, Zoë is an acquired taste and has more issues than *Jet* magazine, but there is a side to her that most others don't get to see."

Kyle stood in front of me with hands on hip, looking like he wanted to shake the shit out of me. "For instance?"

"Look at this." I extended my arm and showed him the Movado Zoë had given me earlier at lunch.

Kyle examined the watch, trying his best to appear unimpressed.

"Humph, with all her money, is that the best she can do?" he asked, letting my arm drop. "I'm just saying . . . it's not like it's an Audemars, or Patek Philippe, or something really *grand* along those lines."

Kyle was being a hater, but I gave him a pass. It was my birthday, and continuing to defend my friendship with Zoë with him would only lead to an even bigger argument. *Spreadlove. com!*

"I don't think we're ever going to see eye to eye when it comes to Zoë, so let's just respectfully agree to disagree," I said. "Besides, if we started dropping friends on the basis of flaws, then you and I would have parted ways a long time ago, darling."

"Don't be preposterous! No one walking this earth is as perfect as I am. Flaws? Please! Name one!"

"Remember that time you stole the guy I was dating right out from under me?"

"Chile, please, that boy clearly preferred beef over fish, so you should consider that an act of love," Kyle explained. "Plus, he didn't turn out to be worth a damn anyway, so—"

"So, you see, you're *not* perfect," I retorted, checking my reflection in the mirror from all angles. I was dressed for the party in the best Roberto Cavalli had to offer, and looked chic and elegant if I must say so myself. "Neither is Zoë, but she is a helluva lot of fun to hang out with."

"Miss Eva, you're getting to be a full-grown woman now, and it's time you learned that 'fun' should not be the basis for a friendship. How about someone who's trustworthy and has your back no matter what goes down?"

"That's what I have you for," I said, playfully squeezing Kyle's face until his lips puckered like a blowfish. "Now give me shuga!"

Kyle obliged by giving me a peck on the lips, then spun me around and zipped my dress up in the back.

Along with everything else he meant to me, Kyle was also my self-appointed stylist and social escort whenever I needed one. For the most part, he had always been on hand to assist me in getting dressed for big events. We had grown up in the same neighborhood, and it was a tradition that started back in Chicago with my very first junior high school homecoming dance. Back then, there was no money to buy a new dress, so Kyle and I came up with the bright idea to make one. The pattern we picked out at Joann's was for a poufy floor-length gown that we decided to make with white lace and shiny pink taffeta.

Neither of us knew how to really sew, but it took the two of us just a few days to piece the dress together, with mostly safety pins, fabric glue, and a whole lot of prayers. The dress turned out cute, though, and back in Chicago on my grandmother's mantel, were the pictures to prove it.

"There, now!" Kyle said, stepping back to take a full look at his handiwork. We both looked in the mirror, admiring my reflection, and I did a twirl to make sure everything was just so. Thanks to Kyle, who had a way with the curling iron, my hair was full and curly, and my makeup was beat to perfection.

"Gorgeous as always." Kyle fluffed my hair a bit more to increase the volume. He really was a dear, sweet friend, and even though Kyle had a live-in boyfriend, and a busy life of his own, he always took time out of his packed schedule to drop in and make me feel as if I was the most important thing in his world.

Thinking about what he means to me made me teary-eyed and sentimental.

"Thanks, Kylie-Poo. You are *everything* to me!" I said, giving him a big hug. "That's why you and me, we must never part. Promise?" I held up my pinky, and we pinky-swore, which for some reason made Kyle sentimental as well.

"Love you too, pumpkin," Kyle said, looking verklempt. "Happy birthday!"

"All right, now let's get this party started, shall we?"

I went over to the iPod docking station, where I found my favorite song, pressed play, and cranked up the volume.

Biggie's voice came booming through the speakers, and Kyle and I danced to "Juicy," a song that had become a tradition for us to play on either of our birthdays. Plus, the song was quite personal to me because it summed up perfectly how my life had played out so far.

An Affair to Remember

At eight PM sharp, Donovan and I arrived outside 30 Rocke-feller Plaza in a white, chauffeur-driven Bentley Continental GT. Right before we got out of the car, he slyly sent someone a text message, which I assumed was to alert our waiting guests that we were on our way up to the Rainbow Room.

"You look stunning tonight," Donovan said as he took my hand and helped me out of the car.

"Why, thank you, Mr. Dorsey," I said in a Southern belle accent. "And I must say that you look quite dashing yourself this fine evening!"

Donovan laughed and we walked arm-in-arm into the Plaza, both dressed to the nines and looking very coupelicious, him in a rich, dark brown Armani suit with a peach buttoned-down shirt and matching pocket square, and me in my black Cavalli number, accented by diamonds galore.

We complemented each other perfectly.

In the elevator on the way up to the sixty-fifth floor, Dono-van made small talk, trying to lead me to believe that we were just having a simple dinner.

"I think I'm in the mood for surf 'n' turf, tonight," he said, caressing the nape of my neck. "How about you?"

"Hmm, I'll have to check the menu, but steak and lobster is always good," I said, hoping I sounded innocent and clueless.

Donovan escorted me off the elevator, and we were met by a violin quartet who were all dressed in formal attire and playing 50 Cent's ode to birthdays: "In Da Club." *Go Shawty it's ya birthday!"*

"Wow, what's all this about?" I asked, trying to keep a straight face.

Donovan, also trying to appear clueless, said, "Good question. . . ." Then he opened the doors to the banquet room where 150 of my closest friends yelled "Surprise!"

I dropped my jaw and gave them the wide-eyed, deer-in-headlights look that I had practiced in the mirror all afternoon.

The Rainbow Room is already gorgeous on its own on an ordinary day, but walking into it that night felt like walking into a dream.

I surmised that the theme was pretty in pink, because everything in the room, from table linens and napkins to the bouquets of peonies that adorned each table, was decorated in various shades of pink, from bubble gum to fuchsia, which all blended well together.

I spotted floral designer Preston Bailey standing off to the far side of the room trying to be inconspicuous, and knew that it was his talent and sheer genius that was responsible for creating such a breathtaking atmosphere. Donovan must have paid him handsomely for his services.

Everyone was there. Well, everyone besides members of my biological family, but Zoë, Sandra, Giselle, Janine, Penny, Sherry, Katrina, Kyle, Pilar, Kelly, and Helene, my stylist, were all in attendance, looking shiny and beautiful. But the biggest surprise of the night was that my girl Tameka had temporarily emerged from the rock she'd been hiding under to come show love and celebrate my special day.

The party was wonderful.

Pre-dinner cocktails were pink grapefruit margaritas and a signature drink created especially for me called Eva's Raspberry Supreme, which was a tasty concoction of champagne and raspberry-flavored vodka with a hint of grenadine, garnished with a skewer of fresh raspberries.

Dinner was course after course of all my favorite gourmet foods, and instead of the usual birthday cake, there was a lavish cupcake tower with a huge array of flavors, my favorite being tropical coconut cake with mango sauce.

People made great toasts to me, we all danced, and good humor flowed as freely as the champagne.

Then John Crosby showed up.

John was Donovan's friend, colleague, and mentor. He was twenty years older than Donovan and had carved out a career for himself at Goldman Sachs. From the minute Donovan came on the scene, fresh out of business school, John took him under his wing, and the two would eventually come to be like father and son.

In addition to attending dinner parties and countless other social functions with John and his wife, Carol, Donovan and I vacationed with them at least twice a year, so I knew John well, and was happy to see him.

Donovan, on the other hand, looked nervous when John entered the room, and knowing him as I did I sensed that he was reluctant to go greet his friend and welcome him to the party.

I nudged Donovan and whispered, "Aren't you going to go say hello?"

"Of course," he said, forcing a smile and kissing me on the forehead. "Enjoy yourself. I'll be back in a few minutes."

I turned my attention back to my guests who had formed a Soul Train line and were cutting up something serious to Young MC's old-school cut "Bust a Move."

"Come on, Eva, get in here, girl!" Tameka dragged me out to the dance floor, and I was so glad to see she had let her hair down and was having a good time despite her personal woes.

"Hey! It's my birthday, it's my birthday . . ." I went down the middle of the Soul Train line doing a combination of old-school dances starting with the pop lock, which segued into the robot, and then the cabbage patch.

Forget that the guest list was exclusive, and was a veritable who's who of New York African-American society; we were turning the Rainbow Room out! Then I heard John Crosby yell something about wanting his fucking money and wanting it NOW!

All eyes shot across the room to where Donovan and John's quiet conversation had taken a wrong turn and become heated. John looked wild-eyed and full of rage, which was disturbing to me because he was normally such a nice, mild-mannered guy.

"I wonder what's up with that?" Zoë mused aloud, as I excused myself to go see what all the ruckus was about.

Donovan and John were around the same height, but when I joined the two men Donovan looked like a little boy being admonished by his father, plus there were beads of sweat on his top lip, a sure sign that he was under duress.

"Excuse me, gentlemen," I said. "But you two aren't talking business at a time like this, are you?"

"No, just a small misunderstanding," Donovan said. "Everything is all cleared up now, right, John?"

"Yes, for now." John had lowered his voice, but his body still reverberated with anger. After giving Donovan a long, hard look, he then turned to me with a smile and a warm hug. "Happy birthday, Eva. This is quite the party, isn't it?"

"It is! Donovan always goes all out, so it is definitely one to remember."

"Good deal, but because life has a way of changing on a dime, be sure to really take it all in, and savor the moment. . . ." said John, whose face was friendly, but his tone was cryptic as hell.

Okay . . . Thanks for weirding me out on my birthday . . .
Creepyguy.com!

"Well, sorry you can't stay longer, John, but please give Carol our best," Donovan said, walking John to the door.

Afterward, the good energy returned, and the party went on for a couple more hours as if nothing had ever happened.

I danced with my guests in the middle of the revolving dance floor, which after a while started to feel like being on one of those tilt-a-whirls at the amusement park.

Tons of pictures were taken, and I came away with a haul of birthday presents that you wouldn't believe. I received so many gifts that I couldn't even open them all. Donovan had anticipated that would be the case, so he'd arranged to have them delivered to our apartment by van.

That was my Donovan, always thinking of everything.

Around two AM, waiters offered warm chocolate chip cookies along with shots of cold chocolate milk, then passed out goodie bags filled with random but great gifts like Ojo Personal Video Phones, gold pave bracelets by Gabriella Francesca, Laura Mercier candles, an assortment of gourmet snacks from Dean & Deluca, and a bottle of Rutherford Cabernet Sauvignon 2000.

I waited until the end of the night, when Donovan and I were back in the Bentley, to ask the question.

"So, what was that situation with John Crosby all about?"

"Nothing for you to worry your pretty little head over," he said, loosening his tie. He avoided my eye contact, and I knew he was lying. I could have pressed further, but decided to let the matter drop. Besides, if he had explained in detail what the deal was with John, it would have probably just gone over my head.

Donovan could be so technical at times. He was so passionate about his career, and the day-to-day activities associated with it, that he often failed to realize that not everyone shared the same passion or interest.

While Donovan was taking off his tie and suit jacket, I got comfortable as well.

I had danced almost the entire night, and my dogs were barking something ferocious. I unstrapped my heels, sunk my feet into the plush lamb's wool rug, and reflected on the night.

Putting the incident with John aside, it was one of the most memorable birthdays ever, second only to my twenty-third, when Donovan took me to Bermuda, where we stayed at the five-star Cambridge resort for a week and had private beach dinners for two, every night.

I snapped out of my reverie upon noticing that Thaddeus, the driver, had taken the exit into LaGuardia Airport. "Why are we heading to the airport?" I asked Donovan, who looked like he had been deep in thought himself.

"I told you to be up for anything, remember?"

"Yeah . . ." I said with anticipation

"Well, we're going to Paris, baby!"

"No way!"

"Have I ever lied to you, Eva? Seriously, we're hopping on the jet and we're leaving tonight—right now as a matter of fact."

I screamed like a little girl on Christmas morning. Paris was, and will forever be, the fashion capital of the world, and since I was a fashionista through and through, Paris was to me what Mecca is to Muslims. A pilgrimage that the seriously devout make every year without fail.

I stopped screaming when I realized that I didn't have one essential thing. "Donovan, wait, I don't have my passport."

He reached inside his suit jacket and flashed both his passport and mine. And the screaming continued.

"I should have known!" I planted kisses all over Donovan's face. "You always cover every base!"

I was beyond excited. I had expected to perhaps spend the night at a ritzy hotel, but a trip to Paris was just over-the-top. But then again, that was Donovan for you. It couldn't just be

Christmas at home with just the two of us, it had to be Christmas in St. Bart's on a yacht with several of our friends.

He was impulsive and unpredictable, yet it was always in a good way.

A private jet was one of Donovan's many extravagant toys, so if he woke up and the weather did not suit him, he would say, "Rio is always nice this time of year" or "Shaq is having a party at Mansion tonight in Miami. . . ." which I would take as my cue to start packing for a trip.

"So how long are we going to be gone?" I asked.

"A couple weeks . . . who knows? But, I've been planning this trip for a long time, and the only stipulation is that this be a fun, relaxing vacation with no electronic devices whatsoever, including cell phones."

Huh? I looked at Donovan as if he had suddenly started speaking a foreign language. Leave my phone behind? That caused me great concern. My cell phone was like an extra appendage to me. In fact, it was more like a lifeline, much like the placenta is to a fetus.

I clock a minimum of five hundred minutes on my phone every single day, and Donovan should have known that asking me to give it up was the equivalent of asking me to leave civilization and go backpacking through the wilderness. I could do it, but then what would be the fucking point?

"Donovan, baby, let's be reasonable about this. . . ." I said as if trying to talk him down off a ledge. "I need it to at least check in with Zoë and Kyle every so often."

"No . . . hell, no! I have made up my mind, Eva, and I'm not budging on this. Look, I know that you are the center of all this social activity that you feel you have to keep up with, but surely you can go a couple of weeks without the incessant texting, e-mail, and phone calls about who had an abortion, who hooked up, who wants to hook up, and who is abusing what substances."

"It's not all about gossip, Donovan. I am on the board of some very important committees, remember?"

"Right, how could I forget? Committees that meet every six months only to talk about the next party that you all plan to throw for yourselves. Listen, if it will make you feel any better, I'm giving up my laptop and BlackBerry too."

"Completely? As in you're not even going to take them on the plane with you?"

"Now you're getting it," he said as if I were mentally challenged and had just learned how to tie my shoes.

That was major.

Donovan was constantly working the hell out of his Black-Berry and all of his other electronic doodads, using them to stay on top of industry news, and seal multimillion dollar deals.

If he could do it, I most certainly could too. I would miss my friends and social circle, but at the same time it was a chance to relax and get away from all the hoopla. Donovan was right. The world was not going to catch on fire if I missed a couple of phone calls and text messages. I could check on all the he-said, she-said bullshit when we returned to the country.

Besides, I hadn't brought my charger along with me so the whole issue was really null and void, anyway. I handed my cell phone over to Donovan, which he stowed away in a storage compartment along with his own.

Traveling is great, but there are preparations that have to be made and I hadn't made any.

As the car got closer to the airport, I ran a list of all the pros and cons through my head. The general presidential election was two weeks away, but I had already cast my vote for Barack Obama by absentee ballot, so I was good in that regard.

I had previously RSVP'd to several events that were coming up in just the next week alone.

There was the Stella McCartney trunk show, the launch party for Pilar's vanity line of "luxury" handbags, the ASPCA fund-raising gala, and the premiere of Spike Lee's new joint.

It was also time to start helping Kyle prepare for his annual Halloween bash, which is always an all-out extravaganza.

They were great, lovely events, but they all paled in comparison to a trip to Paris.

Last, being a black woman, my primary concern about going abroad was my hair. Thankfully, I had gone to Helene's hair salon just the day before and had gotten my weave freshly done with a blend of the finest human hair that money could buy. It was also a good thing that I had packed a head scarf and all of the hair products I needed in order to properly take care of it, so with careful routine maintenance and wrapping my "hair" at night like I normally do, then I should be good for up to three months. But I couldn't see us being gone *that* long.

Donovan and I were welcomed onboard his Gulfstream 550 by the flight crew that I had come to know very well. Alex the pilot and Ginger the flight attendant were both as friendly and accommodating as ever, and set us up right away with down pillows and cashmere throws to keep warm.

"Can I get you folks some snacks or refreshments of any kind?" Ginger asked.

"Oh, no, thanks," I said, patting my stomach. "We just came from a party, and I really couldn't consume another thing even if I wanted to."

"Okay, well, call me if you need me." Ginger smiled, then pulled the front curtain closed and disappeared into the cockpit.

Hmm . . . I raised an eyebrow wondering what really goes on up in the *cock-pit* between a hot flight attendant and an equally sexy pilot.

As always, Donovan had thought of everything. He had brought along a comfortable traveling outfit for me to change into, and then we both settled into our plush leather seats.

Once we were in the air I looked down on the city and

blew it a kiss, bidding New York a fond farewell, for now. It was a ritual that I performed with each trip that I took, because besides Chicago, New York was where my heart was, and I missed it terribly whenever I was away for extended periods of time.

I looked over at Donovan and noticed that he suddenly looked more content and relaxed than I had seen him in a very long time. He could pretend that this trip was all about my birthday, but I knew better. He was overworked and needed to take some time away from the grind to de-stress and wrap his head around all that was starting to happen in the financial sector.

From what I had gathered from Donovan and news reports, investment banks were failing, along with long-standing brokerage firms. The failing economy was fueling the presidential debates, and slowly but surely, it was becoming an undeniable fact that investors suddenly had very little money to save, let alone invest in a volatile market.

I reclined in my seat, and sighed.

I hoped that Paris would do Donovan some good, and help bring him back around to his old, happy-go-lucky self.

Caviar Dreams

Seven hours later, around five PM Paris time, Donovan and I arrived at de Gaulle Airport.

We stayed at Le Meurice, an opulent five-star hotel right in the heart of Paris. Decorated with elegant gold-and-white French furniture reminiscent of the Louis XVI era, our four-room suite was luxurious beyond belief.

The soundproofed room offered a private entrance, along with a breathtaking view of the Eiffel Tower.

It was the perfect place for relaxation and lovemaking, and I was looking forward to plenty of both.

Upon our arrival in the city of light and lovers, I assumed that Donovan and I would be swinging from the chandeliers, getting our sex life back in proper order, but our suite was such a haven of quiet and serenity that Donovan slept the entire first two days away, and only awakened just in time for dinner.

Not that I minded. Donovan was obviously sleep-deprived, so while he was at the hotel recharging his batteries, I went out and explored the city on my own.

I had been to France several times before, and while I appreciate progressive cities, I also love that there are ancient places in the world like Rome, Athens, and Paris, where you could go away for one hundred years and return to find that not much has changed. There would still be the same narrow, cobbled streets and the architecture that dates back five to six hundred years.

Our hotel was a stone's throw away from the world-class Louvre museum, where there was so much to take in that I committed myself to spending at least one hour each day browsing the extensive collections.

The Louvre houses many of the world's greatest treasures, including the Venus de Milo statue and Leonardo da Vinci's most famous masterpiece, *Mona Lisa,* hung behind a bulletproof glass barrier just in case some idiots got the idea that they wanted to actually *touch* the painting or, God forbid, steal it again like they did back in 1911.

I studied Ms. Mona closely, wondering if it was true that the painting was actually of da Vinci himself and not some sixteenth-century Renaissance babe whose vamp appeal brought all the boys to the yard.

I detected a faint resemblance. One thing was for sure, though. Ms. Mona Lisa wasn't all that.

I rented a bike for a few hours each day, dipped my toes in the pond at Trocadero Square, and sat in the warm sunshine of the Luxembourg Gardens, just watching the Parisian world go by.

It was a beautiful place to be.

Unlike back home, everyone at least seemed friendly. They were all carrying around long loaves of freshly baked baguettes, and smiling and saying *Bonjour!* all day long to everyone they passed on the streets.

New York is the culinary capital of America, but Paris is the culinary capital of the world.

For lunch, I did what Parisians do and steered clear of touristy spots like the Opera House and the Eiffel Tower.

On our very first trip to France, Donovan had schooled me that "the best food in any city is always where you see more locals hanging out than you see tourists."

It made perfect sense. Tourists can be bullshitted in ways that locals can't.

Sometimes when traveling abroad, I have come across more than a few local business owners that love making a quick buck off of tourists without regard to giving them quality products and service. However, those same business owners dare not disrespect the locals in that way because it will be the local clientele who'll keep them in business long after the tourists have gone back home.

Armed with this knowledge, I went off the beaten path and enjoyed long lunches in quaint out-of-the-way restaurants that served provincial food, recipes passed down from many generations, complemented by crisp, delectable house wines that were not available anywhere else in the world.

Paris's haute couture week was in full effect, which caused the city to be even more electrified than usual. I was desperate to view the spring–summer collections, but try as I might, the shows were impossible to get in to with having called ahead.

I packed a lot into those first few days in Paris, and when Donovan was finally well rested enough, he started rising early every morning to buy me fresh flowers at the nearby outdoor market. Afterward, we would have omelets, croissants, and coffee at one of the many cafes near our hotel, and at night we went out to jazz clubs where we ate steak frites and fresh oysters, and got drunk with the locals who treated us like long-lost cousins.

Donovan looked good in Paris. His smile was broader, he laughed more easily, and the worry lines in his face had all but disappeared.

Best of all, his sex drive had come back with a vengeance, and it was *magnifique! Merci!*

Donovan was passionate and insatiable once again, and all without having to take any of those boner-inducing Cialis pills. The two of us would be out and about, and all it took would be one look at each other and we'd have to make a pit stop back at the hotel for a quickie.

It all started one night when we were getting dressed to go out for dinner. I noticed that Donovan was watching me with a twinkle in his eye. He embraced me from behind and started nibbling on my ear. "You are without a doubt the most gorgeous woman from here to New York City," he whispered, "and I am the luckiest man alive to have you."

I smiled at him through the mirror, and when I turned to face him, it was on and popping. We made love right then and there, and decided to stay in and order room service instead of going out.

The saying that Paris equals romance, and is the best place to revive your love life if need be, is the gospel truth. Donovan was extra attentive, romantic, and so affectionate that I fell in love with him all over again.

Those two weeks in Paris were magical.

Donovan had always been generous, but was even more so on that trip.

I ran through the Louboutin boutique like a kid in a candy store, scoring several pairs of limited edition Lobos that had personally been signed by Mr. L. himself, which transformed them from mere shoes to *keepsakes.*

Some of my fellow fashionistas insist that Loubous are overrated, but to me, they are everything! Especially the pair of five-inch leopard print peep toes that practically glistened in their little red cubbyhole. It was the ultimate gag and swoon moment, and of course I had to have them.

That is what life with Donovan had been like from the very beginning. You covet? You cop it! Simple as that.

We dropped major coins at all the boutiques and design houses along Avenue Montaigne and rue François-Premier, avenue des Champs-Elysées, and rue du Faubourg St-Honoré, all except for Hermes, who I had been personally boycotting since they dissed Oprah by refusing to allow her in the boutique.

I ended up coming away with so much stuff that we also had to buy a full set of Louis Vuitton luggage to take it all back home.

One evening while Donovan and I were walking along the Seine River, I caught a chill because the temperature had dipped down into the 40s. He pulled me close to keep me warm, then quickly hailed a taxi. Speaking in perfect French, Donovan told the driver to take us to J. Mendel on rue St-Honoré where he bought me a chinchilla coat and one of those round, Russian-style hats to match.

It was the most gorgeous coat ever, however, I experienced a bit of sticker shock when the salesclerk rung up the sale and announced that the total was $65,000.

Donovan barely batted an eyelash. "That's not bad," he said, handing the clerk his company credit card.

"Not bad?" I said. "That amount of money could pay off someone's mortgage, send a kid to college, or buy some struggling single mother a nice, reliable car."

"You're right, and it would probably feed an entire African village for the next ten years as well. Do you want to go ahead and do that instead?"

The salesclerk smiled, and waited patiently while Donovan and I went back and forth debating the pros and cons of making such an extravagant purchase.

"I don't know, Donovan. . . ." I felt guilty and selfish, and it really was quite the moral dilemma for me.

"We'll take it," Donovan said to the clerk, who went ahead and closed the sale so fast that it was comical. "Not only do you deserve this coat, Eva, but you're also going to need it where we're going next."

"But babe, it's October. It's not quite cold enough in New York for fur yet."

"I know, and that's why we're moving on to Switzerland," he said, lovingly stroking the pelt of my new coat. "Surprise!"

I gave him the confused puppy look, and waited for the punch line that never came. *Switzerland?*

Lost in Translation

I was in a New York state of mind, and was *beyond* ready to return home. But Donovan seemed so thrilled about extending our trip abroad that I didn't want to spoil his fun, so I kept my mouth shut and went along with part deux of Donovan and Eva's European vacation.

The very next morning after buying the chinchilla, we checked out of Le Meurice and traveled by train from Paris to Switzerland. I would have much preferred to take the private jet, but Donovan insisted that the Bonjour La France rail would be just as fast, and just as comfortable. It wasn't, of course, but the scenic landscape was priceless, and well worth the inconvenience of schlepping all of our luggage along with us when it would have made perfect sense to store some of it on the Gulfstream, which was waiting for us at the airport back in France.

Donovan had long since paid for the flight crew to return to the United States via commercial airline, and had arrangements to fly them back to Paris when we were finally ready to return to New York.

Bern, Switzerland, was picture perfect, with green, wide-open pastures as far as the eye could see. The town was surrounded by high snowcapped mountains, and the clouds were so low that you could literally walk right through them.

Donovan made at least two business trips per year to Switzerland, but this was my first time accompanying him to the country most known for their stellar cheese, chocolate, and ski destinations.

Normally, I don't feel comfortable in countries where you can count the number of black folks on one hand, but the Swiss were friendly, and seemed quite harmless even though they were all tragically unhip.

I felt as if I were on the set of a Ricola commercial, with everyone running around wearing these colorful, elf-inspired costumes held up by suspenders. *Hotdisaster.com!*

To further offend my sensibilities, the women wore their hair in braided plaits that hung down their backs like Heidi, or if they were feeling really sexy, they wrapped the plaits around their heads and wove fresh flowers into them.

We stayed at a superluxurious private ski resort that had endless amenities, but like I said, I was in a New York state of mind and anxious to return home to the United States.

Donovan, on the other hand, was an avid skier, and since the winter skiing season for Switzerland had just started to gear up, he was enjoying the best slopes in the world too much to leave so soon.

France and Switzerland are neighbors, but the two countries are like night and day. Paris had been all glitzy and chic, while Bern was much more rural and laid-back. With "laid-back" being synonymous with boring as hell. The fashions were horrendous, so shopping for clothes was out of the question, and the hottest social activities for the few weeks we were there included: a yodeling concert, which had the town all abuzz; a cow-milking contest; a rock-throwing contest (I kid you not); and a much-anticipated Schwingen match, which was nothing more than two grown men grabbing each other by the seat of the pants in an effort to see who could throw the other to the ground first.

Good times!

However, the good times came abruptly to an end when Donovan left to go skiing one morning and didn't make it back.

I was asleep when he had left, so I assumed he had gone skiing just like he did every morning for the two weeks we had been there. I waited for Donovan to return from sunup to sundown, and when he didn't, I took a cable car up to the slopes a little after nightfall and asked the instructors and other skiers if any of them had seen Donovan on the slopes that day.

As the only black man in town, he would have been easy to spot and to remember, but one after one, the answers were no. Donovan had been there the day before, but no one had seen him up there at all that day.

I got back to our rented bungalow hoping that we had somehow missed each other in passing, but the place was just as empty as it had been before I had left to go searching for him.

I needed to use a telephone, but the room had no means of contacting anyone, not even the concierge. On the day that we first checked into the resort, Donovan had requested that all the telephones be removed from the room so that we could spend quality time together and not be disturbed.

Finally, there was no other alternative but to go over to the concierge's office and have her call around to the local police station and hospital.

"No, Mrs. Robinson, Mr. Robinson is not in the hospital, nor is he being detained by police," she said politely, but I could still detect a hint of suspicion in her voice.

In a sense I was relieved. Donovan wasn't in trouble with the law or seriously wounded, but Mr. and Mrs. Robinson? I know Donovan wanted to get away from it all, but why the alias?

I was so worried; I did not sleep at all that night. Instead, I sat in front of the log-burning fireplace drinking cup after cup of hot chocolate, wondering where the hell Donovan was, and what the hell could have happened to him.

The scenarios that ran through my head were endless.

Maybe he had been kidnapped and sold into the international sex slave trade—no, wait, that only happened to white women.

Or, maybe he had decided to try out a different set of slopes where he crashed into a tree and was walking around with severe amnesia.

Or, there had been an avalanche and he was now out there at the bottom of some mountain buried under miles of snow.

Yes, that was it. Donovan had met an untimely death out on the Swiss Alps doing what he loved to do most in the world besides making and spending money.

I felt such a profound sense of loss and grief that I started to cry. His mother would blame me, I was sure of it. And in a way, it really was entirely my fault. If only I had put my foot down and insisted that we go back to New York instead of continuing on to Switzerland, Donovan would be alive and everything would be fine.

The knock on the door came early the next morning, which startled me even though I half expected it.

I put on a brave front, and opened the door to find the female concierge standing there with a "regret to inform" look on her pale, pretty face. Standing next to the concierge was an older gentleman who wore a crisp navy blue uniform with a starched white collar and bronze name tag that said "Resort Manager" in black letters. He also looked gravely serious.

"Good morning, ma'am," the manager said, looking grief stricken, "we are sorry to inform you that a serious problem has occurred."

I felt my emotions spiraling out of control. I gripped the doorknob, and leaned all of my weight on it for support.

The concierge helped hold me up, and the manager began again. "Yes, well, as I was saying, Mr. Robinson's credit card has been declined for the amount of eight-thousand four-hundred and thirty-six dollars, and fifty-two cents . . ."

The manager handed me documents to prove that what he was saying was true, then went on to say that immediate additional payment was required if we, "the Robinsons," intended to continue our stay at the resort.

It was an outrageous amount of money for a hotel stay. I didn't have any major credit cards in my name, and I only had five hundred dollars in my evening bag the night Donovan and I left for Paris, which was not nearly enough to even make a dent in that bill.

Assumed names and rejected credit cards . . . none of it made a bit of sense.

WHAT THE FUCK WAS GOING ON HERE?

What to do? I needed time to think, but had none.

I followed the manager and concierge back to their office so that I could make a phone call. Before handing over the phone the resort manager asked with a raised eyebrow, "Will this be an international phone call?"

What a dumb-ass question. Of course it was an international phone call.

We were in Switzerland where no other black people were even visiting, let alone residing. Who the hell did he think I was calling, my cousin Peaches who lived around the corner?

I didn't have my cell phone with me, and the only people whose phone numbers that I knew by heart were Kyle, Zoë, and Tameka.

I called Zoë first. After I told her it was me, she responded with:

"What the fuck do you want?" There was a hard edge to her voice, and I thought she was joking around until she cut the conversation short and hung up on me.

Next I called Kyle, who sounded panicked, yet relieved to hear my voice.

"Eva, girl, where are you?"

"I'm in Switzerland. Donovan's been missing for almost an entire day, and things are just a mess right now. . . ."

"Well, things are an even bigger mess back here. . . ." Kyle said, then went on to inform me that a scandal involving Donovan had broken a few short days after we had left the country over a month ago. The Manhattan District Attorney's Office had indicted Donovan for an investment scheme that had swindled hundreds of investors out of $150 million dollars over the last five years—small potatoes in comparison to some of the bigger financial crooks out there, but a thief, whatever the amount, is still a thief.

Donovan's alleged list of victims was a veritable who's who of black America; including John Crosby, Tameka's soon to be ex-husband Jamal, and even my good friend Zoë Everett.

After Kyle relayed all that information to me, I laughed. Among his other outstanding qualities, he had a wicked sense of humor. "Come on, Kyle. I am literally stranded halfway across the world right now, so this is not the time for you to be joking around."

"I wish I was joking," he said grimly, "but I'm as serious as stage four cancer right now, Eva. Donovan is a wanted man. He's on the run right now because the boy done went and got caught up in some serious shit."

When Kyle sniffled and blew his nose, I knew that he was crying, and that's when I knew it was true.

I had been bamboozled, hoodwinked, and led astray.

Donovan, if that was even his real name, was a world-class fugitive, and he had taken me along for the ride.

Welcome to the Matrix

The transatlantic flight back to America was a miserable, not to mention humbling, experience.

When you're used to traveling by private jet or first-class at the very least, it is exceptionally hard to accept a downgrade to economy class.

Talk about culture shock. I had no idea that coach was such a zany, zoolike atmosphere. I've heard horror stories, but you know. . . .

The one and only other time I had flown coach was when I was eleven years old and traveled with my grandmother from Chicago to North Carolina for a relative's funeral. I remember it being a pleasant experience, probably because in those days people dressed up nice for travel, and for the most part were courteous and acted like they had some damn sense. Nowadays, not so much.

First, since when did passengers have to start paying for snacks and beverages? And why are there always at least three howling babies onboard, placed strategically throughout the cabin so that they can collectively get on everybody's damn nerves?

There was no leg room to speak of, and the flight attendants quite obviously saved all their smiles and friendliness for the folks up in first class.

It was way janky, and I have never felt like such a second-class citizen in my life.

To make matters worse, I had the middle seat, and was sandwiched in between what looked to be the Unabomber's identical twin brother, and a ginormous woman whose bad body odor and expansive flesh kept infringing upon my personal space. How she was able to get onboard without having to buy two seats was beyond me, but I sighed, shook my head, and decided to sit there and take it like a woman. There was no telling what all I was going to have to face once the plane landed in New York, so I had better start toughening up ASAP because newspapers were all over this scandal.

In one paper, a leading socialite who reportedly lost two million dollars of her inheritance in the scheme spoke under condition of anonymity and was quoted as saying, "I'm willing to bet that girlfriend of his has something to do with this, too. Eva Cantrell is a known opportunist and something like this has her fingerprints all over it."

Now, who does that sound like to you? If I had to venture a guess, I would say that the unnamed and anonymous socialite was none other than Zoë Everett. That sounded exactly like something she would say, and it was just like her to make an inflammatory statement like that and not have the guts to sign her real name next to it

It was the ultimate sucker punch, and an outright lie.

An opportunist in my book was someone who sought out relationships for the sole purpose of exploiting them to further their own agenda. I was nobody's opportunist. It just so happened that I fell in love with a wealthy man, who as it turns out was a con-man. See the difference?

The Unabomber's twin started snoring before the plane even taxied down the runway. I looked over at him, all scruffy and content, and thought that it must be nice not to have something weighing so heavily on your heart and mind that you couldn't fall asleep even if you wanted to.

* * *

After a long, tortuous eight hours, my flight from Switzerland touched down at JFK Airport on a beautiful, sunny Tuesday afternoon. Despite everything that was going on, I was so happy to be back in New York that I would have kissed the ground if it wasn't so grimy.

I emerged from the gate, and was pleasantly surprised to see that Tameka was there waiting for me. I sighed with relief, happy at last to see a smiling, familiar face.

She had proved to be a true friend in my time of need. And to think, I was scared to call Tameka at first, but she had come through like a champ.

For Donovan to leave me stranded in another country with no concern as to what would become of me was the lowest of low.

The thought of skipping out on the ski resort bill crossed my mind, but it would be nearly impossible to escape undetected with all that luggage I was carrying around. Besides, I was pretty sure that nonpayment for services rendered was a crime no matter where you are in the world, and I didn't want to add sitting up in a Swiss jail to my growing list of problems.

I needed roughly twelve thousand dollars to take care of the ski resort bill, and to get a one-way plane ticket back home. There were less than five people in the world I could call for that kind of money. Donovan and Zoë had been among them, but now they were off the short list, for obvious reasons. Kyle, who normally would have given me his right arm, just plain didn't have it, which I was sure had something to do with Irwin, his new high-maintenance lover.

"Give Tameka a call," Kyle had suggested. "I know she's good for it."

"No, her and Jamal are going through a divorce and she's having a hard enough time getting child support out of him as it is," I said, "plus Donovan got Jamal for some money too, didn't he?"

"Mmm-hmm . . . that's what they say."

"Well, that's out of the question. She's probably mad at me just like Zoë."

"Yeah, but Tameka genuinely loves you like I do. I haven't talked to her about it, but I'm sure she knows that what Donovan has done has nothing to do with you."

I made the phone call, and Tameka picked up after the sixth ring. The connection was a bit staticky, but I could clearly hear her sons in the background, yowling like three wild banshees. We spoke for only a few minutes, but I hung up relieved, and thanked God for Tameka Monroe-Harvey.

"Pack your things and go to the Swiss Air counter at the airport, where they should have your boarding pass," she had said. "Now pass the phone to the concierge or whoever I need to give my credit card number to in order to clear up those outstanding charges."

As Kyle would say, it was an act of love.

Except for asking to borrow twelve thousand dollars, I didn't have to explain much to Tameka. I didn't have to. Donovan J. Dorsey, Wall Street golden boy turned shiesty-ass crook, was the talk of the town. Just like Kyle, Tameka had read enough in the newspapers and seen enough on various television news reports to have the full picture. And at that point, they both knew much more about what was going on than I did.

"Welcome back," Tameka said as I kissed her on both cheeks and hugged her tight. It was an expression of both gratitude and fear for the unknown that would undoubtedly overtake my life in the months to come.

"Girl, I can't thank you enough," I said. "I don't know how soon I'll be able to pay you back, but I'm going to pay you back every dime. I swear."

"You're my girl, and I love you," Tameka said, "so don't worry about all that right now, Eva, it's cool."

That would be easier said than done. I hated being indebted to anyone for anything.

Tameka and I stood at the baggage carousel for almost an hour, and the only bag I had received out of a total of eight bags was the garment bag containing the chinchilla coat that Donovan had bought for me in Paris.

"You said you had *eight* Louie bags?" Tameka asked, pointing out the obvious.

"Yes, plus these two," I said, indicating the train case that held my makeup and the duffel bag that I carried on, which contained my jewelry, digital camera, and other valuables I didn't want to lose.

And that is exactly what had happened to all the other bags I had checked with the airline. They got lost.

It was Murphy's Law in full effect. Whatever could go wrong was most certainly going wrong.

Apparently, lost luggage happens all the time and is no big deal. At least that's the impression I got from the folks in the lost and found department. More than a hundred thousand dollars' worth of missing items and all I got after filling out a baggage inventory form detailing the contents of my lost luggage was a receipt with the reference and contact number of the Swiss Air lost and found office, and a terse "We will be in contact with you after the central baggage tracing office in Bern conducts a thorough investigation."

The ride from the airport to the Central Park West co-op was uncharacteristically quiet for both me and Tameka.

Usually whenever we rode in the car together, the music was bumping and the conversation was loud and rowdy. Not that day. Tameka had the volume on the radio turned down so low it might as well have been off.

It was just as well, because I didn't feel much like talking anyway.

Instead, I stared out the window watching the multitude of nameless people on the street as they went about their respective days.

Bike messengers deftly maneuvered through traffic on their

bicycles, food cart vendors served their waiting customers, and traffic cops stood in the middle of the street taking their jobs way too seriously, making manic, exaggerated gestures.

We passed the Naked Cowboy standing on the corner happily strumming his guitar in his tighty-whitey drawers. He was wearing a full-length brown sable coat over his underwear, but it was mid-November, and starting to get too damned cold for that gimmick. I wondered what he does in late December and January, in the dead of winter. If he had any sense, he'd keep the hustle going by packing up his guitar and going down to south Florida.

Some of the people on the street looked happy. Pedestrians walking in twos, holding hands and laughing like life was oh-so-grand and carefree.

Even the bums seemed happy-go-lucky.

I was jealous of them all. Mainly because no matter what their personal problems were at that moment in their lives, they weren't nearly as big as what I had suddenly found myself having to contend with.

I could only imagine what Gwen would say about all of this. My mother's voice was suddenly in my ear, very loud and extremely ghetto. "Eva, girl, it looks like you have really gone and stepped in it now! But it serves your ass right. . . . Didn't I always tell you to keep your own everything so that the quality of your life doesn't depend upon the actions of some damn man?"

Uh, no. . . . That was *grandma*.

The only useful advice Gwen had given me up to that point was to "cross at the green and not in between," and not to eat yellow snow.

Growing up, Gwen was never a constant presence in my life, which was why I preferred to call the woman who had given birth to me by her first name, instead of mom, mommy, mama, or ma dukes.

Gwen's voice was the equivalent of fingernails on a chalkboard to me, so I tuned her out and fished my makeup compact out of my bag so that I could fix my face.

I pulled the sun visor down, flipped open the vanity mirror, and winced at my reflection. I looked like death warmed over. Tired, bloodshot eyes with dark circles underneath. My eyebrows needed to be waxed, my makeup had melted, and a huge, stress-induced pimple had popped up all of a sudden on the tip of my chin, causing me to resemble the Wicked Witch of the West. I leaned forward to examine the zit, which was so hard that it hurt.

Yeah, like powder is going to help that look any better right now.

Disgusted, I snapped the mirror closed, just as Tameka slammed on the brakes so hard that we both would have sailed through the windshield if we weren't wearing our seat belts.

Riding with Tameka was always an adventure because, quite frankly, she was the world's worst driver. I gripped the overhead assistant handle for dear life as she swerved recklessly through congested rush-hour traffic. She raced through yellow and red lights, cut other drivers off, and switched lanes without using her signals

"Girl, will you slow down?" I said. "Why are you driving like a bat outta hell, anyway?"

"I'm late picking up the boys. I should have been there over an hour ago," she said, gunning down the West Side Highway at a high rate of speed. I made the sign of the cross and said a silent prayer: *Lord, please let me get home safe and in one piece. . . .*

When we were only a couple of blocks away from my building, I breathed a deep sigh of relief. *Ah, home, sweet home.*

Even though I was angry with Donovan, the Funderburk was still my home, and I planned to stay there at the penthouse until we had a long talk about this mess he had somehow gotten himself in and made a definite decision about the future of our relationship. That was, if he decided to man-up and come back from wherever he was to face the music.

I had no idea how I was going to be able to afford the monthly maintenance fees, which were close to thirteen thousand dollars a month, but what a joy it would be to finally get back to the serenity of my superdeluxe apartment and sleep in my own bed.

Out of the corner of my eye, I noticed that Tameka kept sneaking peeks over at me as she drove.

I sensed that she was keeping something serious from me. "What's up, Tameka?" I asked.

She gave me a solemn, closed-mouth smile, and then reached over and grabbed my hand.

"No, I prefer that you keep both hands on the wheel," I said, placing her right hand back on the steering wheel. "Whatever it is, just say it. I mean, what's the worst that can happen at this point?"

Tameka sighed heavily, like whatever she was holding in was causing her a considerable amount of pain. Then she spilled her guts in one big blurt.

"I'm not sure if you have a home to go back to. The feds raided the apartment while you were gone, and now word on the street is that Donovan's mother has already sold the place."

Oh, so that's the worst that can happen at this point.

If what she was saying was true, I had officially fell down a rabbit hole, into an alternate universe.

I closed my eyes and laid my head on the tan leather headrest. "Please tell me you're joking. . . ." I pleaded. I opened my eyes and looked over at Tameka, who shook her head sadly, letting the silence speak for itself.

With everything that I'd had to process in the last ten hours, the status of things at the penthouse honestly had not even crossed my mind until Tameka brought it up. Was it really possible that I was now homeless, along with everything else I had to deal with? Tameka pulled up in front of the Funderburk, and I was out of the truck and in the lobby before she'd even come to a complete stop.

"Ms. Cantrell, can I speak to you for a moment?" It was Clarence the doorman, with his nosy, backbiting ass. He was a short, pudgy black man in his late fifties, and had been a fixture in the building since long before I moved in. I cut my eyes at the sight of him. It was rude, but it was a knee-jerk reaction that I couldn't help at that moment. My primary concern was getting upstairs to see what had gone on in my home while I was gone, and the last thing I felt like dealing with was a self-important doorman who gossiped like a bitch.

I had always been cordial to Clarence, tolerating his compulsion to tell me which tenants were into swinging and wild orgies, who was having money woes, and who had out-of-control sexual perversions and/or drug habits.

However, this was not the time.

"Not now, Clarence," I said over my shoulder as I ran for the elevator bank.

"You're trespassing!" he said in a loud, commanding tone that I had only heard him use with service people who failed to give him his due respect, and sightseers who really were trespassing on the property.

The words *you're trespassing* made me stop dead in my tracks. They were like daggers in my back, serving as further proof, just in case I needed it, that my life had unequivocally changed. And not for the better.

I straightened my back and turned to face Clarence the doorman with steely resolve.

"I'm sorry, but what did you say?" I had heard him right, but I was just stalling for time. Wishing and waiting for someone to suddenly jump out and say, "You've been PUNKED!!" and that everything I'd been through in the last twenty-four hours was all part of an elaborate hoax.

That would have been too good to be true, which is why it didn't happen.

"There's no need for you to go up there," Clarence said, in

a kinder, softer tone. "The locks have been changed, and the place has been cleaned out and sold."

"Sold by whom?" I asked tightly.

"By Mrs. Dorsey, of course. I mean, after all, she is the rightful owner of the apartment—well, she was until last week when the new tenants closed on it."

I felt my mind and emotions spiraling out of control, as my once-friendly neighbors briskly passed me by as if they didn't know me from a can of paint. The fact that Donovan had registered the apartment in his mother's name was news to me.

Without being asked, Clarence went into great detail, repeating much of what I had already heard from Kyle and Tameka.

The federal authorities had shown up at the co-op with a search warrant just two days after Donovan and I had left the country. Since Mrs. Annette Dorsey's name was on the deed, the building manager called her to come over and handle the situation.

Clarence bore witness as authorities carted away everything that they perceived to be evidence in Donovan's wrongdoings, including computers, a safe, and an entire file cabinet full of documents. "Word is, Mrs. Dorsey got so spooked that the feds could possibly seize the penthouse that she quickly sold it to the highest bidder, even though she had to sell it at a huge loss," said Clarence.

What was worse, Clarence went on to say, was that he and many of the tenants in the building had been hounded mercilessly by hordes of photographers and by journalists looking for a quote or a scoop, and it had taken weeks to get the situation completely under control.

"You should have seen 'em out there, camped out like they were waitin' on a Michael Jackson concert or something." He shook his head, clearly still awed by the memory of it all. "Stuff like that doesn't usually go on around here," he said, his voice dripping with accusation.

By the time Clarence had finished relaying all that information, Tameka had joined me in the lobby, claiming that she was now pressed for time and was late picking her kids up from the babysitter's.

"So where are my things?" I asked.

"Well, everything had to be moved out to make way for the new tenants," Clarence said as if that alone should have satisfied my curiosity.

"That still doesn't answer the question," I said, feeling rage threatening to overtake me. "I had closets, and drawers full of my personal things. Where are they?"

Clarence had Warren, the building maintenance guy, man his post for him while he took me a couple of floors down, into a dark, dank storage room that prior to that moment I hadn't even known existed.

There was an unmistakable *my how the mighty have fallen!* expression on Clarence's face as he pointed to several large trash bags. "This is it," he said, "everything that Mrs. Dorsey left for you."

Perched on top of one of the garbage bags was a bundle of mail addressed to me, which was held together by a rubber band.

There was also a note from Donovan's mother.

Dear Eva,

Unfortunately, I had to sell the apartment along with a number of Donovan's assets, because there is no telling what creditors will want to seize and liquidate.

As you may know, the property was worth $8.6 million, but since real estate properties involved in scandal rarely go for the asking price, I had to scale the price down to $5.9 million.

And I am sure that a huge sum of that money will be needed for Donovan's bail and defense.

In any case, these bags contain everything you came into my son's life with.

Good luck. Annette Dorsey

"Everything you came into my son's life with . . ." Just how the hell would she know *what* I came into her son's life with?

I ripped the letter apart and tossed the pieces on the floor, which Clarence clearly did not appreciate, because more than likely he'd have to clean the mess up.

Rest assured that if Annette Dorsey were within my grasp at that moment, I would have torn that old, pretentious bitch apart, starting with that gaudy, *gaud ugly* bleached-blond head of hers.

I didn't have to look through the bags to know that my personal belongings had been significantly reduced down to one-fourth of what I had actually owned. I had no idea what Mama Dorsey had done with all of my things, but I did know that Donovan wasn't the only thief in the family. He had gotten it honestly.

Downward Spiral

The nameplate on the closed office door read VANCE MURPHY, ATTORNEY AT LAW. I barged into the office unannounced, and with a frantic and very pregnant receptionist on my heels. "Excuse me, miss, but you can't go in there without an appointment!" said the frowzy frump in a navy blue polyester pants suit.

Vance was Donovan's attorney.

I went to his office in midtown Manhattan because, looking back, I recalled that Donovan had conferred a hell of a lot with Vance during the weeks before the scandal broke. There were countless secret meetings, and phone calls outside of business hours that Donovan all of a sudden found necessary to take in another room behind closed doors.

So in light of all that, I did not doubt that there were questions only Vance could answer.

When I walked in on him, Vance was seated behind a stately wooden desk, poring over a stack of legal briefs.

"I tried to stop her, but obviously there's some dire emergency that needs your immediate attention," Vance's receptionist said in a snippy manner that I felt was unprofessional and uncalled for. The Blind Boys of Alabama could see that I was in distress. Where the hell was her compassion?

"It's all right, Sonya. I'm pretty sure I know what this is

about, and I'll take care of it," Vance said, signaling for Sonya to leave and close the door behind her. He came from behind his desk and helped me to a chair opposite his desk. "Eva, I heard you were back in town. . . ."

"Yes, for better or for worse, I am. . . . Now, if I had known all of this was going on, I would have kept my ass in Switzerland and become a milk maiden or something like that."

Vance chuckled as he went and sat back behind his desk, which was framed by a large plate-glass window that looked out over the city skyline. Behind him, the Chrysler and Empire State buildings served as a backdrop.

I had known Vance socially for years, but this was the first time I had ever been to his office, which I noted was filled with expensive paintings, sculptures, high-tech gadgets, and lots of glossy bonded leather furniture accented with brass studs.

Everything in his office spoke to the fact that the brother was very good at what he does, and was being compensated accordingly.

"Have you talked to Donovan?" I asked anxiously.

"Unfortunately, the last time I spoke with Donovan was a few days before he fled the country. While I can't go into specifics due to client confidentiality, I can say that it is as bad as it looks."

"I have heard a lot of different things from different people, but I want to hear straight from you just what it is that Donovan has supposedly done."

"How much time do you have?" Vance laughed, but I didn't crack a smile. My patience was too thin for corny-ass jokes. Vance took the hint and continued.

"Well, I can't say too much, but it's hard not to get a God complex when you're used to people constantly patting you on the back, telling you how brilliant you are. Sooner or later, you mistakenly start to believe that you are invincible, and that if you say five plus five equals a thousand, then everybody is supposed to believe you."

Without saying anything directly, Vance had said a mouthful. And it made sense.

Donovan was an intellectual snob who always assumed that he was the smartest person in every room he entered. He loved the game of chess, which he said was a good way to relax while also sharpening his mind and strategy skills. Donovan termed everything he did as either "a chess move" or "good business."

For instance: paying for expensive lunches and dinners with clients was good business. Doing favors for colleagues was good business. Buying expensive gifts for people he was in business with, or who he wanted to be in business with, were chess moves that he fully expected to pay off later down the line, which would then result in good business.

"Life is nothing but one big game of chess," Donovan had said once, while teaching me the game, "and the trick is to always anticipate your opponents' moves, and to stay at least five steps ahead of them at all times."

All of those traits, along with his considerable charm, is what I had always thought made Donovan such an outstanding leader in his field. I had no idea that he had a dark, evil side lurking within him. One that could mastermind such a diabolical scheme that so far looked like it just may have been the perfect crime.

I listened intently as Vance explained the basics of a "Ponzi scheme" to me. In a nutshell, Donovan pretended to be buying blue-chip stocks but never did.

Meanwhile, the money was pouring in, and investors were happy and none the wiser, because they received monthly statements that showed that their "investments" were growing by leaps and bounds, but they had no idea that the statements were bogus.

"It is essentially a house of cards that continues to grow, as long as people don't start cashing out all at once," Vance said, then gave me a colorful analogy: "Say you're a sports bookie, and you have all these people coming to you with a minimum of a hundred dollars, all wanting to bet on the Knicks to win over the Los Angeles Lakers. Now, as the bookie you know damn well that the Knicks aren't going to win, so instead of turning in all those bets to the big boys, you pocket everybody's money and nobody is none the wiser as long as the Knicks actually *lose* the game. Now if the planets should all line up and the Knicks should happen to *win*—"

"—I, the bookie, have to pay all those people, all that money, which more than likely I don't have because it has already been spent supporting my lavish lifestyle."

"*Exactly!*" Vance leaned back in his swivel chair and laced his hands together behind his head. "Or maybe you do have it, but instead of paying everyone what you owe them you'd rather keep the money hidden away in various offshore bank accounts."

"So what about the apartment? Donovan and I lived together for almost three years! Can his mother just swoop in and sell the place out from under me like that?"

"Unfortunately, she can. You have no recourse because you and Donovan never legally married, and the state of New York does not recognize common-law marriages. Also, Annette is Donovan's trustee, meaning that she is legally authorized to act on his behalf, and at her discretion she can do whatever she wants in regards to his assets and personal property, and that includes the sale and liquidation of said assets."

Vance saw the confused look on my face and added, "In layman's terms: if Mrs. Dorsey wants to evict you and put the penthouse up for sale, then there ain't nothing you can do about it."

My worst fears had come true. It was all so surreal that I felt outside of myself, like I was watching myself star in a tragic movie and no amount of shouting at the screen would help change the outcome.

The name of the movie was *LIFE: Starring Eva Cantrell,* and it was one part comedy, with some melodrama and suspense thrown in for good measure. I didn't know how the ending would play out, but quite frankly, it was turning out to be one of the scariest movies I had ever seen.

It was so scary, in fact, that I began to howl as if I were in mourning, which in a sense, I was. My life with Donovan as I had known it was over. I felt like Cinderella after the ball. The clock had struck midnight, and I was back to rags, and back to being nobody, as if it were a beautiful and elaborate fantasy that had been just too good to be true.

It was a surreal moment, one that left an indelible impression in the depths of my soul.

The thought of going back to Chicago crossed my mind, but I quickly banished the thought. That was definitely not an option. While I loved my family dearly, New York was my home now. Besides, I refused to be like all the Cantrells before me who had gone off to various other big cities vowing to make it big, only to end up back in the projects mere weeks, months, and in Uncle Booney's case, within days of their departure.

Vance came out from behind his desk and handed me Kleenex after Kleenex as I cried. I had no home to call my own, no job, no money, and no prospects for any of the above. Staying with Kyle was out of the question because I couldn't stand the sight of Irwin, his live-in lover, and the feeling was quite mutual. If we were to force a co-habitation situation, surely one of us would be either dead or in jail in less than twenty-four hours.

What would become of me now? Would I inadvertently be sucked into the New York underworld, out on Hunts Point Avenue having to do something strange for a little bit of change?

Would I be reduced to living in squalor in some condemned flophouse in the Bronx? Ragged and filthy, scrounging for food outside of fast-food restaurants, and taking dumpster chic to a whole new level of realness. My signature scent of Prada Infusion d'Iris would be replaced with a new fragrance. One with top notes of old garbage and stale urine accented by undertones of human musk.

Or, since liquidating seemed to be what was in vogue, maybe I should sell off what few possessions I had left, cash in my chips so to speak, and get the hell outta Dodge.

It was common knowledge that the Bloomberg administration wanted to reduce the city's homeless population so
badly that they were actually buying one-way plane and bus
tickets for the homeless to leave the city.

Puerto Rico? Paris? Oklahoma? Fine, just pack up your
cardboard box and go be dead weight someplace else. Maybe I
should take the mayor up on his offer and head out to the West
Coast. After all, it was late fall. Winter was right around the
corner, which is definitely not a good time to be homeless in
New York.

Coincidentally, I'd seen a news piece several weeks earlier
that claimed Beverly Hills was the best place on earth to be
homeless.

Not only is the weather great all year-round, but the homeless in that area have direct access to rich people who can afford to be pretty generous. One street dweller boasted that
handouts can go as high as a thousand dollars, and the segment
backed up the guy's claim by showing the wealthy pulling up
in their expensive cars and offering trays of leftover gourmet
food, unwanted jewelry, and last season's designer clothing.

Yeah, that sounds like a plan. . . . I thought as I snapped the
last Kleenex out of the box and blew my nose long and hard.
It might not have been much, but it was the only plan I had.

"What am I going to do, Vance?" I asked simply.

"Well, I can put out a press release first thing in the morning letting everyone know that you weren't complicit in what
Donovan has been accused of doing, and to essentially back
off," he said hopefully, but totally missing the point.

"I appreciate that, Vance, but where am I going to *live?*"

It was the multimillion dollar question, which hung in the
air for what seemed like an eternity before Vance replied. "You
can stay at my place, at least until you get your bearings and
find a more permanent living situation. Okay?"

I smiled for the first time all day, and jumped up and
hugged Vance so hard that he started to cough.

Damsel in Distress

In just a matter of hours, I had gone from being "TUF," The Ultimate Flyygirl to "TUF," The Unfortunate Fool.

I was officially a charity case, but at least I had a roof over my head—for now.

Vance's TriBeCa apartment was spacious and very well appointed, even though the building itself was an unassuming red brick high-rise that could have easily been mistaken for a warehouse.

The building paled in comparison to the Funderburk, but at least there was a doorman downstairs, which was a pretty good indication that the building had other great amenities to offer as well.

Inside, it was a bachelor's pad, to be sure. And while Vance had good-enough taste, his apartment was in desperate need of a woman's touch. The walls were plain, stark white, with no artwork, and very few accent furnishings that help make a house a home.

There was no theme to speak of. Just a mishmash of offbeat and unusual furnishings, like a leopard-print ottoman, a large Buddha statue, and various artifacts that Vance had obviously gathered from his travels around the world.

I admired the high ceilings, exposed brick walls, tall windows, and glossy, pinewood floors; however, it was clear that cleaning was not one of Vance's strong points.

Dirty laundry was scattered all over the place, and judging by the smell, the garbage needed to be taken down to the incinerator ASAP.

Clearly, Donovan and Vance were worlds apart in terms of taste and style. A stickler for order and cleanliness, Donovan had no problem cleaning up after himself even though we had a housekeeper who came in five times a week. Nothing in Donovan's world was ever disorganized or in disarray, and no matter how late it was, he would not go to bed before everything in the house was cleaned and in its proper place.

In contrast, Vance may not have been a neat freak, but to his credit, he was for sure a stand-up guy.

After agreeing to let me move in with him for the time being, he was kind enough to take time off from work long enough to load my things from Tameka's vehicle into his, then took me to his apartment where he brought all of my bags upstairs for me and gave me a spare key.

"It's not much, but it's all yours for as long as you need it," Vance said, showing me to his "guest bedroom," that in all actuality was just his home office with one of those disastrous, floral pull-out couches. Whose idea was *that?* I wondered, but kept my mouth shut so as not to bite the hand that was helping me out. It wasn't the W Hotel or the Ritz Carlton, but it would certainly do in favor of a shelter or the cold, hard streets.

"I really appreciate this, Vance. This is like, going above and beyond the call of duty," I said. "And I'll tell you just like I told Tameka: I don't know how, or how soon, but I promise I'm going to pay you back one day."

Vance shook his head and waved me off. "No repayment necessary, and you're more than welcome. Donovan is one of my best clients, and I would like to think someone would do the same for a loved one of mine if she needed it."

The words "Fuck Donovan!" came to mind.

That conversation to determine the future of our relationship was no longer necessary, because as far as I was concerned, we were over. He had practically left me for dead in a foreign country, with no way or means of getting back home. It was best for him to stay on the run, because if his punk ass ever returned to New York, he would have more than the law to worry about.

But if Vance wanted to think that he was doing Donovan a favor by letting me stay with him, then so be it.

"Now, there isn't much in the way of groceries around here, but write down what you want and need, and I'll swing by Zabar's tomorrow and do some grocery shopping."

"Oh, no," I said. "Don't go out of your way on account of me. Beggars can't be choosers, so whatever you have or decide to get is fine with me."

"Okay, well, I'm sorry I don't have time to give you the grand tour, but I'm running late for a dinner date. . . . Are you going to be okay?"

"Yeah, I'll be fine." I tried unsuccessfully to stifle a yawn. "Ooh, excuse me! To tell you the truth, I'll probably just sleep. You go ahead and enjoy yourself."

Before leaving, Vance gave me a pillow and a blanket, which I intended to put to use immediately.

I was so jetlagged and emotionally drained that I didn't even have the energy to take the cushions off the sofa and pull out the mattress, or to call Kyle and let him know that I was back in town.

Ugly as the couch was, I curled up on it and slept for more than twelve hours.

No Money, Mo Problems

I woke up the next day disoriented. For a brief moment, I didn't know exactly where I was, but one look down at that disastrous floral couch I was laying on and it all came rushing back to me. I rubbed my eyes trying to make it all go away, but unfortunately, this was my new reality. Instead of waking up on my Sleep Number bed in my luxurious bedroom on Central Park West, I was at Vance Murphy's apartment in TriBeCa.

Damn.

I had slept soundly, but I'd had a vivid, violent dream in which I was a medieval queen sitting on a throne, being fed peeled grapes by a muscular manservant. In the dream, the entertainment for the evening was watching Donovan and Annette Dorsey get their just deserts, which included waterboarding and being flogged with a cat-o'-nine-tails. After they had been sufficiently tortured, I shouted "Off with their heads!" And the mother and son duo were carted off to the guillotine where they were beheaded. Their eyes bulged in their severed heads, which were tossed to an angry mob that got satisfaction out of kicking them around like soccer balls.

If only it were true. That would have been great!

I got up and ventured out into the apartment. It was quiet, without even a television or radio playing. I called out, "Vance, you home?" but got no response. No wonder. The clock on the microwave in the kitchen read 12:32 PM. It was the crack of noon, so like most people with thriving careers, Vance had probably been at work for a few hours already.

I was famished. I went through the refrigerator and kitchen cabinets, and determined rather quickly that Vance's disclaimer about there "not being much around here in the way of groceries" had been modest. There clearly wasn't a whole lot of home cooking being done around there, because the only thing Vance had the makings for was a grilled cheese sandwich, which I ate with a bowl of Campbell's Chicken Noodle soup.

It had been a while since I'd had to do it, but I was no stranger to making something out of nothing.

My ability to adapt was like a superpower. No matter what the circumstances, I may bend, but I never break. At least I haven't so far, but what I was facing then was the ultimate test in strength and resourcefulness. I emptied the last of a carton of orange juice into a glass and sat down at the kitchen table to eat. It was far from the glamorous gourmet meals that I was used to, but it was still tasty, and it got the job done.

Vance had left that morning's *Times* on the table, so I browsed the classifieds hoping against hope that there were some great editing jobs available, or at least a decent freelance writer position.

I had heard about the restructuring, the hiring freezes and massive layoffs in publishing and print media, but the pickings were so slim it was ridiculous.

Apparently, the industry was not only struggling, it was on life support.

There just weren't very many jobs to be had, and unfortunately, that's the way the cookie crumbles. When the economy is bad, people put themselves on budgets, and the first things to go are the magazine subscriptions.

There were, however, plenty of openings for: nannies, CDL drivers, bike messengers, "dancers," and escorts. I grabbed a nearby pen and put big X's through all the job listings that weren't for me, and added detailed commentary such as No! No! No! *Hell,* no! And hell fucking no!

I tossed the newspaper aside, cleaned up the dishes I had used, and then went to check out the lay of the land.

Vance hadn't taken the time to give me the grand tour the night before, but I've learned that sometimes the best tours are the ones that you give yourself.

I started poking around in the living room, which usually says a lot about a person. Vance's living room said that he was a music man, to the core. Off in the far corner of the room there were two three-foot-tall conga drums, a steel pan drum set, and an acoustic guitar. "Who does he think he is?" I wondered out loud. "Wyclef Jean?"

For sure, Vance's musical tastes were as eclectic as I have ever seen in one person's personal music library. He had some jazz, techno, gospel, a little bit of country, and a little bit of rock 'n' roll. There were just as many vinyl albums as there were CDs, and I'm not talking about just old school albums either. He had plenty of new stuff too, like the latest from Georgia Anne Muldrow, Oumou Sangare, Kid Cudi, and some Canadian kid named Drake.

After taking care of some business in the bathroom, I took a peek in the medicine cabinet and found it full of shaving cream, Sportin' Waves hair pomade, Mach3 razors, a nose hair trimmer, dental floss, an unopened box of contact lenses, Crest Pro-Health mouthwash, and oh . . . ! What do we have here? A box of Just for Men in the shade of "natural black." It's a bad habit, I know. "Rambling" is what Mama Nita called it, and I don't know why I do it, except for the fact that you can find out pretty much all you need to know about a person by rifling through the medicine cabinet.

For instance, before I met Donovan, during my single, girl-about-town days, I dated a guy named Eric who I was really into. Eric was a successful concert promoter, and we always had a great time whenever we hung out. Well, when Eric in-

vited me over to his modest co-op in Park Slope for the very
first time, and when I made the inevitable trip to the bathroom, what did I find in his medicine cabinet? Zoloft, plus
Xanax, plus Paxil, which added up to be just plain fucking
crazy! No more dates with that one. Trust me, I've learned.

Vance's master suite was huge. The shades were closed so it
was cool and dark inside, and the room smelled liked Carolina
Herrera's 212 cologne. There wasn't much to see in there except a giant four-poster bed that needed to be made, and a
closet full of the standard lawyer uniform, consisting of dark,
three-button suits, striped shirts, and insanely expensive suits
that contributed to Vance's GQ mystique.

The second bedroom was fit for a princess.

Almost as big as the master bedroom, it was an explosion
of all things pink and frilly, and was the exact prototype of the
kind of bedroom I wished I'd had growing up. There was a
canopy bed made of bleached-blond wood, with matching
dresser and nightstand, a large toy chest, and a teeny-tiny vanity table and mirror.

I smiled, thinking that Vance's little girl was lucky to have a
daddy who obviously loved her very much.

If only I had been so lucky.

Bernard, my own father, had been doting as well, but he
had vanished from my life when I was around six years old,
and his absence from my life was an issue that still baffles me.
How could someone who took you everywhere he went and
made sure you had the best of everything just turn and walk
away from you, never to be seen or heard from again?

Whenever I had asked Gwen where my father was, she
would either ignore the question or laugh and suggest that
maybe he had been abducted by aliens. That was typical Gwen.
Crude and rude, and so self-absorbed that other people's feelings were of no concern to her.

Vance's living room was dominated by a sliding glass door

that led out to a patio large enough to host a party for about twenty to thirty people, and it also had an awesome view of the Hudson River.

The apartment was on the twenty-third floor, and for a split second, I thought of flinging myself off the terrace balcony. In less than one minute my problems would be over and I wouldn't have to worry about any of it, but the thought left as quickly as it came, because I was far too vain to end it all in such a horrific manner.

Like the great poet Pat Parker once said, "Black people do not, Black people do not, Black people *DO NOT* commit suicide!" It was such a selfish, cowardly act, and was definitely not an option, so I wiped those thoughts from my mind and chose instead to focus on the best way for me to move forward.

I had spent the last two years totally absorbed in a lifestyle that didn't really belong to me. Hell, it didn't even belong to Donovan, because it was all bankrolled on stolen money.

Now, literally overnight, I was expected and required to get on a path of independence and self-sufficiency, and the sooner the better.

I know, cue the violins, right? I only had myself to blame, because I should have never gotten off the path in the first damn place.

Looking out over the bustling city, I recalled one of the first articles I had written for *Flirt* magazine, where I had started out as a staff writer.

> *When in a pinch for cash, fashionistas in the know head to the Upper East Side, where in comparison to any other area of town, the most money is offered in exchange for gently used clothing and accessories. . . .*

I went back into my "bedroom" where I dumped the contents of the trash bags containing my belongings right in the middle of the floor. I needed to access what was what, and it was just as I suspected.

There were so many of my things that were unaccounted for, it was downright criminal. And the missing items weren't limited to just the things that Donovan had bought, like Annette had implied. Gone were the expensive investment pieces that I had worked for, and paid for myself, like classic Chanel blouses, cashmere Prada sweaters, and neat little jackets from Cavalli and Isabel Toledo.

It takes years to create a look that works and build a complete wardrobe. Mine had been immense.

My designer bag game was proper, and my shoe game was mean. . . . *Grrr!* Gucci, Christian Dior, Fendi, Missoni—you name it, I'd had it. And now it was all gone, including all of the gifts that I had received on my birthday from the two celebrations.

All that was left were my underwear, several pairs of jeans, a couple of pairs of shoes, a few lousy tops, and the large stuffed elephant that Donovan had won for me the first time we'd gone to Coney Island together.

Insult was added to injury when I discovered that my jewelry box was nowhere to be found.

I sorted through what was left of my former life, and tried my best to keep the tears back, but regardless of my efforts, they flowed like running water. Annette Dorsey was a scandalous old crow who was proof that the apple does not fall far from the tree, and that you can take the woman out of Queens, but you can't take Queens out of the woman.

I was livid, and I refused to take that woman's abuse lying down.

Wiping my tears, I grabbed a cordless phone off of Vance's desk and dialed a number. Blanche, Annette's housekeeper, answered on the other end.

"May I speak to Mrs. Dorsey, please?" I asked Blanche, sounding very friendly and businesslike.

"I'm sorry, but Mrs. Dorsey is hosting a luncheon at the moment and can't come to the telephone. Is there a message?"

"No, no message." I smiled at her through the phone. "Thank you!"

Taming the Shrew

The first thing Donovan did with his first ten million dollars was to buy his mother a home in the prosperous suburban enclave of Scarsdale, NY, which with traffic is about forty-five minutes away from the city.

It was a little after one PM on a Wednesday afternoon, so traffic was light. Add that to the speed demon way I was driving Vance's black E-class Mercedes coupe, and I landed on Mama Dorsey's doorstep in thirty minutes flat.

Technically, Vance hadn't exactly given me permission to borrow his car. I had noticed that there were a couple of sets of car keys hanging on the key rack in the kitchen, and seeing as how this was an emergency, I was certain he wouldn't have minded.

Besides, it wasn't like the Benz was Vance's only means of transportation. He had three vehicles, two of which were just sitting in the underground parking garage collecting dust. I grabbed the set of keys with the Mercedes Benz emblem, but when I got to the garage, I was surprised to see that there were all kinds of Mercedes parked down there.

Vance's neighbors were also doing very well for themselves, because there were Mercedes trucks, sport wagons, coupes, convertibles—you name it. Thank God for modern technology. Otherwise I would have never known which one of those vehicles belonged to Vance.

I pressed the alarm button on the remote key and viola! There it was. Luckily, the E-class had a full tank of gas, which was plenty to get to Scarsdale and back. The plan was to replace whatever gas I ended up using, and have Vance's car back before he even knew it was missing.

Annette's sprawling, ivy-covered mansion sat on several acres of manicured land and was surrounded by poplar and pear trees.

The house was rumored to have been owned by Nicky Garofalo, the legendary goodfella who had wisecracked to the media years ago during his racketeering trial that there were multiple bodies buried deep beneath the property. I'm not sure how true the story is—it could just be hearsay—but I am certain that Nicky Garofalo and Annette Dorsey were cut from the same cloth and would have gotten along very well.

Blanche hadn't lied. There really was some kind of social function going on, because Annette's circular driveway was filled with dozens of expensive vehicles. Several uniformed chauffeurs milled around outside smoking cigarettes and shooting the breeze with each other to pass the time until their employers were ready to leave.

My bet was that it was a luncheon to benefit whatever cause Annette wanted to kiss the ass of that particular week. Her social standing was very important to her, and she was constantly writing checks and throwing elaborate functions in an effort to keep herself relevant and in the good graces of the social hierarchy powers that be.

Blanche, who I placed at around 108 years old, led me into the massive living room that looked like a page straight out of *Architectural Digest,* which is great if you like your home to have the look and feel of a museum.

Everything inside, including the lady of the manor, was overwhelmingly ornate, overstuffed, and antique. The decor was personally not my style or taste, but was the old-money style that Mama Dorsey cultivated, with her nouveau riche ass.

The thing about Annette Dorsey was that she was so snotty and relentlessly high-minded that one would never know she was born and raised in Hell's Kitchen and that she was once a short-order cook, and also sold Avon in order to make ends meet.

Annette's living room was dominated by women, so it was clearly an intimate girls-only luncheon, and they had all dressed exquisitely for the occasion, some of them in elaborate Mad Hatter–style hats. The Grande Dame herself looked resplendent dressed in a fire-engine-red Escada pantsuit and so many sparkling diamonds that she looked like a walking Christmas ornament.

Annette was shocked to see me, but she played along nicely as if I were an invited guest that she had been expecting and was thrilled to see.

"Eva, sweetheart, it is so good to see you!" Annette said, calling me over to introduce me to the group of women to whom she had been talking. There was the wife of this mogul and that, a celebrity or two, and the heads of several notable charities and foundations.

"And everyone, this is Eva Cantrell, a dear, dear friend of the family. . . ." Then she stage-whispered, "She's a piece of work. . . ." out of the corner of her mouth, which caused a few titters.

"And it certainly takes one to know one. Right, Annette?" I tittered a couple of times just like they had and then stopped abruptly, sending the clear message that I wasn't there for idle chitchat, or to play games.

It was an awkward moment for Annette. But she sailed through it gracefully by straightening her back and smiling broadly. "Eva, dear, can I have a word with you in private?" she asked.

"But of course!" I said in a voice that matched her theatrics.

She had some nerve. Carrying on as if *I* were the one who'd stolen millions of dollars of other people's money, money that more than likely helped pay for her home as well as this little afternoon shindig for which she had pulled out all the stops.

Mama Dorsey smiled and said, "Pardon me for a few moments," to her guests, and I followed her down a long hallway into her cherry-paneled private study.

Once the door was shut Annette whirled on me like a fire-breathing dragon. "Why are you here?" she snapped

"I think we both know the answer to that."

"No, actually I don't." she said, giving me a steely-eyed stare. "But I must say that this was certainly a pleasant surprise."

"Pleasant? Really?"

"Yes, really. I've always enjoyed having people show up at my doorstep uninvited."

Annette was being facetious, but I knew how to play that game as expertly as she did.

"Right, and I just love being robbed of just about everything I own by someone who is certainly old enough to know better."

She nodded. Now that she knew exactly why I was there, she seemed to relax a bit. Like a predator who had caught its prey but wanted to play with it before devouring it.

"Do you have any idea what this last month and a half has been like for me?" Annette asked quietly, reaching into her desk drawer and pulling out a pack of Newport Menthol 100s. She lit a cancer stick and inhaled the smoke deeply as if it were both calming and refreshing. "While you and Donovan were off traipsing around Europe, I was here, from day one, right in the eye of the storm. . . ."

I could have sworn I heard violins playing as Annette sadly filled me in on how life had been for her since the scandal broke.

"You're so lucky that you and Donovan never married. You'll move on and put this behind you one day, but can you imagine what it's like being the mother? The stench of this is going to be with me for the rest of my life, and I know full well that none of those bitches out there are really my friends. I know that at this very moment, they are all out there laughing and talking shit about me behind my back. . . ." Annette daintily dabbed at the corners of her eyes. "And do you know that the turnout for this luncheon was much lower than expected? I can't get anyone on the phone anymore, and this is all just too much! I worked so hard to get here, only to have it snatched away in the blink of an eye. . . ."

It was pure, unadulterated drama. Mama Dorsey had certainly missed her calling as an actress, because I was on the verge of feeling sorry for her until I noticed that she was wearing a large pair of Deco Dome diamond earrings that looked alarmingly familiar. I would recognize them anywhere, because they were mine.

"Nice earrings, Annette," I said, casually. "Where did you get those?"

She was busted and she knew it.

And it was interesting to watch her eyes go from lukewarm to ice cold in a matter of seconds.

"Let me give you a bit of advice, Eva," Annette said, furiously smashing her cigarette out in a crystal ashtray. "What I've done may seem unfair and unethical, but when the ship goes down, it's everyone for themselves."

That was all the confirmation I needed that the rest of my belongings were stashed away somewhere in her mausoleum. I saw red, and it wasn't just from the loud pantsuit she was wearing.

I advanced toward Annette calmly, without saying a word.

Reading my mind and body language correctly, she made a run for the intercom built into the wall and frantically pressed a call button: "Gary, get in here NOW!!" she screamed as if she were about to be killed.

Gary was Annette's butler-slash-bodyguard-slash-part-time-lover, and by the time he made it into the room, I had tackled her to the floor like Ray Lewis and it was Queens versus Chi-Town round one. *Ding-ding!*

To his credit, Gary didn't throw me out as forcefully as he could have. Instead, he scooped me up into his big, solid arms and carried me outside, past all those expensive-looking broads who were watching and whispering out the sides of their mouths.

God Bless the Child

Lucky for me, lawyers keep notoriously long hours and Vance hadn't made it home from the office yet by the time I returned to the city from Scarsdale. I parked his car in the exact spot I'd found it and walked out onto the avenue headed to the post office over on Canal Street. There, I forwarded my mail from the Central Park West address to the new P.O. box that I paid thirty dollars to rent for six months.

Afterward, I wandered into the super-deluxe twenty-four-hour CVS that people were so excited about and couldn't seem to get enough of. I went in there for just a couple of personal items like apricot body wash and carrot oil for my scalp, but ended up going on a mini, and I mean *very mini,* shopping spree in the cosmetics/skin care aisle. Sephora it wasn't, but hell, lip gloss is lip gloss, and the Cover Girl Queen collection has some awesome shades of eye shadow that really compliment my skin tone.

I also bought one of those cheap pay-as-you-go cell phones. It was a far cry from my beloved iPhone, which I considered to be the best invention since Spanx and the oxygen facial. But it was now function over style, whereas before, it had been the other way around.

You know you're doing bad when a purchase of $78.52

hurts your pockets. My attempt to retrieve my stolen goods from Annette Dorsey was futile, and still left me with next to nothing to sell toward helping me get back on my feet.

Four hundred and forty dollars was all I had left to my name, so the HELP WANTED sign in the window of a bakery where I distinctly remember a pizzeria used to be the last time I'd been in the area really caught my attention.

Watching my grandmother work as hard as she did gave me an appreciation for the almighty dollar, and luckily I had never been one of those people whose pride would not allow them to perform certain jobs they felt were beneath them. The truth is, you have to crawl before you can walk.

A bell dinged overhead as I stepped inside the small mom-and-pop establishment, whose only customer was a guy seated by the window drinking coffee and working a *Reader's Digest* crossword puzzle.

"Welcome to Belle's Bakery, how can I help you?" asked the man behind the counter. I was taken aback for a moment when I saw him, because black-owned businesses were a rarity in this part of town.

"Hi. I actually came in to inquire about the sign in the window."

"You sure I can't get you something else?" he asked, laughing at his own joke. He was tall, good-looking, and shall we say "fluffy" the way most bakers tend to be, which was probably due to an overabundance of carbs. "Seriously though, do you have any professional baking experience?" he asked.

"No, but I'm a fast learner and I'm really good with customers."

"Oh, yeah? And I'm sure you have a *brilliant* personality too, right?"

Again with the jokes. One thing was for sure, if I got the job he would be fun to work with.

He said his name was Steve. Belle was his mother, and she had been out on sick leave for a few weeks due to a mild heart attack. God willing, Belle would return to work within the next month or so, and she would make the final decision as to who would be hired.

After filling out a job application Steve looked it over and said, "You haven't worked in almost three years? Is this right?" He was judging me. And that made me not want to tell him the truth, which was that I had been luxuriating on an extended vacation thanks to a wealthy boyfriend but was now forced to fend for myself.

So I lied. "I'm just coming out of a marriage, and yes, it is time for me to support myself. . . ." I said wistfully, and rubbed my eyes as if trying to hold back tears.

Steve backed off, and even gave me a sympathetic pat on the back. "Hey, I know what that's like. . . . You're gonna be fine, trust me."

I left Belle's Bakery with a spring in my step. No, Steve didn't hire me on the spot, but I still came out with more than I had going in, which was a concrete and tangible prospect.

"I still have a few more interviews to do, but we'll let you know something one way or another within the next couple of weeks" were Steve's parting words to me.

Good enough!

Before, everything looked either black or gray. But now that I was in a better mood, it was like I could see color again. The oranges, pinks, and purples of the setting sun, and the red, yellows, and electric blues of neon signs on the avenue, which was vibrant and alive with activity.

I wasn't ready to go back to Vance's apartment just yet, so I decided to take the longer, scenic route. I crossed the street at Franklin and Hudson streets, quite sure that Robert De Niro had just passed me in the crosswalk. I did a double take and although I couldn't see his face, the body language said that it was DeNiro. Love him! Not only for his stellar acting talent, but also because he has always been unabashedly down with the swirl.

I actually used to stomp through this part of town quite regularly back in my early days in New York, and found the TriBeCa neighborhood to be quite charming. Cobblestone streets, quaint shops, and a world-class restaurant on every corner. What's not to love?

Oh, and they make movies around there too, which explains why there are goo gads of movie theaters to choose from.

I walked past the Landmark Sunshine Cinema, my favorite because they offered a variety of options from old classics and international films to documentaries and cutting-edge independent films.

Donovan and I had gone to the Landmark once to see *Sometimes in April,* and he'd made it a miserable experience, because he viewed hanging out downtown as slumming it.

Even though he had been born and raised in Queens, Donovan J. Dorsey had eventually evolved into a bona fide snob. He hated being around what he called "pretentious artsy motherfuckas" who dressed as if they were literally starving artists, with their paint-splattered clothing, ripped jeans, plaid shirts, and those damn black Fedoras with the red feather stuck in the band.

Donovan avoided downtown like the swine flu, and identified more with the uptown crowd who lived in their own exclusive world—the one he had introduced me to after we had met. It was a world of fashion mavens, socialites, entrepreneurs, and people who were on the fast track in the music industry and corporate America. In hindsight, even that had been a "chess move" for Donovan, because uptown was where the big money was.

Speaking of that night at the Landmark, Donovan had also gotten on my nerves because he swore that there were rodents running rampant throughout the theater. "Did you see that?" he had whispered every two minutes, pointing in the direction where he'd supposedly seen a mouse or some other creature whiz by. I didn't actually see the alleged varmints, but there was an undeniable squeaking sound that proved Donovan's claims had some merit.

Continuing my little sightseeing adventure through the TriBeCa neighborhood, I passed a bar called Tutti Fruity where a brawl had spilled out onto the street. Burly chicks in flannel shirts were shoving each other around and trying to smack each other in the face. A little farther down from the fray was a rough-and tough-looking female wearing a white wifebeater, Timberland boots, and a doo-rag. There was a toothpick stuck in her mouth, which she took out to lick her lips and say, "Sup, Ma?"

Security!

No judgments, I'm just saying . . .

I read the novel back in high school, and to be honest, I'm not the least bit interested in playing around in another woman's *Rubyfruit Jungle.*

After passing a couple more clubs, I found the name Amanda Sardi had popped into my head. Amanda was a former roommate who since the days when we roomed together had managed to make a name for herself as the "empress of nightlife" after opening several successful clubs throughout the city. She was also the darling of all the New York papers, and while we weren't BFFs, we were close enough that I knew that I could count on her for a favor if I needed one.

Since my contact numbers for Amanda had been lost along with my iPhone, I stopped at a corner pay phone and asked information for the address and phone number of each of Amanda's clubs: Visions, Compound, and the ever popular Chateau.

After writing down the information, I called Compound first.

"Hi, is Amanda Sardi there by any chance?"

"And who wants to know?"

"This is Eva Cantrell, an old friend of hers."

"Hold on. . . ."

That was a good sign. Amanda was always on the go, and hard to track down because she had this nervous, frenetic energy that suggested she'd already had the nervous breakdown but was too busy to notice. After putting me on hold for several minutes the person on the other end of the line came back and said, "Amanda said to tell you that she's on her way over to Visions—you got a pen? I'll give you her cell number."

Visions

Visions was only about three miles from the pay phone where I had made the call, but my feet had started to hurt so I hailed a cab for the short ride over to the meatpacking district where Amanda had told me to meet her.

As my taxi pulled up in front of the club, I saw that Amanda was standing outside the club smoking a cigarette. She was not what you would call a conventional beauty, but she was striking nonetheless at 160 pounds and close to six feet tall. Amanda Sardi was a big girl, but she was also a sweetheart who would give you the Dolce & Gabbana blouse off her back. The first thing she did when she saw me was smile, flick her cigarette in the gutter, and run over to give me a warm hug.

"Eva! Omigod, girl, how have you been?"

"I'm good, but I've been better," I said, kissing Amanda on both cheeks. "You're looking good!"

Dressed in all black with gold accessories, Amanda was as hip as always in skinny jeans, Balenciaga gladiator heels, and a short, fox-fur jacket over a sequined halter top.

"You too cute as ever!" she said, fluffing my weave, which I knew good and well was a hot mess. I had gone to sleep a couple of nights in a row without wrapping and covering my hair properly, and it had disintegrated into a frizzy, tangled mess.

I usually got my hair done at least once a week, but due to my extended overseas rendezvous with Donovan, it was way past time to sit down in Helene's chair and have my weave tightened up.

The problem was, I couldn't afford it.

Helene's arm-and-a-leg prices were now way too rich for my blood, but my hope was that my meeting with Amanda would change all that.

"C'mon, let's go kick it like old times," Amanda said, as she took me by the hand and led me inside Visions where Cuban music pulsated into every nook and cranny.

Visions' nightclub was one of those exclusive, bottle-service-type clubs with a star-studded crowd, super-tight security, and flat-screen televisions mounted all over the place. It was a large lofty space with brick walls, red leatherette chairs, and slate tiled floors.

Amanda's personal table was perched high up on a balcony overlooking the rest of the club, where we sat drinking key lime martinis and eating spicy Indian food that her in-house chef had prepared.

Clearly, being boss lady has its privileges.

"So," I said. "I'm sure you've heard what's going on with Donovan, right?"

"Yeah, I read the papers, but look . . . Regardless of what anyone else believes, I don't think you had anything to do with it. I tell everybody, 'I know for a fact that girl has a heart of gold, and she doesn't have it in her to be in on a scam like that.' "

"Awww, thank you, Mandy," I said, "That's sweet!"

Amanda shrugged. "Hey, I'm Italian, and when you're a friend of mine, you're a friend for life. So as a friend, how can I help you out?"

"Well, long story short, I need a job . . . *and* . . . I was think-

ing that it would be a win-win for both of us if I started promoting parties at your clubs," I said.

Party promoting is very lucrative, and one of the few legit-
imate ways that I know to earn a substantial amount of cash in
a short amount of time.

The deal is that the club owners let promoters use their
club to invite friends and other partygoers to party for the
night, and in exchange the promoter gets a certain percentage
of money from the night's profits. It would be like forming a
partnership, and my money woes would be over.

Amanda took a sip of her cocktail, then looked at me in
the most loving and sympathetic way. "Eva, I love you and all,
but absolutely not. First of all, my clubs are hot all on their
own. And second, who would come?"

"I have tons of friends with money, and what I could bring
to the table is the more flavorful urban element that love to
pop bottles and buy out the bar."

"Look, I'm Italian, but I'm no racist. It's just that, I'm not
so sure I want that make-it-rain type of element in my clubs.
We tried it already, and the shootings, and the fights, and the
lawsuits—" Amanda sighed as if the very thought of an "urban"
crowd wore her out. "Trust me, I've learned that a mixed, bal-
anced crowd works best for everybody. Besides, promoting is
based mostly on popularity, and no offense, Eva, but you're
popular right now, but not in a good way."

"I've been out of the country and out of the loop for a
minute, but dayum! The streets are talkin' like that?"

"Yeah, it is what it is. People talk," Amanda said, "but the
good thing about stuff like this is that people eventually forget.
I mean, look at Eddie Murphy. No one looks at him anymore
and automatically thinks transvestite hooker."

We continued to debate for a few more minutes before
striking a deal. I would be a party hostess at Visions where it
was possible to make upwards of two thousand dollars a night.

l breathed a sigh of relief and hugged Amanda, happy that she was willing to help me get on my feet.

She was always super-cool, which is why the biggest conflict we had back when we shared a two-bedroom in Chelsea was that she literally said, "I'm Italian" fifty times a day, and her inflections ranged from pride to where you weren't sure if you were being threatened or not.

"We Italians are as thick as thieves. . . ."

"I'm Italian, Fuhgeddaboudit!"

"Hey, I'm Italian, whaddaya want me to do?"

"It's an Italian thing, you wouldn't understand. . . ."

I couldn't take it. Being proud of your heritage is great, but at least once a week I would have to scream, "Okay, you're Italian! Sheez . . . I get it!" Amanda and I toasted to old times, and to the fact that we would be working together starting Friday night. Salute! (That's *Italian,* you know.)

Truth or Consequences

The next afternoon, I met Kyle for lunch at Cornelia Street Café in the West Village. It was his treat, of course, because the lunch I could have afforded would have included the words *value menu*.

"See! I had no doubt whatsoever that you were a resilient bitch!" Kyle said, raising his glass in a toast. "And when I say bitch, I mean that in the fiercest, diva definition of the word."

"Cheers!" I said as we touched glasses.

It was my first time seeing Kyle since the night of my birthday party at the Rainbow Room, so we had a lot of catching up to do.

"And I truly believe that's why Amanda has been so successful, because she has a kind heart and is a true friend," said Kyle, "but that heifer Zoë is another story, honey."

"Why do you say that? What have you heard?" I asked, despite the fact that I didn't want to be reminded of how someone I thought was a friend could turn on me so quickly, but as the old saying goes, "You knew it was a snake when you picked it up."

"It's not what I've heard, it's what I know! Look at this. . . ." Kyle pulled out his cell phone and showed me a message that Zoë had sent out on Facebook to all of our mutual friends.

There is no doubt that you all have heard about the enormous investment scam that our so-called mutual "friend" Eva Cantrell has been involved in along with her fraudster boyfriend, Donovan Dorsey. I, as well as many of you, have been a financial victim of Eva's deceit, which just goes to show just how disgusting a human being that she really is. Subsequently, I have removed Eva from my entire network. Clearly, she is no friend of mine.

You being a mutual friend, both in real life and on Facebook, would mean that I would still have some connection to Eva Cantrell, and I will not allow that. So this message is my request that you decide by Friday whose side you're on, and who you want to be friends with. It's either team Zoë or team Eva. There can be no riding the fence on this one. Your friendship means a lot to me, but Eva Cantrell needs to be removed from the picture altogether, and if you choose to remain connected to her, then I must sever you from my circle of friends as well. Please decide on this at your earliest convenience, because I will promptly begin removing people still connected with Eva ASAP.

Thank you, your friend (I hope!)

~ Zoë

"Oh, she is really tripping!" I said, handing the phone back to Kyle.

"But the tragic part is, it worked. Have you checked your Facebook page lately?"

"At a time like this? Facebook is the last thing on my mind," I said. "I haven't even thought about it, truthfully."

"Well, FYI, you're down to about thirteen friends. There's me and Tameka, of course, and the rest are your friends and family from back home."

"Thirteen! When I had over two thousand?" Kyle scratched his bald head and avoided eye contact. "You should see some of the comments that were left on your wall as they exited," he said. "Vicious!"

It wasn't surprising. I knew that Zoë had it in her to be so immature and nasty, and when she dislikes someone, she expects everyone else to fall in line and hate them too.

Clearly, my mistake was in thinking that we had a truly solid friendship. Never in my wildest dreams did I ever expect to be on the receiving end of Zoë Everett's hatred.

And speaking of Facebook, it's probably unnecessary to change my relationship status to "It's complicated" since I'm sure everyone knows that by now.

"But forget about all that mess, how are things working out with you and this Vance Murphy?" Kyle asked.

"So far, so good. He works long hours and the only time we really see each other is when we run into each other in the bathroom, or the kitchen."

Which reminded me of the incident that occurred earlier that morning.

I had jumped up early and got dressed to go get some coffee and a couple of lemon bars from Starbucks. I thought it would be a nice gesture if I checked with Vance to see if he wanted anything, and when I knocked on his bedroom door, it swung wide open. I peeked in the room and saw that Vance had just gotten out of bed and was stretching, with his body chiseled and ripped up like Adonis.

He was also butt-naked, and his morning wood was enormous. Oh, my *God,* what a big ego! Vance looked over and saw me standing in the doorway, and we were both so shocked that I just said "Sorry!" and closed the door behind me.

Kyle laughed after I relayed the story to him. "And that's how you left things?" he asked.

"Yeah," I nodded, "pretty much. . . ."

"Well, it should certainly be interesting when you two see each other again!"

"I know, right? Akward.com!"

"Hmm . . . so is that a situation you wouldn't mind getting to know better?" Kyle asked with a cheeky grin.

"Who, Vance? Oh, hell, no! He's a decent-looking guy and everything—very kind and thoughtful, but he's totally not my type."

"And why is that?"

"I don't know. . . . stuffed suit, kinda dry . . . and even if there were some chemistry there, which there certainly is not, the fact that Vance is a friend of Donovan's automatically rules him out."

"Wait, stop the damn presses!" said Kyle, holding his hand up. "It's because of Donovan's thoughtless, greedy ass that you're living under a cloud of suspicion, and without two quarters to rub together. *Now* you're running around here with your weave all busted up—yet you're still loyal to the man?"

I patted my head self-consciously, hoping my tracks weren't showing because they sure as hell were slipping.

"Look, my lack of interest in Vance has less to do with loy-alty to Donovan and everything to do with having morals and values. My motto is: If I have ever slept with anyone you know, and vice versa, then you and I can never be. So there, Mr. Man, take notes and *learn!*"

"To each his own, but as for me, I would definitely take it on a case-by-case basis," Kyle joked. "So what are you going to do when they track Donovan down and bring him back to face the music? Are you going to support him through the whole court process or what?"

"Wow . . . I don't know. I've been so busy trying to figure

out how to pull myself up out of this mess that I haven't thought about it. I still care about Donovan and I don't want anything bad to happen to him, but if I do support him during the trial, it will be as a friend and not his girlfriend," I said. "I mean . . . why? What even possessed him to take all those people's money like that?"

"Yeah, that was some cold, calculated shit that he pulled," Kyle said. "And with a smile on his face too."

"And don't think that white America isn't saying, 'See what happens when black folks get in these positions of power?' "

"We told you they can't be trusted!"

"Which is just one of the reasons why I'm so pissed at Donovan," I said. "Because we had countless discussions on what he perceived to be the black man's burden in corporate America, which is when they open the door and give you a seat at the table, you can't fuck it up. *We* have to represent so that *we all* can go further. And what did he do?"

Kyle said it with me. "He fucked it up!" Donovan had the golden opportunity to go down in history as a brilliant financial wizard. Instead, he would forever be known as the biggest *black* Wall Street swindler of all time.

After lunch, Kyle and I walked over to Greer's clothing store, where I watched with envy as he was measured for a custom-made leather jacket with a rock star vibe.

"I remember what that's like," I said wistfully as I browsed through the racks that were full of exotic, one-of-a-kind pieces.

"You need to go ahead and sell that fur coat," said Kyle. "You ought to be able to get at least five grand for it."

"For a sixty-five thousand dollar coat?" I asked incredulously. "I would be a bona fide fool to take a loss like that. Besides, I have been checking in with Swiss Air every day. Hopefully they'll find my luggage soon, and I can sell some of those things instead."

Kyle smirked, trying not to laugh in my face. "Eva, girl, not to be insensitive or anything, but you might as well write that luggage off. Some Swiss bitch bought your stuff hot and is walking around the town square sharper than a porcupine's spine, honey."

"Don't say that," I pleaded. "I can't stand the thought of all those beautiful things out there somewhere, lost to me forever. I mean, you should have seen all the stuff I copped in Paris, Kyle. It really was quite impressive."

Kyle and the tailor looked at me with concern all over their faces.

I had become emotional without even realizing it, and was on the verge of tears.

"Believe me, sweetheart, I understand," Kyle said quietly, and I sensed that he might have been a bit embarrassed for me, so leave it to Kyle to bring humor to a tense situation. "Now, I know that you don't have that many clothes left, but fear not, 'cause, girl, I still have some things left over from my old drag days—some fabulous pieces that you will just die for!"

That made me smile. "But Kyle, sweetie, you're six foot four, two hundred and twenty pounds. What am I supposed to do with that?"

"Alterations, darling!" the tailor said dramatically, and we all laughed.

"Besides, clothes aren't a huge deal. You can always get more clothes and look fabulous in anything you put on, even a flour sack if you so choose," said Kyle, "but what are we gonna do about this hair?"

"You know what? You have one more chance to crack on my weave, and it's gonna be me and you!" I laughed. "Now, if it's that bad, why don't you help me do something with it? You know you've always had a way with my hair."

"Oh, baby, I wish I could, but I have to be at rehearsals with Killjoy in about an hour, and you know I mustn't keep the children waiting. Besides, Keith, you know how those little homo-thugs can be, don't you? They just might cut me!"

Keith the tailor laughed, and nodded in agreement. "Yeah," he said. "They do act like they have something extra to prove."

"Nuh-uh, Kyle, I don't believe you!" I said. "Are you saying that the members of that cute little teeny-bopping boy group are gay?"

"First of all, don't be fooled, because those aren't teenyboppers, those are grown-ass men in their twenties who are very well versed on the art of sixty-nine."

"Ugh, enough, TMI!" I said. "Way too much information and I don't even want to visualize it!"

"What? Don't kill the messenger, I'm just stating facts," Kyle said. "And since you're all queasy with sensitive ears, I won't go into any more detail, but let's just say that if all those swooning and adoring female fans only knew what takes place before and after the curtain goes up, those boys would have an entirely different audience. The gays!"

Kyle was a dancer who had both the New York City Ballet and Alvin Ailey dance troupe listed on his resume. He also danced lead in several big Broadway productions, such as *The Lion King* and *Cats,* and *The Nutcracker.*

These days, at the ripe old age of twenty-nine, Kyle was leaning more toward the choreography side of things, working with veteran recording artists like Janet and Mary J., and on down the line to newbies like the R&B boy-band, Killjoy.

Kyle's revelation about Killjoy made me wonder just how much of the world's population was living some kind of illusion, whether it is their lifestyle, marriage, sexuality, finances, and the list goes on and on.

Perception was not always reality, and what you do in the dark really does eventually come out to the light. Donovan J. Dorsey was proof of that.

Clash of the Titans

After lunch with Kyle, I went back to Vance's apartment and took a long, hard look in the mirror.

Tired of random cracks about the state of my raggedy-ass weave, I wondered just what to do to remedy the situation.

Should I spend my last few coins on a nice lacefront wig, or take my chances and go to Supercuts. Hell, does Supercuts even do weaves?

I used several of my pay-as-you-go cell phone minutes to call Helene for an appointment for a full weave. No, I still did not have the funds to afford her services, but she owed me one. I remembered how she was always saying that because of all the clients I had helped bring into the salon by way of referral that I was entitled to a complimentary hairdo—free of charge.

I do not know if it was just something for Helene to say at the time, thinking that I would never actually hold her to it, but it was time for her to pay up.

"I'm sorry, Eva, but Helene is booked solid for the next three months, but we will definitely call you if an unexpected opening comes up in her schedule," said Liz, Helene's receptionist and right-hand woman.

"What? That's new! Since when has Helene ever been too busy to squeeze me in?" I asked. "Hello?"

I didn't get an answer, because Liz had hung up on me, which was also a first. What the hell was going on?

If I hadn't known better, I would have thought that I was being blackballed from the salon, but I gave Helene the benefit of the doubt since she had been doing my hair for years. Not only was I a good, paying customer, but the total sum of money that I had given her over the years was more than enough to have paid for that new shiny Lexus that she recently bought.

Convinced that it was all just a misunderstanding that would be cleared up once I got to the salon, I borrowed Vance's car once again.

Helene Lamar's Hair Studio is a loud, lively place, but when I walked in all the chatter came to an abrupt halt. Including staff and clients, there were about thirty women in there, most of whom I had chatted with on several occasions, and they were all giving me the stank-eye as if I had personally done something wrong to each and every one of them.

"Nobody speaking today?" I asked jokingly, and I could have sworn I heard crickets.

The tension was so palpable, you could dip it with a spoon.

Liz was manning the front desk, and became so nervous when she saw me that she spilled her coffee all over her work area. Liz averted her eyes and wouldn't even look me in the face as she mopped up the mess she had made. She was an older woman in her late fifties and brought to mind one of those fraggles from the *Fraggle Rock* show that was on back in the day.

"How are you today, Liz," I asked cheerfully. "Is it the coffee that has you so jittery?"

Finally, Liz forced herself to smile and meet my gaze head-on.

"Oh, Eva, hey . . . !" she said as if she had just noticed me standing there. "I'm sorry you made a trip up here for nothing, but like I told you on the phone, Helene is booked up so far into the future that I have no idea when we can get you in."

"I understand that." I smiled. "And that is exactly why I want to speak to Helene myself."

Without further ado, I marched back to the private room where Helene works her magic and walked in to find her with needle and thread in hand, sewing hair into Zoë's head.

"I told you that she was the type of bitch who couldn't take a hint." Zoë sneered, looking up at me through the weft of hair dangling in her face.

"You're damn right, Zoë, and since we're all here why don't you tell me what it is you think I need to know."

"Okay, cool! I think you're a basic, bottom-feeding bitch, and I can't *wait* until you and your shyster-ass boyfriend get everything you deserve!" Zoë said, practically foaming at the mouth. "I should have known better than to let some common, trashy bitch like you infiltrate my clique."

"Let me tell you something, you shallow, idiotic bitch! I considered you a friend, and there is no way that I would have allowed you to invest with Donovan if I had known what he was up to. The truth is, you made a bad business decision and now you're looking for someone else to blame besides yourself and Donovan," I said, taking note that everyone in the salon was ear-hustling, and some women had even come out from under their dryers to listen to the exchange I was having with Zoë. "For the record, I didn't have anything to do with that shit, and I'm as shocked and pissed off as everybody else. Now, all you nosy, backbiting heifers go run and tell that!"

Zoë jumped up and swung at me, barely grazing the side of my cheek with her fist. It didn't hurt. Love taps is what we call them back in Chi-Town, but it did make me angrier. I grabbed a handful of Zoë's hair, twisted it around my hand, and pulled for all I was worth.

Helene is a big, strong woman, so she was able to break up

the tussle single-handedly. Without breaking a sweat, she pinned my arms behind my back like an arresting officer and hustled me out of the salon and onto the sidewalk.

As a teenager, I was kicked out of school a couple of times, out of movie theaters, and even a city bus for being too rowdy with my little friends, but this was a new, embarrassing low.

"Look, Eva, I'm sorry about all this because I believe you, I really do, but you have to understand that this situation that your boyfriend is involved in is deep. It's like September eleventh, where if you weren't affected personally, then you at least knew someone who knew someone else that was," Helene said. She went on to say that not only had Zoë invested and lost her entire trust fund to Dorsey Capital Management but that Zoë's parents also invested heavily with Donovan and have also been so financially ruined by this that they refuse to discuss it publicly and have quietly put Zoë's grand apartment in Manhattan's Turtle Bay on the Sotheby's auction block.

"That's absolutely horrible," I said, "because I love Zoë's parents and I love her too, but this is some bullshit, Helene. You mean to tell me that I can't even come here to get my fucking hair done?"

Helene sighed, looking like she was literally stuck between a rock and a hard place.

"Unfortunately, that's just the way it has to be right now, because I can't afford for my business to be tainted by having fights all up in here like what just occurred," said Helene, parting my scalp with her fingers to access what was going on with my head.

"It's a mess, right?"

"Mmm-hmm . . . but listen, maybe when things settle down and are all sorted out, say in about a year or two, then you can come back and I'll welcome you with open arms, because you know, you my girl!" Helene laughed, trying to bring some humor to the situation that was anything but funny.

Helene gave me a farewell hug and left me standing on the

sidewalk. I felt lost and alone, like a little girl abandoned in rush-hour traffic. Figuratively speaking, it was like yet another death. Helene and I had been more than just hairstylist and client. We confided in and supported each other through our ups and downs, highs and lows.

I had dutifully brought Helene organic chicken soup from Whole Foods after both of her fibroid removal surgeries, supported her through the death of her father, and was a shoulder to cry on when Luis, her Latin lover, maxed out all her credit cards and then left her for Kitty, who had been one of her top stylists at the salon.

No worries. My stress levels were at an all-time high, and my self-esteem was at an all-time low, but I was not going to cry, and I damn sure wasn't going to let these people break me. I jumped back in the Benz and drove over to Essence Hair Salon, a Dominican spot up on Flatbush Avenue and Eastern Parkway, where I had heard that Liza, the owner, was legendary for whipping hair into a frenzy.

She did not disappoint.

After a lengthy consultation, I told Liza to do what she does best as far as cut and style goes, and she immediately went to work.

None of that sitting around leafing through magazines for an hour before Helene even bothered to touch my head.

It cost me fifty bucks and two hours of my time for Liza to take down my old, busted-up weave and to wash and deep condition my natural hair and cut it into a bone straight, asymmetrical side-swept bob that was tapered in the back, which was a look I would have never asked for but was glad she decided that's what was best for me. My new hair was a mixture of contemporary rocker chic and was reminiscent of Salt-N-Pepa in the "Push It" video. It was low maintenance, but still cute and stylish.

It was freeing for me. One less thing to worry about and I loved it!

Oy Vay!

I felt good after getting my hair done, and was excited about my party-hosting debut at Visions later that night, but the feeling did not last long. I pulled Vance's Mercedes into his building's parking garage and was horrified to see that the white Nissan truck that he used as his everyday vehicle was parked in the empty spot that the Mercedes should have been in.

I was so busted.

Vance worked long hours and usually did not make it home at least until around eight PM, and it was only a little after six o'clock. I didn't know Vance that well, but I figured something major must have happened to cause him to come home early.

I let myself into the apartment and walked in on Vance pacing back and forth, furiously waving a magazine around, and yelling into his cell phone. "That's not my problem, Roger, it's yours. You know as well as I do that this story on Donovan is full of lies and half truths, and I want a retraction in next month's issue, or you can expect a lawsuit. . . . You're damn right I'm going to file it on my client's behalf!"

Vance handed me the magazine he had been holding, and I immediately saw what all the fuss was about.

It was the latest edition of *Black Enterprise Magazine,* hot off the presses with the cover story "The Rise and Fall of Donovan Dorsey."

There was a nice photo of Donovan on the cover, one the magazine had obviously taken from a photo shoot with Donovan a year before for a feature named "Leaders in Business." In the photo, Donovan was dressed in an immaculate black cashmere suit with a lavender tie.

His crossed arms portrayed confidence, and he stared into the camera with a cocky, one-sided smile that some people could have interpreted as condescending. And they would have been right, because it was.

While Vance raved and ranted on the phone, I sat down on the sofa and read the article from beginning to end.

It was all standard stuff, and it all seemed pretty factual to me.

"What's the problem with this?" I asked Vance when he had finally finished with his phone call.

"Nothing, but it wouldn't have looked good for me to sit back and not say anything," Vance said. "Donovan has the deck stacked high against him right now, so the best way to create doubt of his guilt in people's minds is to deny, deny, deny, and object to *everything*."

"Good strategy," I said, even though I was thinking that lawyers were some shrewd, two-faced sonofabitches. Mama Nita always said that they could not be trusted as far as you could see them.

"So, how was your day?" asked Vance in a way that let me know he was about to lay into me about taking his car without permission.

"Hey, I'm sorry about not asking to use your car before taking it, but an emergency came up and I had to get there as quickly as possible," I said, which was the complete truth, because my hair emergency really was quite critical.

"Okay, well, this is a good time for us to set some ground rules since we are roommates, in a sense. First, no more borrowing any of my cars without permission, and second, all closed doors are to be knocked on *before* entering."

"Gotcha!" I said, "But you should know that I did knock on your bedroom door this morning, but I evidently knocked harder than I intended to, and it just flew open."

"Yeah, that door doesn't catch all the way sometimes, but from now on, I'll make sure that it's closed all the way, and locked on top of that."

"Same here, but it's not like I'm going to sneak into your room in the middle of the night and molest you."

"Well, one can never be too sure," Vance said cheekily, which cut the tension and made both of us laugh. "By the way, I like your new haircut. It becomes you."

I ran my hand over my newly shorn locks, and smiled. "Why, thank you," I said. "And since you're in a much better mood than when I came in, can I borrow your car tonight for my first day of work at Visions?"

"Visions, the nightclub?"

"Yeah . . ." I said expectantly.

"Oh, no, that's out of the question. I don't even drive my cars to nightclubs because that's when they are more likely to be stolen or damaged in some way," Vance said, always the lawyer. "As a matter of fact, can I have my car keys, please? I need to go check Lola for any dents or scratches."

"Lola?" I raised an eyebrow as I dropped the set of keys in his hand.

"Yeah, I name all of my cars. The Mercedes coupe is Lola, because she's hot and sexy. The Nissan truck is Brenda, because she's so dependable, and the old-school Chevy is Pauline."

"Men and their damn cars," I said, shaking my head.

"It's no different than women and their hair. Especially black women," Vance said. "Now that's an obsessive, love–hate relationship right there!"

"Touché!" I said. "Well, while you go check on Lola, I'm going to go rest up a bit before my shift. Do you mind if I take a catnap in the princess room? It looks so much more comfortable than that cramped little couch—no offense!"

"You mean Sydney's room? Yeah, I guess it's okay, as long as you don't wet the bed."

Rimshot, ka-boom!

Vance's cornball lawyer humor was wearing me out even more than I already was. The first half of the day had been very eventful, starting with my fight with Zoë, and then getting kicked out of Helene's hair studio and pretty much banned for life. That was enough to put anyone's energy levels on low.

"I assure you, I'm housebroken," I told Vance before he walked out to go check on his precious car.

Just as I was about to go down for my nap, the house phone rang so loudly that it almost quite literally scared the shit out of me. There was no way that the phone call could be for me, but I picked it up on the second ring, just to get the noise to stop. "Hello?" I said, trying not to sound hostile, but failing.

"Hi, who is this?" chirped a friendly female voice on the other end of the phone.

"This is Eva; I'm a friend of Vance's. . . ."

I heard the woman taking in a long, deep breath as if she were trying to keep herself calm. "Are you now?" she asked, her voice no longer friendly. "And just how good of a friend are you to him?"

I knew where this was going. I had had the same conversation with other females in the past, but this was Vance we were talking about, so I couldn't help but laugh. "Oh, no, it's not anything like that!" I chuckled. Vance had a body like Terrell Owens and was a good catch for someone, but . . . come on! The guy had zero swag as far as I was concerned. "Vance is just being a sweetheart and letting me live with him temporarily until—"

"Wait a minute, *live* with him? And whose fucking idea was that?"

Me and my big mouth. I had said way too much, and I didn't

even know who I was talking to. "Look," I said, "I really think you need to talk to Vance—"

"I damn sure will be talking to Vance about this!" she said, before hanging up in my face.

I clicked the off button on the handset, thinking that whoever that chick was, Vance had his hands full dealing with her. Whoo! Attitude and drama times ten! I didn't know if she was his girlfriend or what, but Vance had my sympathies, because in just the short amount of time I had talked to her, she had managed to irritate the hell outta me and give me a throbbing migraine.

I could only imagine what it was like dealing with her face-to-face for more than two minutes.

Afterward, I went into the room fit for a princess, where the bed was as comfortable as I had hoped it would be, and fell fast asleep shortly after my head hit the pillow.

I don't know how long I had been asleep, but when I woke up there was a mean, angry mug standing over me shouting, "Vance, I knew you were lying! I thought you said she looked like Forest Whitaker with a bad weave!" I could tell by the voice that it was the same snitty chick I had talked to earlier on the phone, and I thought *here we go again!* As if I hadn't already had enough drama for one day.

It would be my third physical altercation in less than a week, and none of them were fights that I started. Well, except for Mama Dorsey, and I am sure we can all agree that one was completely justified.

"Think about it, Candace," Vance said. "If anything was really going on between Eva and me, don't you think she would be lying in my bed instead of Sydney's?"

"And that's another thing!" shouted crazy Candace. "Why the fuck is she laying bare-ass naked in *my* daughter's bed? Oh, you best believe that I'm burning these sheets!"

Oh, so she was the baby's mama. Poor Vance, having to deal with her deranged ass for the next fifteen-plus years.

I had taken my jeans off and was standing in front of those two wearing just a thong and a T-shirt, so technically, I wasn't bare-ass naked.

"Listen, Candace," I said. "Vance is a really great guy with a big heart but we are not physically attracted to each other, and believe me, there will *never* be anything between us on that level."

Candace must have believed me, because she smiled and said that she just did not want Sydney coming over to visit an unsafe and unwholesome environment. "A mother can never be too careful, you know," she said.

"It's all right, all is forgiven," I said, "but if you two will excuse me I have to get ready for work."

It had been a while, and I didn't realize how much I missed saying those words until I said them. It felt good. I was about to start raking in some major cash, so hopefully it wouldn't be long before I was able to get my own place. That in itself would be a dream come true, because the only real security there is, is that which you can provide for yourself.

Hostesss with the Mostess

Since Vance selfishly refused to let me borrow his car to get to work, I had no choice but to take the bus. As luck would have it, I only had to wait several minutes before the number 6 bus came along to take me down to the meatpacking district.

It had been years since I had stepped foot on a bus, and I had no idea how much it cost, which pissed off the people behind me waiting to get on.

"How much is it?" I asked the driver, who jerked his thumb toward a laminated sign that listed the fare as $2.25, coins and metrocards only.

I didn't have a metrocard so I rummaged through my purse for change.

"What's the fucking holdup?" shouted one of the people behind me.

"I'm looking for change!" I shouted back, which caused some of the more seasoned riders to snicker and shake their heads.

Ahhh . . . public transportation.

I hate everything about it, from the stickiness and the germs to people looking warily at each other, wondering where they were going and what their story was.

The most annoying thing besides the various body odors

coming at you from all directions is that everyone, and I mean everyone from the oldest to the youngest, is yakking on their cell phones all at once.

And in the day and age of iPods and other MP3 devices, there is still at least one Radio Raheem toting around a ghetto blaster cranked up to the max, playing disparaging, woman-hating lyrics.

Bitch this, ho that, suck this, and get down on the floor and crawl like a dog . . . Exhausting!

Sometimes it feels as though the black man has waged war against us. After all that we have done for them, and all we've been through together, this is how they treat us? How about lifting us up, singing our praises, and calling us "Queen"? Then again, I guess that wouldn't sell very many records, now, would it?

No one says a word, unless it's something nasty like, "What the hell are you staring at?" or "Hey, you just stepped on my fucking foot!"

Instead, everyone takes turns sighing impatiently until the bus finally reaches their stop. My stop was one block away from Visions, because I didn't want anybody to see me getting off.

"Hi, you must be Eva!" said a cute, perky blonde who introduced herself to me as Heather. Heather and I had arrived at Visions' employee entrance/the back door, at the same time.

"Yes, I'm Eva," I said. "Nice to meet you."

"Same here," Heather said. "We're gonna make tons of money tonight. Did you see that crowd?"

I had. Out front, there was a long line of well-to-do hipsters waiting to pay the cover charge of fifty dollars for men, and thirty dollars for women.

Heather rang a doorbell, and seconds later a tall, thin guy with a shiny bald head and a goatee opened the door.

"Hey, Paul," Heather said. "This is Eva."

"Ah, Miss New Booty!" Paul said with a laugh.

"Poor girl," said Heather. "She hasn't been here for a full minute yet, and she's being sexually harassed already."

"I'm only joking, of course. This is a fun place to work, so you'll find that we laugh and joke around a lot here," Paul said to me. "Come on in, ladies. The pre-shift meeting is about to start."

I followed Paul and Heather into a large office that had MANAGER marked on the door. There were five other women waiting inside, and I noticed that they were all wearing the same skimpy outfit: black short-shorts and a tight black T-shirt that had VISIONS written across the front in purple.

"Everybody, this is Eva," Paul said. "She's our new VIP hostess, and the friend Amanda told us all about."

The other ladies smiled and waved, but the energy I got from most of them was *Great, just what we need around here, another bitch taking tips away from me!*

After Paul introduced me to everyone, he ran down the half-price drink specials for the night, which were vodka and cranberry juice, Ciroc and Red Bull, and three hundred dollars for a three-liter bottle of champagne.

There had been a huge awards show earlier in the evening, and all of the VIP tables were reserved by some serious heavy hitters. Paul dropped names like Bono, Diddy, and Lenny Kravitz, and some of the other ladies went gaga over just the mere mention of some of the names.

I wasn't impressed. I had met plenty of them before and had concluded that some of the biggest assholes in the world were celebrities. Except when it comes to Prince Rogers Nelson, I just don't get fan worship. At all. They were just regular people whose jobs just so happened to have landed them in the spotlight.

After the other girls left, Paul had me stay behind so that he could give me my uniform and a crash course on how to be a successful and popular party hostess.

Basically, my job was to get the party started and to keep the party going by persuading customers to buy bottles of champagne and liquor. The bigger the bottles, the better it would be for my pockets at the end of the night. Not only was I working for tips, but as a special favor to me Amanda had agreed to give me 12 percent of the total of my combined bar tabs at the end of the night, compared to some of the other hostesses who were only getting around 8 percent.

Since everybody loves to show off their club pictures these days, I was also expected to play photographer and party with my guests by encouraging them to dance and whoop it up.

It sounded like so much fun, I could hardly wait to get started.

Paul showed me to a small locker room where I changed into my uniform, which I must admit I filled out very nicely. I followed Paul out into the club, where it was so dark and crowded, you could not tell the famous faces from just the average Joe.

Paul's parting words to me as he left me in my section of the VIP area was to "Keep smiling, keep your energy up, and have fun!"

My party hostess cherry was broken by a bachelor party of six who were all great guys and excellent tippers. Four hundred dollars just to smile and look pretty and keep the drinks coming? I could get used to that!

Overall, my first night working at Visions was successful. I raked in a little over three thousand dollars, but like Donna Summer said, I worked hard for that money. From eleven PM to four AM, I'd had to deal with folks who should have been popping Altoids instead of more and more bottles of alcohol, and I'd had to deal with a few touchy-feely assholes who obviously thought that buying out the bar entitled them to grab all the ass and tits that they wanted.

"This ain't that type of party, sweetheart!" I told one boozed-up loser, who thought it was funny to lift my skirt up every time I passed by him. I threatened him with my pepper spray, which he thought was even more hilarious. Having had enough of him, I signaled for the bouncers to take care of the guy, which they did, immediately.

My pockets were definitely fatter by the end of the night, but I came away feeling like there was a whorish quality to being a party hostess.

There was no sex involved, of course, but I still had to show off my body, stroke egos, make people feel good, and pretend that I was dealing with the most wonderful and interesting people in the world, yet in the back of my mind I was counting my dough.

Start Snitching

I spent Thanksgiving day with Tameka and her three boys. Besides the noise and the multitude of toys underfoot, Meka had a beautiful five-bedroom townhouse in Gramercy Park that I couldn't believe that Jamal was trying to force her and the kids out of—the heartless bastard. He was really taking Tameka through unnecessary changes, talking about selling the townhouse and setting her up in a smaller, much cheaper apartment.

Tameka can't put a decent meal together to save her life, so she hired a caterer to do all of the cooking for the holiday. Being that she was from High Point, North Carolina, dinner was a Southern feast that included Cajun turkey with wild mushroom and oyster stuffing, green rice, yeast rolls, and Waldorf salad. Scrumptious! I could get with everything on the menu except for the chitterlings, which Tameka insisted were delicious when doused with hot sauce and accompanied by cole slaw.

"No, thanks!" I said, moving the proffered plate of pig guts out of my face.

"Girl, where I'm from, this is good eatin'! You just don't know what you're missing!"

"Yes, I do," I protested. "I've had chittlins before, it's just that my grandmother made me stay up half the night cleaning forty pounds of that disgusting mess for Thanksgiving one year, and I vowed right then and there that nary a chitterling would ever pass my lips again."

"How old were you?"

"About eleven."

"Umph!" Tameka shook her head as if I had her deepest sympathy, then proceeded to devour the chitterlings herself. "You sure you don't want a bite?" she asked, with chitterling juice running down her chin.

"Yeah, I'm good." I frowned, and it was a comical moment, with both of us sitting there shaking our heads at each other as if we just didn't get the other's point of view.

After dinner, Tameka took the boys to go see the latest animated Disney movie, and I went back to Vance's place to shower and get ready for work. I certainly didn't feel like catering to a bunch of rambunctious drunks, but since the gravy train had come to a screeching halt, it was imperative that I keep the coins rolling in by any means necessary.

After working another shift at Visions, it was around 5:30 AM when I got back to Vance's apartment. He was in the kitchen fixing Sydney a bowl of Fruity Pebbles, and even though it was our first time laying eyes on each other, she smiled when I walked through the door, as if she knew exactly who I was and was thrilled to see me. Five years old and cute as all get-out.

"Good morning!" I said, smiling at Sydney and trying hard not to stare at Vance's pecs and biceps, which flexed inadvertently when he moved. He was shirtless, and wore nothing except a pair of Burberry pajama bottoms.

"Hey there," said Vance. "How did it go?"

"It went well enough to make almost three grand," I said, waving the cash in the air for him to see.

"Great—"Vance said, but was interrupted when little Sydney asked, "That's your friend, Daddy?"

"Yes, Syd, this is Eva," he said. "She's the friend that I told you would be staying here for a little while."

" 'Cause she in trouble?"

Kids say the darndest things, don't they? Vance looked caught, and I wondered just what he had said to his daughter about me.

"Umm . . . eat your breakfast, Sydney, all right?" said Vance. "Then we'll get dressed and go to the museum, how's that sound?"

"Kay!" Sydney wiggled excitedly in her chair, and slopped up her cereal, letting milk run down her chin. Vance wiped her mouth, and then gestured for me to follow him into the living room.

Once we were out of Sydney's listening range, Vance said, "I have some not-so-great news for you."

My heart dropped. "Is it Donovan?"

"Well, yes and no. I got a phone call from the district attorney's office, and they want to talk to you about Donovan."

"What? And why would they contact you about me?"

"Apparently they got wind of that press release I sent to the media on your behalf, and obviously assumed that I was your attorney."

I suddenly became a nervous wreck, but Vance remained calm, cool, and reassuring.

"You don't have a thing to worry about, Eva. You were close to Donovan and were the last person to see him before he disappeared, so I'm sure they just want to ask where you think he might be right now."

I remained a nervous wreck for the rest of that week. I worked at Visions on both Saturday and Sunday nights, but I felt like Rosie the Robot, just going through the motions.

★　★　★

Monday morning could not have come fast enough for me. Vance and I rode together to the district attorney's office in lower Manhattan.

Ronald Nash was a mountainous man with cold, piercing gray eyes. When Vance and I walked into his office, he wasted no time with niceties or pretensions. "Well, now, if it isn't Eva Cantrell. Just the woman I wanted to see," he said. "Did you have knowledge of Donovan Dorsey's illegal business dealings but just chose to turn a blind eye?"

"Not at all," I answered truthfully.

Without pause, Nash proceeded to grill me for almost two hours, not asking, but *demanding* that I reveal Donovan's whereabouts.

I told him I had no idea where Donovan was. He didn't believe me.

"You're playing dumb right now," Nash told me. "You don't get a bachelor's degree from the University of Chicago majoring in journalism and English if you're not highly intelligent."

"You've obviously done a background check on me, so you should have concluded that I am as shocked about all this as everyone else," I said.

"Actually, I have concluded the opposite," Nash said with a crooked smile. "You see, more than a few people have stepped forward to say that you were a feeder for Dorsey Capital Management and that they never would have invested with Donovan if you hadn't practically bullied them into doing so."

"That's an outright lie!" I said. "Donovan had a very exclusive client list and was selective about who he took on as a client, so people came to me all the time asking if I could somehow persuade Donovan to let them open an account with them. I never once solicited or 'fed' anyone to invest with Donovan's company."

"Well, the jury is still out on that," Nash quipped, grating on my last nerve. "What I do have so far that is undeniable is the two foreign bank accounts that list you as the trustee."

I gasped sharply. It was all news to me, and I was blown away by the fact that Donovan had constructed such a complex and diabolical scheme that on paper made me look just as guilty as he was.

"How much money are we talking about here?" Vance asked.

"Seventy million dollars," said Nash, "which leaves eighty million still unaccounted for. Where's the money, Ms. Cantrell?"

"What? You can't be serious!" I said, feeling as if I was in the perfect storm with no means of escape. The whole situation was absurd and unreal. Nash's brutal, relentless interrogation made all of my other problems pale in comparison.

"That money is out there somewhere, and we're going to find it," Nash said, "but Ms. Cantrell, you could save us all a lot of time, and the taxpayers a lot of money, by just telling me where that eighty million dollars is buried."

"Okay, that's more than enough—Eva, don't say another word," Vance said. "Mr. Nash, this meeting is officially over, on the grounds that my client may inadvertently incriminate herself."

"Ah, so soon?" Nash whined sarcastically. "We were just getting started!"

"I'm sure you were," Vance said. "Have a good day."

"We'll be in touch!" Nash shot back as Vance and I left the office.

Out in the hallway, my knees were so weak that I almost collapsed.

"This is not a joke; these people really want to send me to jail!" I said, with my voice echoing through the hallowed halls of "justice."

Vance put his arm around my waist to keep me steady. "Calm down," he said. "I don't think it's nearly as bad as he tried to make it seem. Honestly, I think Nash was bluffing a bit, hoping that you would crumble and lead them to Donovan."

"And I wish I knew where he was hiding out, because I swear I would drop a dime on his black ass in a heartbeat."

Later that day, news crews filed into a conference room at Vance's firm, where he made a public plea for Donovan to turn himself in.

Shortly afterward, the district attorney's office put a two hundred and fifty thousand dollar bounty on Donovan's head.

Enter the bounty hunters. From that point on, anybody anywhere in the world essentially had the go-ahead to track Donovan down and bring him to justice.

What Would Jesus Do?

The next Sunday rolled around, and I got my behind up bright and early in order to be front row and center at the Bread of Life Christian Academy, which was a church that Tameka credited with helping her keep her faith strong while she was going through her painful divorce from Jamal.

They say if you're scared, go to church. And facing a long stint in prison for something you are innocent of will definitely make you seek the Lord more diligently.

The Bible says, "Raise a child up in the way they should go, and they will not depart from it." However, I had. Growing up, I stayed in church, and was in attendance pretty much every time the doors opened. However, the only saints I had been acquainted with in the last couple of years were Saint Bart's, Saint Lucia, Saint Thomas, and Saint Maarten, and I had visited the Virgin Islands rather than the Virgin Mary.

It was shameful. Mama Nita would have a fit if she knew, but fortunately or unfortunately, she may never know the details of the circumstances I had found myself in, because Alzheimer's disease was ravaging her memory.

From the minute the news broke about Donovan, I had longed to hear my grandmother's voice and get some guidance and advice on what I should do, but the last few times I called back home to Chicago to talk to her, she had no idea who I was. She kept calling me "LeAnn," the name of her oldest daughter who had died in a car wreck when she was just two years old.

As far as the rest of the family goes, they were all crazy as June bugs in a bottle of liquor, so I could not call any of them for good, sound advice.

The only one I could turn to was God, who unfortunately I hadn't realized was all I needed until God was all I had.

After getting dressed, I went downstairs and waited in front of Vance's building in what I felt was my not so Sunday best.

Since I did not have much to choose from, I'd had to make the best of a bad situation, and was wearing a recession-inspired number that consisted of a Diane von Furstenberg wrap dress from two seasons ago and a pair of flip-flops. It was late November, and my feet were freezing. I was thankful that Tameka had agreed to let me borrow a pair of her heels, because I just could not bring myself to enter the house of the Lord with my bare feet exposed.

Again, Mama Nita would have had a fit. "Don't you *ever* let me catch you going to church dressed like some bummy orphan!" she had told me years ago after noticing that the dress code in churches was becoming much more lax than it had been in her day. "Folks coming in any kinda way, with their toes all out, wearing jeans, and doo-doo rags on their heads. . . ."

"They're doo-rags," I said.

"Doo-who?"

"Doo-rags! That's what they're called, Grandma. Not 'doo-doo rags.' "

"Well, whatever it is, it's a mess!" she said. "As for me and mine, we shall serve the Lord, and we shall enter the house of worship with some respect and dignity!"

Amen.

Shortly after I had walked outside, Tameka pulled up to the

curb and I was dismayed to see that she had brought her rug-rats along with her.

Now, I love Tameka's three boys, the youngest of which is my godson, but they are not the best-behaved children in the world. Six-year-old Jamal Junior was the oldest, and the first thing he said to me when I got in the car was, "Ooh, you ball-headed!"

See what I mean?

"Boy, watch your mouth!" Tameka said, reaching back to swat J. J. on his legs. "And Eva's not *bald,* her hair is just a lot shorter than you're used to seeing her wear it. By the way, girl, you are rockin' that new 'do. It's fierce!"

"Thanks, Meka, I like it," I said, sticking my tongue out at J. J., which made him laugh.

"She looks ball-headed to me!" said four-year old Chavez, and that comment earned him a couple of swats on his legs as well.

Tameka had barely touched him, but the boy started yowling as if she had whipped him within an inch of his life.

I shook my head and thought, *This should be fun!*

Going to church with small kids in tow was distracting to say the least, what with them fidgeting, whining, having to pee every five minutes, and playing peek-a-boo with the people in the row behind them. With Tameka's kids, I was certain it would be all of that times twenty-four, but I made up my mind right there in the car that I was going to tune out all of the distractions and stay focused on receiving the word.

The Bread of Life Christian Academy was a megachurch, similar in size to Madison Square Garden. As someone who is used to much smaller, intimate church settings where everybody literally knows everybody, it felt less like a place of worship and more like a concert hall.

Master Prophet Bishop Londell Gordon was the man in the pulpit, and was nicknamed "The Hip-Hop Reverend" be-

cause of his large following of rappers and other music industry moguls.

He was a dark-skinned man in his late forties, and not only
was he gregarious and handsome, but Pastor was buff, too!

Instead of the usual pastoral robes, the Master Prophet wore
black slacks and a matching vest over a white short-sleeved
shirt that showed off his bulging biceps and well-developed
upper body.

Hello, sexy hip-hop reverend! Not for me, mind you, but
looking at the faces of some of the women around me I could
tell that they were feeling his vibe, despite the fact that he was
a married man of God.

When Tameka and I walked in with the boys, service had
already begun and the Master Prophet Bishop was berating
people for not paying their tithes, offerings, and love gifts like
they were supposed to.

"Listen now," he said like a stern daddy. "I know times are
tough all over for everybody, but no matter how little you have,
you must give *GOD* his share. It is an act of faith that *GOD*
will provide for you and bless you with supernatural favor and
abundance. But you must first give unto him, as he has already
given unto you!"

At that moment, about fifty ushers sprang into action and
started passing silver collection plates around. Tameka wrote
out a check for two thousand dollars, and when she passed the
tray to me, I saw that it was filled with plenty of other personal
checks written for large amounts, and there were a lot more
fifty and hundred dollar bills than there were any other de-
nomination. I added my little twenty dollars to the collection
plate thinking it might as well have been fifty cents.

The day's sermon was on Ezekiel and the dry bones. "No
matter what you may be going through, brothers and sisters, I
serve a God who provides hope in the midst of hopeless situa-
tions, even if we are left for dead!" The mothers of the church
cosigned by moaning, *Mmm-hmm!*

"Whatever your trial, and whatever your dilemma, it's all about faith," continued the bishop. "You will be tried and tested in ways you never imagined. But oh, ye of little faith . . . put your breastplate on, strap on your helmet, and fight the good fight of faith!"

I took a small notepad out of my purse and wrote down, It is all about faith! Hold on to it even when you think things are dead and hopeless.

It was a good word, one I hoped that I would remember as I tried to dig myself out of the hole I was in.

After church, Tameka dropped her kids off with her soon-to-be-ex-husband in front of FAO Schwarz, and I stayed in the car while they made the exchange. Tameka had said it had come to that, with her and Jamal dealing with each other only in public places to keep verbal and physical confrontations to a minimum.

To me, Jamal Harvey looked like a six foot six almond, with his bald, shiny head and dark brown skin. It was well past Labor Day, but he was dressed in a white linen shirt and pants and wore Carolina blue Florsheim shoes made of alligator skin. With no socks. A hot swamp disaster.

Jamal fancied himself a ladies' man, but he was country to the bone. Tameka kept the exchange brief. She kissed each of the boys good-bye, and as she made her way back to the car, I could see anger and tension in her face.

"Ooh! He makes me sick, I can't stand him!" Tameka said through clenched teeth when she got back in the car. "Smiling all in my face like he doesn't own me almost three months' worth of child support and money to pay the bills. I am literally living on credit cards right now, me and his kids just might be out on the street soon, but oh! He can take some barely legal eighteen-year-old white girl on a ten-day vacation to Turks & Caicos, though!"

Tameka was seething, and I could totally see where she was coming from. I had heard all the rumors and seen all the items in the press about how Jamal was tricking dough on groupie hos like it was going out of style. According to the grapevine, Jamal was splurging on expensive jewelry and all-inclusive trips, and just recently, one chick even got an Escalade.

Meanwhile, little Chavez had just had his fourth birthday and all Jamal could manage to spring for was an afternoon at Chuck E. Cheese's, which was a long way from the elaborate party that Tameka had planned for him.

Jamal had simply refused to pay $15,000 for the party, and that was that.

"Ooh! If I hadn't just come from church, there were some words I would have loved to say to him."

"Yeah, but you two have got to develop some kind of friendship for the sake of your kids," I said. "Maybe it would help if you kept in mind that you were madly in love with him at one point and time."

"And now I would just *love* to see him floating facedown in the Hudson River."

I looked over at Tameka and saw that she was dead serious.

That really blew my mind, because Tameka and Jamal had been college sweethearts back at the University of North Carolina, and until just a few months ago had been totally co-dependent, joined at the hip like Siamese twins.

Socially, you just did not see one of them without seeing the other, and now she wouldn't mind if he were pushing up daisies? Scary.

"Girl, don't say that. Jamal is the father of your children. I know you guys are going through it right now, but to wish death on him? It's not that serious."

Tameka stared straight ahead as she drove, looking almost as if she were in a trance. "You know, I was watching that show *Snapped* the other day, where these women just went off one day and killed their boyfriends and husbands.

"Okay, now you're *really* starting to scare me. Will you stop talking like that?" I laughed nervously. "Besides those women on *Snapped* are stupid, and you're a smart girl. I know you wouldn't do anything to jeopardize your kids' future."

Tameka looked over at me and smiled. "No, Jamal is definitely not worth me being locked up in prison and away from my children, but I'm just saying, I don't condone what those women did, but I do understand."

From FAO Schwarz, we headed over to Bubby's restaurant in Brooklyn, which, surprise, surprise, was actually open that day. *Gasp!*

Bubby's had one of the best brunches in town, and it always felt like eating at Grandma's house, but the eatery didn't bother keeping regular, set hours, so all the regulars knew that it was a fifty-fifty chance that they would be open on any given day.

Luckily, they were open that Sunday, and Tameka and I had a long, leisurely brunch. My treat. Since I was making decent money working at Visions, I wanted to start paying Tameka back the money I owed her, money that as I was finding out she could not afford to loan me in the first place.

"It's not much compared to the grand total of my debt, but I want you to have this," I said, sliding three one-hundred-dollar bills across the table. "And thank you again for coming through for me the way you did."

"We're friends." Tameka shrugged. "You would have done the exact same thing for me if I needed it."

I certainly would. And if I didn't have whatever she needed, I would try to move heaven and earth to get it, because that is just what real friends do for one another.

Looking at Tameka just then, I realized that life is too short to waste time with superficial friendships.

People like Zoë Everett do not know the meaning of the word, and only want to be connected to you if the association can raise their profile and status in some way.

Just in the relatively short time that I had been in that circle, I had seen many a "friend" come and go, acquired and discarded the way most people go through toothbrushes. Every two to three months, it's time for a new one.

When it came to chicks like Zoë, there was no such thing as BFF, only BFFN (Best Friend For Now)

Sure, she had been a blast to hang out with, but like Kyle said, friendships should have more depth to them than just hanging out and having fun.

Genuine friends like Tameka and Kyle added depth to my life and were irreplaceable. They also served as reminders that true friendships continue to grow, even over the longest time and distance, and we don't have to change friends if we understand that friends change.

Survival of the Fittest

Because I needed as many jobs as I could get for the time being, I stopped in to Belle's to check the status of my application, and to pick up some tasty treats for my coworkers at Visions. Call it bribery, sucking up, or whatever you want, but when you are the new girl in any situation, bringing in fresh baked goods is a great way to win friends and influence people.

On my way in, I noticed that the HELP WANTED sign was no longer in the window.

"Welcome to Belle's Bakery, how can I help you?"

This time it wasn't Steve who asked the question when I entered the bakery, but a short, pretty woman in her early fifties who I assumed was Belle herself.

"Hello, my name is Eva Cantrell, and I applied for a position a couple of weeks ago. Has the position already been filled?"

"Yes, my son Steve told me about you, and you're every bit as cute as he said you were," she said, offering me her hand. "Hi, I'm Belle."

"Nice to meet you!" I said, shaking her hand.

"No, sweetie, the position hasn't been filled and it won't be filled after all," Belle said. "You see, all of that was Steve's doing. I had a little heart trouble, and he wanted to bring somebody in and train them so that I wouldn't have to work so hard, but the truth is, I don't know how much longer I'm going to be able to keep the doors open around here."

There was so much pain in her eyes when she said those words that I instantly wanted to reach out and give her a hug. I only stopped myself because I know that everybody is not the 'hugger" that I am.

"I'm so sorry to hear that," I said. "You have a great place here, and I would really hate to see you go."

"Well, thank you, sweetie. This little bakery was a lifelong dream of mine, and I never saw losing it this way, I'll tell you that." Belle went on to explain that she was a widow whose husband had left her a substantial insurance policy. Per her husband's stipulations, Belle opened the bakery with part of the money and invested the rest with Dorsey Capital Management. One million dollars. Gone.

Belle's money woes, she believed, were the direct cause of her recent "heart trouble."

And it was all because of Donovan Dorsey.

Standing face-to-face with one of Donovan's victims was surreal, and the magnitude of what he had done hit me in a devastating way.

Not only had Donovan stolen from the super-rich, he had also stolen from a sweet, hardworking woman whose first, and probably only, million came from the death of her husband. I thought of how utterly unfair it was for Donovan to have swindled this poor, sweet woman out of her husband's legacy, and I started to cry.

"Oh, no, don't cry for me, sweetie," Belle said, coming from around the counter to give me a comforting hug. "I'm going to be all right, because God doesn't give us more than we can bear. Besides, I got family down in North Carolina where it is much cheaper to live. But if I can give you a bit of advice, it's never put all your eggs in one basket."

"But I just can't stand how the rich keep getting richer and it's almost always at the expense of decent, hardworking people who are just trying to make it for themselves and their families."

"Unfortunately, it's the way of the world, at least it's been that way since I can remember, and I've been around for a while," Belle said, "but you just have to remember that you can't control what happens to you, but what you can control is your reaction to what happens to you. Remember that, all right?"

I nodded and dried my eyes. "I'm sorry to fall apart in the middle of your shop like this, but I'm going through some things myself, so I've been overly emotional lately."

"No, no, don't apologize, that's fine by me. I have found that it's best to cry if you need to, when you need to, for as long as you need to," Belle said. "Holding it all in is what gets you in trouble."

I felt so much genuine warmth coming from her that I gave her a hug before I left and promised to drop in on her from time to time, just to say hello.

Frenemies

"Well, well, well . . . look who we have here, hustlin' drinks like the two-bit barroom bitch I always knew you were," Zoë said when I approached their table. It was her, Bianca, Sandra, and Pilar, and they had come to Visions specifically to give me a hard time.

"Is this your dream job?" Sandra snickered, with her titties hanging all out as usual.

"Your mother must be so proud to have a cocktail waitress in the family," Bianca said, with her suspect ass.

I kept smiling, determined not to let my temper get the best of me.

"Good evening, my name is Eva and I will be your server for the evening. What can I start you ladies off with?"

"You can start me off with two million dollars, bitch!" Zoë said, causing her cronies to laugh at my expense.

"Anything else?" I asked cordially.

"No, that's it," Zoë said, folding her arms and staring me down. "I'm just going to sit here and wait patiently for my money, because I know you have it stashed away somewhere. Now run along!"

Then the heifer snapped her fingers at me, like I was her dog or indentured servant.

Still, I sucked it up and let it slide. When I turned to walk away, I was pelted with ice chips, and when I turned back around, they were all sitting there as if nothing had happened.

I didn't know which one of those bitches threw the ice, but I did know who was responsible for all the unnecessary animosity toward me. I grabbed an ice bucket and dumped the cubes right on top of her 30-inch Indian Remy Body Wave in Jet Black.

It was an involuntary reaction, it really was, but Amanda was not the least bit sympathetic.

"I still got love for ya, Eva," Amanda said. "But I'm *Italian,* and I'd fire my own mother if she fucked up my money the way you did tonight!"

And that was the end of my career as a party hostess. Grand opening, grand closing.

Imitation of Life

"Don't tell me you lost that damn job!" said Kyle after I explained the ordeal that had just unfolded. "How you gonna let Zoë, of all bitches, mess with your money like that?"

"Anyways." I sighed. "I didn't call to get fussed at. You're obviously at home, so I'm on my way over."

"Uh, wait a minute, Miss Girl. How do you even know I'm in the mood for company?"

"I'm not company, I'm family."

"If you insist. . . ." Kyle sighed like he was being put upon. "But I'm starving, so please don't come empty-handed."

"I'll bring the food if you have the wine."

"Done."

It was close to midnight when I left Visions, and bitterly cold. I caught a cab uptown to Talay Restaurant where they serve the perfect fusion of Thai-Latin cuisine. Figuring that Kyle and I would share everything like we normally do, I ordered the crispy shrimp and plantains with sweet chili aioli, crab cakes with Thai basil mayonnaise and baby greens, and the Thai-Mex chicken quesadilla. Nothing quite eases the pain of being fired like stuffing yourself with good food and good drink.

Kyle lived in Harlem, in a renovated tri-level brownstone on 119th and Third. He greeted me at the door dressed in burgundy silk pajamas, looking like a black Hugh Hefner, only gay.

"Aww, my baby got fired?" he asked, kissing me on both cheeks.

"Yeah," I pouted. "I figured this was the best place to come to lick my wounds."

"Well, come on in, girl! You're just in time—*Imitation of Life* is about to start."

"Which version," I asked. "Black-and-white or color?"

"Black-and-white, of course! Now, I love both versions, but Louise Beavers and Claudette Colbert served the drama back in nineteen thirty-four, honey!"

"I beg to differ, only because black-and-white films are like visual tryptophan to me. There's just something about them that make me sleepy."

"Well, not tonight, because if you fall asleep on me I'm gonna put hot sauce in your mouth like we used to do back in the day."

"Ooh! You remember that? Our sleepovers used to be so much fun."

"Yeah, those were the days. Ah, to be young and carefree again."

"I don't know what you're talking about, because I'm still young, but carefree? Now *that* would be nice."

I loved visiting Kyle's place, which is very warm and welcoming when his partner Irwin isn't home, which fortunately he wasn't. The two of us never quite hit it off. Probably because when he and Kyle started dating, Kyle always referred to Irwin as "trade" and was initially only interested in him because he was a sales associate at Bergdorf's men's store and could get deep discounts on clothing, label whore that he is.

Now, just three months later, Kyle claims to be genuinely in love. I don't buy it. Irwin is five years younger than Kyle, and I always thought he was using Kyle for his nice home and stability. In that case, they were using each other, and a fair exchange ain't no robbery, but in my eyes, Irwin is still trade, and trade does not deserve respect.

When his dancing and choreography days are officially over, Kyle plans to reinvent himself as an interior designer, which he certainly should because his home was an oasis of serenity and a showplace of refined tastes.

Kyle had a lot of Japanese-inspired furnishings, and had decorated the brownstone in neutral tones of chocolate brown and peach, with gold and red accents.

"Oh, and you brought the good stuff!" Kyle said, looking thoroughly delighted that I had brought food from Talay's. "You always did have good taste."

"I guess you taught me well after all, huh?"

"I helped, but you've always had it, my dear." Kyle patted me on the cheek like Glenda the Good Witch. "You may have needed a little guidance here and there, but trust, you've always had it."

Kyle took the bag from me while I took my coat off and hung it in the hall closet. I followed him into the living room where there was a warm glow coming from the brick fireplace, and he had already set up place settings on the large glass coffee table, along with a bottle of white wine.

We sat down Japanese-style on soft, comfortable floor pillows and watched the classic mother–daughter drama unfold on TCM.

"I'll tell you one thing," I said when the movie got to the part where the daughter kicks her poor mama out of her life, "that Sarah Jane sure was one ungrateful-ass bitch!"

Kyle just nodded, trying to hold back the tears.

I had seen the movie several times before, and every time I always came away wishing that I had a mother like Annie. She loved Sarah Jane more than oxygen, but all Sarah Jane wanted to do was pass for white, even if it meant never having anything to do with her mother again.

Sarah Jane did not realize how lucky she was to have such

a loving mother until it was too late and Annie was dead, while I had a mother who, for all she knew, could have had a dead daughter.

Hanging out with Kyle that night reminded me of the old days back in Chicago when we would eat and watch movies together. Only, instead of eating gourmet, it was always some ghetto-ass meal like chili mac with melted cheese, or hot dogs and pork 'n' beans. I was twelve and Kyle was around fifteen when we really started hanging out.

The two of us bonded over the fact that we were both orphans whose biological parents had left us to be raised by relatives. Kyle always was a wise old soul, and whenever I would break down and cry to him about my missing parents, he would comfort me with, "Just remember, Eva, when your mother and father forsake you, the Lord will take you up." At the time, I wasn't exactly sure how that Bible verse applied to me and my situation, but as Kyle broke it down to me, I imagined that because Gwen and Bernard had walked away and left me, God put a force field of protection around me, and no matter how bad things got in life, somehow, someway, I would be sustained and I would always land on my feet.

Hell up in Harlem

I awoke the next morning to find a big brown cat perched on the arm of Kyle's sofa where I had slept. "Hey, kitty-kitty . . ." I said, wondering exactly when it was that Kyle had gotten a cat.

I stretched, and wiped the sleep from my eyes. Then I froze. Kyle doesn't have a cat, because he's allergic to them.

I took a second look, this time noticing that the kitty cat had beady red eyes, a pink pointy nose, and a long skinny tail with no fur on it.

A chill ran through me as I realized, *That ain't no damn cat!*

I jumped up and screamed at the top of my lungs. "*Kyle!* Get in here, quick! Help!"

I started throwing magazines, pillows, the remote control—everything I could get my hands on at him, but Mr. King Rat just looked at me like he didn't get what all the fuss was about. And he sure as hell wasn't scared of me.

Finally, the humongous rodent jumped down off the couch and walked off. Mind you, this particular rat did not scurry away like most of them do. He simply walked off as if he had seen all that he had come to see, and was over it, and buh-bye!

I had heard that the rats up in Harlem are a different breed. By all accounts, they are larger and more ferocious than you would normally find in other parts of the city, and like their human counterparts, the rodents in Harlem have their own distinct swagger.

Kyle came running downstairs wielding a baseball bat and a pellet gun.

"What is all the screaming about, somebody break in?"

"No, it was a supersized rat! He was on the other end of the couch when I woke up—just chilling!"

Kyle looked at me and laughed. "Chile, all that noise over a little old rat? Hello! This is Harlem, baby. You're gonna see a rat or two every now and then. It comes with the territory."

"Well, hell, I didn't expect for him to wake me up and practically ask what's for breakfast!"

"There he is . . . ," Kyle said, noticing that Mr. King Rat was under the dining room table. He raised the pellet gun, aimed carefully, and popped him a couple times in the side. Only then did the rat *scurry* away like rodents were supposed to "Ha ha, got him! I betcha his ass won't be back! Now, you want grits or oatmeal?"

For breakfast, Kyle made smoked turkey sausage, cheese grits, and toasted slices of walnut raisin bread.

We watched the Channel 7 news while we ate. According to the meteorologist, a cold front was moving in from Canada and snow was in the extended forecast.

"And to think," I said, buttering my toast. "This time last year I was packing my bags for an island Christmas. Now there's not even going to be a Christmas this year."

"Girl, hush, there's always a Christmas. It's just up to the individual to count their blessings and remember the reason for the season."

"That's easy for you to say because you have a great career, and this big, beautiful home," I said. "And by the way, what are your plans for the holidays, Mr. Man?"

"I'll be in Miami. . . . " Kyle winced as if he expected me to punch him.

"Miami! See?" I reached across the table and playfully rung Kyle's neck. "Talking about 'count your blessings and remember the reason for the season' when you're gonna be shaking your jelly all up and down South Beach on Christmas Day."

"No, honey, you got it twisted. Killjoy has a concert and a video shoot, so I will be working."

"In the sunshine, enjoying the palm trees, and kicked back on the beach, and yachting in eighty-degree weather with a cold, frothy cocktail or two. . . ."

"Well, hell, work is work no matter where you do it!" Kyle laughed. "But seriously, Irwin isn't even coming with me, so right there you know that should tell you that this is not a pleasure trip."

"Where is Irwin, by the way?"

Kyle sighed and shook his head. "Your guess is as good as mine. He didn't call or come home last night, so I suspect that he's back up to his whorish ways and is somewhere laying up with rough trade. That is the way he likes it, you know."

"Hmm, moving on!" I said. "You know, I've been doing some thinking, and if I can get the money together, I just might go back home for Christmas. I want to see Mama Nita even if she doesn't recognize me."

"That's wonderful, but just make sure you come back," Kyle said. "And don't go hooking up with that Jayson Cooper, and settle down and start having babies."

"Wow, I haven't heard that name in years," I said. "But Jayson was my first love, so I'm single, and if he's single . . . you never know."

At that moment, Irwin came through the door super-sloshed, hammered, drunk as the proverbial skunk.

Irwin saw me and slurred, "What the hell is this broke bitch doing up in here?"

And the lovefest began.

"That's funny, because I was just about to ask the same

thing about you, boo!" I said. "Enjoy your rough trade last night? *Trade!*"

"Hey, knock it off you two. It is way too early in the morning to be going at each other's throats the way you tend to do."

"Your so-called man started it," I said. "With his trifling ass." Irwin gave me the finger, and less than a minute later, he was crying.

"What the hell?" Kyle and I said at the same time.

Irwin slobbered and slurred his words, but was eventually able to get out that he was fired from Bergdorf's men's store the day before for sliding free merchandise to his buddies. He didn't come home because he knew that Kyle would be mad at him.

"You're damn right I'm mad!" Kyle said. "I told you to cut that shit out before those needy, greedy bastards ended up getting you fired, and now look!"

"I know. . . ." Irwin sobbed like a little boy who just got his butt whipped. "I'm sorry!"

I said my good-byes to Kyle and quickly got out of there before Kyle blew his top and the real fight got started.

I sympathized with them, but hell. I had my own problems. I had just been fired myself, and was once again back at square one.

The Fun Zone

The rest of my day was spent updating my resume, and registering at Internet jobs sites like Monster.com and Career-Builder.com.

Afterward, I got the idea to track down some of my colleagues in the publishing industry. My hope was that at least one of them would hook me up with a job, or at least provide me with a lead or two, but it was rough going, because without my iPhone, I was lost.

There had been way more than four hundred contact listings stored in that phone, and now I had to sit for hours racking my brain trying to recall the names of my old college buddies and industry colleagues, and where they had last worked.

Between the white pages online and 411, I was able to round up the numbers of several folks I was sure would do me a favor if it was possible for them to do so.

I got on the horn, and after a few phone calls, I found it amazing and tragic that nobody was where they used to be. Melissa, Lee, and Lorraine had all respectively been let go from *Conde Nast, Time Inc.,* and the *New Yorker,* and I had known a fair amount of folks at *Cosmo Girl, Radar,* and *Men's Vogue,* which had recently ceased publication.

My beloved publishing industry appeared to be down for

the count. The death knell had sounded, and it was all over except for the shouting. It was depressing. Kinda like witnessing the slow, agonizing death of a loved one, and there is nothing you can do about it.

The writing was on the wall: it was time to forge a new career path. But what? Writing was what I had gone to school for, and what I knew for sure that I could do well without hesitation.

Seeking answers, I took one of those online career assessment tests and the end result was: *You are artistic, creative, and best suited for a career that will allow you to display your analytical and writing skills. . . .* Hmm . . . Yathink?

Later that evening, I was in the living room yelling at the clueless woman on *Wheel of Fortune* who'd had the chance to solve two puzzles with a huge amount of money in the bank, but was wrong on both of them.

"It's Rumpelstilskin, dummy! Say 'R' . . . 'R'!"

The woman said "A," was dead wrong, and ended up losing yet another puzzle.

Note to self: Check into getting on Wheel of Fortune. *Potential for revenue—extraordinary!*

At that moment, Vance walked through the door with Sydney in tow. He was home from work earlier than usual, and I couldn't have been more embarrassed to be caught watching television and looking like a freeloading slacker.

To counteract any bad feelings or misconceptions, I told Vance everything that had transpired since I last saw him. Getting into it with Zoë and her goon squad, getting fired, and waking up to a rat staring me down over at Kyle's place.

When I was done, Vance asked his daughter, "What do you think we should do to cheer Eva up, Syd?" Sydney put her forefinger to the side of her head and appeared to be giving it some deep thought. "Dave and Buster's!" she said with such glee, you would have thought she just solved the economic crisis.

"Well, what do you say, Eva, do you want to go to Dave and Buster's with us to have a little fun?"

Sydney looked up at me with enormous doe eyes, filled with so much hope.

And a little child shall lead them. . . .

Dave & Buster's in Times Square is an overpriced tourist trap if there ever was one. It reminded me of the arcades that used to be all the rage back in the 80s, before malls started going bankrupt and every household had its own gaming system like PlayStation and Nintendo.

It was my very first time at D&B, and I must admit that I loved the concept and the energy of the place. It was like an indoor carnival with decent food, jumbo-sized adult beverages, and all the latest games. Fun! Sydney, Vance, and I stuffed our faces with an assortment of junk food like bar burgers, Buffalo wings, and cheese sticks, and then hit the gaming area with a vengeance.

Vance supervised Sydney as she played Crazy 8's and Dance Dance Revolution, while I was drawn to my old-school favorites like Donkey Kong and Ms. Pac-Man.

I felt almost like a kid again, running around sticking my power card in every game that looked like a good time. But, oh! I almost lost my mind when I saw the row of Skeeball machines.

"Ooh, Daddy, look at all those tickets she got!" Sydney said when she and Vance joined me, fifteen minutes into my hot streak. I was in my zone, rolling the Skeeball and hitting the $500 hole three and four times in a row. The machine was going crazy spitting out those yellow tickets.

"Eva's all right, Sydney, but Daddy can get you way more tickets than that," Vance teased.

"Uh, hello! In case you haven't noticed, I'm kinda like a

big deal over here," I said, indicating the small crowd that had formed to watch me do my thing.

"Yeah, but you throw like a girl." He laughed, doing his best to get under my skin. It was working.

"Is that a challenge?" I asked.

"Direct, and in your face, lady!"

I sighed. "Now why do you wanna embarrass yourself like that in public?"

"Don't you know that me and Skeeball go back like fried bologna and government-cheese sandwiches?"

"Oh, yeah? Well, that's nothing, because me and Skeeball go back like Jheri curls and Thriller jackets."

"Ooh, you got me on that one!" I said, giving Vance a high five. "But c'mon and put your power card where your mouth is."

I hated to do it, but Vance got his butt whipped two games in a row in front of his daughter. I felt so bad that I purposely let him win the next two so that he could redeem himself in Sydney's eyes.

By the time we were finished playing, we had enough combined tickets for Sydney to go crazy over in the redemption center, as if she didn't already have enough toys and stuffed animals.

"You guys make a good-looking family," said the woman behind the redemption center counter, as she handed over a stuffed Shrek doll.

Vance and I looked at each other and laughed.

"We're just friends," I said, "and that's his daughter, not mine."

"Well, you can't tell it just by looking at you," the woman said knowingly, and winked.

What the hell is that for? I wanted to ask her, but quite honestly, it did almost feel like we were a family.

Especially once we got back home, and Sydney invited both Vance and me to watch her favorite DVD with her, *Lady and the Tramp.*

Again, how could I say no when she asked in such a sweet and endearing way? "I'm in, what about you?" I asked Vance, who was obviously also unable to refuse any request his daughter made because he was already setting up the DVD. "Of course," he said, "anything for my princess."

The three of us settled down on the couch with a bag of Act II popcorn. Vance and I on opposite ends of the couch, and Sydney in between us. When it came time for Scamp to take Lady out to dinner, Sydney looked up at me and said, "He gon' give her summa his spaghetti, watch Eva!"

Awww . . . *Heartmelt.com!*

That night, I started to look at Vance in a different way. He wasn't the boring, corny stuffed suit I thought that he was. Now that I had gotten to know him a bit better, I found him to be charming and sweet, and could see that he would make an excellent boyfriend. Not that *I* was interested. I'm just saying.

America's Most Wanted

The following Saturday, Donovan was profiled on *Most Wanted Fugitives*. Sydney was with her mother, and Vance and I were just about to walk down to Nobu for a bite to eat, when he got a call on his cell phone to turn to the program. Vance was all over it. He pressed record on the DVR, jotted down notes from beginning to end, and periodically grunted his disapproval.

"Devious, calculating, genius, crook—that is how federal investigators and the Manhattan district attorney's office describe Donovan J. Dorsey, who seems to have pulled off the perfect crime . . . " said Simon Chandler, in that intense and earnest way of his. *"Donovan Dorsey understood the odds. His mother was a short order cook at a popular soul food eatery in Harlem, and his father was never around. Despite the deck being stacked against him, Dorsey rose from humble beginnings to become one of Wall Street's highest rollers Dorsey lived a jet set lifestyle, and seemed to live only for the day. Now, Donovan Dorsey is accused of gaining the trust of hundreds of investors, then swindling them out of close to one-hundred million dollars. . . ."*

Several of Donovan's victims spoke on camera, and some in the shadows, about how the scam had negatively affected them and their financial futures, and what they wished would happen to Donovan as a result.

"One step ahead of the law, Dorsey cashed in his chips a couple of months ago, and said a hustler's good-bye; fleeing the country with his gorgeous, longtime girlfriend. . . ."

They inserted a picture of me dancing on a table at Butter, back when it was one of the hottest spots in town. The photo was clearly from the private collection of someone who had known me personally, and I wondered which one of my former friends had so willingly provided the picture. Bitches.

"Eva Cantrell has since returned to the U.S., claiming no knowledge of Dorsey's whereabouts or fraudulent activities—which certainly remains to be seen!" Simon said snidely, making me wish that I could reach through the television and choke him with his own black leather jacket. *". . . phone records have run cold, and the man that has wreaked financial devastation in the lives of so many has all but disappeared into thin air. America, let's bring this scumbag to justice. If you know where Donovan Dorsey is hiding, please call 1-800-FUGITIVE. . . .*

I didn't appreciate having my name put in it, but overall, I thought it was a good piece. Donovan's capture would be the first step toward clearing my name. Simon Chandler and *MWF* mean serious business, and once they put the word out on you, you are as good as got.

I was optimistic that it would be any day now.

Hi! My Name Is . . .

In her continued quest for emotional healing, Tameka joined a support group that called themselves Ladies in Transition.

"I'm telling you, Eva, those are some of the strongest women I have ever met in my life!" said Tameka, her eyes flashing with excitement. "You should come join us."

And so I did, mainly because I was curious as to who and what was responsible for causing Tameka to do almost a complete one-eighty when it came to dealing with Jamal Senior. She no longer flew off the handle at the mere mention of his name, and there was no more crazy talk of "snapping" on his ass, even though he now had the audacity to question the paternity of Montell, their youngest son.

"Hello, my name is Sarah and I'm here because ever since I lost Charley, my life just hasn't been the same!" sobbed the blond waif seated next to me. It was my very first Ladies in Transition meeting, and we were at the part where the facilitator goes around the room and makes everyone introduce themselves and tell how and why you came to be there.

I always hated that part. Especially back in high school when forty pairs of eyes bore through me, picking my appearance apart from the unflattering mushroom haircut that was my trademark to my corny, unfashionable outfit that Mama

Nita swore there was nothing wrong with. Yes, hard to believe, but I was not the ultimate flyygirl back in my school days. I wanted to be, of course, but there was just no extra money for all that.

"Charley meant the world to me, and I just don't know how to get past it—" The waif's voice broke, and she covered her face with her hands as she burst into tears. A sympathetic chorus of "Oooh"s went around the room. Including Kate, our hostess, there were eight of us in the room. Women of various colors, races, and ages, seated in a circle on brown folding chairs, each of our faces displaying various degrees of distress and bewilderment.

None of us looked like we had anything in common other than the fact that we were "evolving," moving from one stage in our lives and chartering new, unknown territory.

Kate crossed the room and draped a comforting arm around Sarah's shoulders. "Oh, Sarah, we're all so sorry to hear about Charley. . . ." Kate said, patting Sarah's back in the same manner as if burping a baby.

While she took care of Sarah, Kate smiled at me, and nodded for me to continue with the introductions.

"Good evening, ladies, my name is Eva Cantrell and I'm here tonight for support in dealing with financial ruin caused by a recent breakup," I said.

"Welcome, Eva, keep coming back!"

There were eight women in attendance that night, and it was an amazing and diverse group of women ranging in age from early twenties to late fifties and every color, race, and religion, but what we all had in common was that we were each struggling to overcome devastating personal hardships.

There was Irene who was dealing with the sudden, tragic death of her only daughter, and Bethany the hoarder who had a very hard time throwing anything away.

Tameka was there, as was Tiffany the pre-op transsexual, and Mitzi, who cried and carried on the entire time because

just that day she and her hedge fund fiancé were forced to post-
pone their wedding indefinitely because of rumors that the recession was expected to deepen, and last for at least three more
years.

When it comes to support groups, anyone can start one.
There aren't any required credentials or prerequisites, and there
are no boards or committees to apply to. No. All you have to
do is set some chairs in a circle and spread the word.

If you start it, they will come.

So in light of that, I didn't quite know what to expect of
the meeting, certainly no more than a bunch of women sitting
around griping about their problems and crying on each other's
shoulders, but my first Ladies in Transition turned out to be
more helpful than I had thought it would be.

Kate had brought in an expert who gave us all tips on how
to start getting our lives back on track.

I took lots of notes, but what really stuck with me was:

1) Write down one area in your life, whether it is your finances, marriage, health, career, in which you feel insecure, un-
easy, or frustrated. What one thing can you do right now to
improve your situation? What can you do tomorrow and the
next day?

Answer: Liquidate my few remaining assets, including chinchilla and diamond necklace.

2) Procrastination and fear often block our progress. What
task have you been avoiding for at least a month? Why are you
putting it off?

Answer: Liquidating my few remaining assets, including
chinchilla and diamond necklace. Why? Good question.

Recessionista

It was a frigid Thursday afternoon, and I had just left Dalyah on Fifty-eighth Street, where I sold the diamond necklace Donovan had given me for my birthday for three thousand dollars.

The jeweler had gotten over like a fat rat, but I couldn't argue with the fact that the recession had hit so many people so hard that I wasn't the only one trying to unload my baubles for extra cash. Dalyah's display cases were filled with OPJ (Other People's Jewelry), and I was told that there was plenty more of it in the back.

Still, I was happy to have gotten even that small amount of money, and next up for sale was the infamous chinchilla coat.

I was ashamed of the amount of time that it took me to come around, but the fur was the most expensive thing I had left over from my life with Donovan, and I had been reluctant to give it up for that very reason.

I guess you could say that the coat was my trump card and as long as I had it in my possession, I felt like I was somebody, even if in reality I was a poor somebody who was living in the guest "bedroom" of a man I hardly knew.

Plus, it was just time. Not only did I desperately need the money, but karma-wise, I needed a clean slate. The fur coat, the diamonds, the designer this and that—none of it ever truly belonged to me, because every last one of those things was bought with ill-gotten gains.

And bad karma was more than likely the reason why my entire set of Louis Vuitton luggage had been lost in transit, and I had completely given up hope that I would ever see any of it again.

Of course I hated to give it up, but there would be other furs. Ones that I would buy for myself, with my own hard-earned money.

With the decision made, the only thing left to do was find the right furrier, who would give me a fair price for the coat. If I played my cards right, I could walk away with at least twenty-five thousand dollars. Easy.

If that was the case, I would be able to pay Tameka the twelve grand I owed her and have enough left over to repay Vance's kindness and get myself an apartment.

My thinking was, J. Mendel was where the coat came from, and they would probably be the best place to start. I was so confident that I would make the sale that I had stuffed a jacket into my tote bag so that I would have something warm to change into.

After leaving the jewelry store, I headed down Madison Avenue, on my way to J. Mendel. I looked like my old self, which was a well-pulled together fashionista with the world at her fingertips.

I strolled through my old stomping grounds wearing the full-length chinchilla and matching hat that Donovan had bought for me in Paris, and a wicked pair of black Balenciaga boots that Anne Dorsey hadn't stolen, for whatever reason.

Probably because they were thigh-high with spiked six-inch heels, and had a definite dominatrix look about them. They weren't for everybody, that was for sure.

I was looking fabulous with nothing but lint in my pockets, but like Holly Golightly, you couldn't tell just by looking at me.

I had a couple of coins in my pocket, but window-shopping, or "window licking" as the French call it, was all I could afford to do. Before the scandal, window-shopping was an activity that I had never understood or engaged in. I never had to. If I went shopping, I did it all the way. If I wanted something, I simply went in the store and bought it.

Now that I was broke, window-shopping was what I had to be content with if I wanted to do any shopping at all.

I had credit cards of my own, and decent enough credit, which would be foolish of me to take the chance of ruining just to satisfy my urge to shop.

It was hard enough to find a decent apartment in the city *with* good credit, so I could only imagine that having a low credit score would make the task next to impossible, which would only lead to additional headaches that I certainly did not need while trying to put my life back together.

As I got closer to my destination, I noticed that there was a milling crowd a little farther down the avenue, apparently some kind of protest demonstration. People with faces red from anger and the cold waved homemade cardboard signs and offered flyers to passersby who more often than not refused to take one.

I didn't think anything of it. People were always marching, picketing, rallying, and just generally raising hell in this town. If it wasn't Al Sharpton taking to the streets, rest assured someone else would take his place. To avoid the surging crowd, I crossed the street and inadvertently ended up right in front of the Chanel boutique, where my heart went pitter-patter longing for the days when I could walk right in there with my head held high and come out with bags galore.

It took every ounce of dignity I had to refrain from pressing my nose up against the glass windows the same way I had literally seen many a low-end fashionista do, while I was on actually on the other side of the glass window getting my shop on.

Just as I was getting into the new quilted Chanel bag that

was prominently displayed in the window, I heard a voice close behind me chant, "Fur is murder! Fur is murder!" I felt something heavy and wet plop against the back of my coat, and turned to see a lunatic holding an empty bucket of paint, with the color red dripping down the sides.

"Fur is murder! Fur is murder!"

I knew what had just happened, but it didn't register until I looked over my shoulder and saw that the entire back of my gorgeous, insanely expensive chinchilla coat had been doused with paint.

Goddamn PETA supporters!

I was so stunned that all I could do for a full minute was stand there looking horror-stricken, like Carrie after being drenched with pig blood, and right before she went berserko and started fucking everybody up.

My paint-can-wielding assailant looked like Peppermint Patty come to life. She had pimply skin, wore horrible clothes, and was clearly of the belief that women looked better *with* facial hair.

"Fur is murder! Fur is murder!"

It was thirty-something degrees, but I stepped out of my ruined coat and commenced to beating the mustache off that blockhead bitch.

Poetic Justice

On the outside, the Fourteenth Precinct is really quite lovely as far as police stations go. But on the inside, it's a shitbox just like all the rest of them. Trust. Even though I viewed my actions as self-defense, I was arrested for assault and thrown in the slammer with a thuggish and ruggish bunch of broads who all looked as though they had been there, and done that, several times over.

After I was booked into the jail, I was allowed to make one phone call, which I placed to Vance at his office. Unfortunately, he was in a meeting and his secretary had to take a message. I was highly disappointed because Vance's secretary and I hadn't exactly met on the best of terms that day when I burst in demanding to see Vance without an appointment.

When she said, "I'll be certain to give him the message," I was certain that she wouldn't. I was in jail without no bail. Payback was a bitch.

Once the iron door to the holding pen slammed shut behind me, I gripped the bars and shook them with all my might, as if I could somehow pry them open and free myself.

An anonymous voice from the back of the holding cell said, "Bitch, if that worked, I'd have been outta here a long time ago!" which elicited a few laughs from some of the other detainees.

A woman with heavy eyelids and crusted scabs on her face sidled up to me and asked, "Hey, sis, what'chu in here for?"

I loosed my grip on the bars and turned to look at my cellmate.

Frankly, I didn't want to be bothered because she was obviously stoned out of her mind on something that was making her feel mellow and itchy at the same time, but I'd heard it was best not to make enemies while locked up in the pokey.

"Assault," I snarled, trying to look hard and tough.

I relayed the story of what landed me in the slammer, and the woman laughed. "Whoo, I bet you whooped her *ass!*" she said with a hoarse laugh that suggested that she was a heavy smoker.

"What about you," I asked. "What got you in here?"

"Girl, sheeit . . . dealin', hookin'—you name it," she said. "I'm probably gonna get sent out to Rikers, but it's cool. I get three hots and a cot, and can kick my habit all at the same time, so I'm good."

"Hey, two for the price of one is always a good deal," I joked, and we both laughed.

"I like you, you good people," she said, looking down at my thigh-high Balenciaga boots that now had splatters of red paint all over them. "You one of Reno's girls?"

"No, hon, that's not my line of business," I said in a lighthearted tone. "No judgments, though!"

The high, itchy hooker shrugged and moved along to make other, more like-minded friends.

I looked around at my surroundings thoroughly disgusted, thinking that this was definitely not on my list of things to do before I die.

It was cold, and stunk to high heaven with a combination of every foul thing you can think of. Heroin addicts suffering from the effects of withdrawal took turns vomiting into a non-working toilet that was already full of shit and stale piss.

In every corner of the cell, there were women curled up on the floor fast asleep as if they were enjoying the most comfortable Sleep Number bed in the world. I shook my head, thinking that I never want to get that comfortable being locked up behind bars.

Peppermint Patty, who had been arrested for assault as well, sat on a wooden bench holding a blood-soaked paper towel up to her nose. I walked over and sat down beside her. "You know that it's your fault we're both in here, right?" I asked.

"I think my nose is broken," Peppermint Patty said as if she were expecting sympathy or an apology.

"Well, you got what you deserved," I said. "What gives you the right to go around vandalizing someone's property?"

"I'll bet you wouldn't want to wear mink if you knew exactly how those coats were made, and how many tortured animals it takes to make just one coat."

"Pardon you, but it wasn't mink, bitch, it was chinchilla. And how presumptuous of you to assume that I don't know how furs are made. It's the food chain, sweetie. I didn't invent it, and like it or not, it is a practice that will still be in place long after you and I are both dead and gone."

"That doesn't make it right," Peppermint Patty said, self-righteously, "and if I had it to do all over again, I would still throw paint on that hideous fur of yours."

"And ditto for the ass whooping, Boo-Boo!" I said. "So minus the twenty to thirty thousand dollars you owe me for the coat, I guess that makes us even, huh?"

We fell into an uncomfortable silence. After giving her the side eye, I determined that Peppermint Patty was probably much younger than I initially thought she was.

"How old are you?" I asked.

"Nineteen."

Wow, and already so passionate about her beliefs.

That caused me to ask myself, Who are you, Eva, and what are you passionate about besides trunk shows and customer appreciation day at your favorite high-end department store?

Before moving to New York, I was not that girl. I cared about looking good, but I was not a slave to fashion, and was definitely not the label whore that I had become.

Had I grown *up* during the time I had left Chicago, or did I grow *away* from my authentic self? The answer was both. Here I was several years older than this girl, yet there was nothing I was as equally passionate about as this PETA supporter who was willing to get her ass kicked for what she believed in? I didn't have the answers just then, but it was definitely food for thought.

In court the next morning, I was sweating like a whore in confessional. Would I be given a prison sentence and sent up to the big house? It was my first time being arrested, and I had no idea how the judicial process worked.

As it turns out, Vance's secretary did give him my message, and he was there to serve as my attorney when I went before the judge that morning.

In court, the PETA supporter wanted money for medical bills as well as pain and suffering. I wanted money for pain and suffering, and destruction of property.

"Miss Marshall, you are hereby ordered to pay Miss Cantrell five thousand dollars for the value of her coat, and I am giving you both eighteen months' probation."

"Excuse me, Your Honor," Vance said, "but my client was essentially the victim in this case, and eighteen months' probation or any probation at all for that matter is excessive and unfair."

The judge regarded Vance with an impatient scowl, but was silent for a few minutes, considering.

"Six months' probation for Miss Cantrell, and that, young lady, is because you went above and beyond what was necessary to stop your attacker. Miss Marshall's nose is broken, and she had several lacerations in two places, and for that, there must be some retribution. Do you understand?" the judge asked me directly.

"Yes, sir," I replied, relieved that I wouldn't be going to jail and that I at least came away with a moral victory, even though I was certain I would never see a dime of that money.

Defining Moments

The first thing I did after getting sprung from jail was to take a long, hot shower. The second was to pack. More than ever, I wanted to get back to Chicago to be around people who knew and loved me.

When I told Vance what my plans were, he recoiled as if I had said I was on my way to Timbuktu. "Chicago?"

"Yeah, Chicago!" I said. "Don't tell me that you're one of those geographical snobs who think New York is the end all, be all of human existence."

"Well, isn't it?"

He was teasing, of course, and I laughed. "Umm . . . no! Although some of you native New Yorkers like to think so, but I assure you there is a world beyond this city."

"So how long are you going to be gone?"

"A couple of weeks, a month maybe. . . . I'm not sure yet, but I do know that I have taken up space on your couch long enough. So, I'll be back to New York, just not here all up in your space."

"Well, I'm sorry to see you go, but my door is always open," Vance said. "And I mean that sincerely."

"Really? Wow! If I didn't know better I would think that you cared."

"Of course I care. Do you think I would have opened my home to you if I didn't care?"

"How should I know? I thought that was something you do for all damsels in distress."

"Only the really special ones." Vance stared at me with an intensity that he had never directed toward me before.

"Well, thanks again for your hospitality and generosity. I don't know what I would have done without you." I felt like I wanted to kiss him at that moment, so I did. But it was on the cheek, and my feelings were purely platonic, of course.

"Will you do me a favor and leave the addresses and phone numbers where I can reach you," Vance asked. "You know, just in case I need to contact you regarding Donovan."

"Yeah, sure. . . ." I said, giving him the side eye. Again, if I didn't know better, I would really think that he cared about me.

Later that evening, Tameka and I met at Allegretti on West Twenty-second Street for cocktails and appetizers. We also ex-changed Christmas gifts. Of course I couldn't afford to do much, but I bought her a box of Godiva passion truffles and a nice, but inexpensive, bottle of Freixenet champagne. It cost me less that fifty bucks total, and either Tameka was an excellent actress or she really was pleased. "Ooh . . . thank you, girl! You know how I love me some chocolate and bubbly, so I will be getting into this tonight." She laughed.

"As you know, my coins took a major hit this year, but I hope you like it" was Tameka's disclaimer as I unwrapped her gift to me, which was a four-piece Thierry Mugler fragrance set complete with perfume, body lotion, shower gel, and a travel bag.

"Aww, thanks, Meka!" I sprayed a little of the perfume on my wrist and sniffed. It may not have been what she would normally give as a gift, but it was thoughtful and it smelled de-licious.

"No problem. I'm gonna miss you while you're gone, but

if anybody can help you put things into perspective, it's your mama."

"Girl, you don't know my mama!" I said. "I love her and all, but we get along best when I'm in New York and she's not."

"Eva, that's cold."

"It's the truth! When I was growing up, that woman didn't have a maternal bone in her body," I said. "Now that she's getting older, she wants to try to rewrite history and come off like she was Claire Huxtable."

"Well, all I know is no matter what differences you two have, you really ought to work them out once and for all," Tameka said. "After all, you only get one mother. Lord knows I wish I had one right now."

Chi-Town

The 747 Airbus thundered down the runway at LaGuardia Airport and up into a sunny, blue sky. With the city spread wide beneath me, I performed my usual ritual of blowing New York a kiss, and bidding it a fond farewell, for now.

While just about everyone in the world, including Vance, was making plans to go to D.C. for Barack Obama's presidential Inauguration, I was headed in the opposite direction to Chi-Town, home of Minnie Riperton, Chaka Khan, George Daniels, Etta James, Jennifer Hudson, Bernie Mac, Chess Records, R. Kelly, Kanye West, Garrett Popcorn, Harpo Studios, Harold's Chicken, and the infamous Cantrell family.

I made up my mind on the way to Chicago not to tell my family any of what I had been through for the past two months. They were hardly a bunch who read four to five newspapers every day, or who kept the television tuned to CNN 24/7, so there was a good chance that they didn't even know what had happened with Donovan.

Not saying that ignorance runs in the family, just that when life is an everyday struggle, then survival tends to be your primary focus and concern. So if they didn't know, I sure as hell wasn't going to be the one to bring it up.

I flew coach, of course, which was a hot disaster, but luck-ily it was a short flight, around two hours and twenty minutes.

O'Hare Airport is one of the busiest airports in the world, but was especially so that day because everybody and their play cousin was traveling for the Christmas holiday.

The weather in Chicago looked warm and sunny, but it was the end of December, so I knew better. Mother Nature was being deceptive that day because the weather looked a lot warmer than it actually was, so I had bundled up accordingly in antici-pation of the brutal Chicago hawk.

That morning before I left for the airport, I called Uncle Booney and told him what time to come pick me up from the airport.

"All right, baby doll. I'll be there with bells on!" he had said, but wouldn't you know that it was Gwen who showed up instead?

It had been almost a year since I last saw her, but there she was, dressed in the flashiest outfit she could find, looking like my big sister instead of my mom.

"There's my baby!" Gwen said.

As we exchanged hugs, I looked over her shoulder and no-ticed a local news crews.

"What the hell is all that?" I asked, and then got my answer when news reporters shoved microphones in my face and asked, "What can you tell us about your time on the run with Donovan Dorsey?"

"Were you complicit?"

"What did you know and when did you know it?"

"Can you explain why there are several offshore bank ac-counts in your name, to the tune of seventy million dollars?"

"No comment!" I said, retrieving my luggage from the baggage carousel.

I looked at Gwen and knew instantly that somehow, some-way, she was in on the whole thing. "Did you call these people and tell them I was coming?" I whispered.

"Not all of them, but there is a reporter from *Hue Magazine* that's willing to pay big money for the exclusive rights to an interview with you."

Same old Gwen. Always working every angle in hot pursuit of the all-mighty dollar.

So much for not letting them in on my little secret.

Irritated, I snapped, "Where are you parked?"

"Wait a minute, aren't you gonna talk to the people?" Gwen asked.

"Are you freaking kidding me right now?" I asked. "What part of the 'no' and 'comment' didn't you understand?"

"Well, if you're not gonna talk to them, then I sure as hell am," she said out of the corner of her mouth like a ventriloquist. "Excuse me, ladies and gentlemen, I'm sorry, but my daughter is fatigued from her flight and won't be answering any questions after all, but I would like to invite everyone who's watching down to the Sugar Shack nightclub to see me perform, from now until the fourteenth of January."

Disappointed, the cameramen turned their lights off and were ready to pack up, but one reporter was apparently determined not to leave without some sort of "story" and urged his cameraman to keep filming. He did so, reluctantly.

"You're a performer?" asked the reporter, who I couldn't believe was actually taking notes.

"Oh, yes, ma'am, I've been performing all my life," Gwen said, hamming it up. "Would you like to hear a little taste?"

The reporter had no sooner said "Please" when Gwen launched into her rendition of the Stephanie Mills classic "If I Were Your Woman."

Gwen can sing, there's no doubt about that, but in the middle of Southwest Airlines terminal B was neither the time nor the place.

I didn't know where she had parked, but I walked away and left Gwen to her one-woman show.

An odd-looking man with a jughead and Harry Potter glasses

trailed behind me. "Excuse me, Eva, I'm Larry Nichols with *Hue Magazine*. Can I have a word with you for a moment?"

"No, sir, you cannot. . . ." I said.

"But I talked to your mother, Gwen, and she said you would—"

"I don't care what she said, I'm not interested—so kick rocks, dude!"

"Well, she has my number in case you change your mind."

"Thanks, but I won't be," I said, and turned around when I heard a smattering of applause.

Gwen had wrapped up her "little taste" and was bowing and blowing kisses as if she were the celebrity she had always wanted to be, instead of the best backup singer who never made it big. Over the years, my mother has sung background vocals for most of the legends in the game, including B.B. King, Buddy Guy, and even Ike Turner for a short time after Tina wised up and left his ass. Gwen's dreams of solo superstardom have eluded her at every turn, but that doesn't keep her from trying and hoping that the next two-bit gig will be the one that will finally land her a recording contract.

"You know, I really didn't appreciate that," I said, once we were finally all settled in Gwen's Chrysler Fifth Avenue.

"What? I thought it was fun!" she said, checking her reflection in her Fashion Fair compact and rubbing lipstick off her teeth.

"As a mother, what would possess you to try to pimp my story out to the media?"

"Well, ain't that about some ungrateful-ass shit? Hell, I figured that I was doing you a favor," said Gwen. "I mean, you do need the money, don't you, or is it true what they say about you having some stashed somewhere for a rainy day?"

I swallowed my exasperation. I couldn't believe that she had gotten started already. "If that were true I wouldn't have been living from pillar to post for the past month and a half."

"And speaking of that, why haven't you called me, girl? I've been worried sick about you!"

"And where was I supposed to call you at, since you don't believe in cell phones, and the last time I talked to you, you were headed to Las Vegas for a gig?"

"That ain't no excuse, you could have called Mama Nita's house—you know Booney is always there," Gwen said, taking my hand. "But that's okay, you home now! You can get your life back on track and forget all about that bullshit back in New York. I know Jayson Cooper is gonna be so happy to see you."

"Kyle said that same thing, but life happens. He's probably married with a bunch of kids by now."

"I don't think so, because he asks about you all the time. He's got a good job down at the hospital, you know."

I laughed long and hard at that one. Did I mention that my mother was an amateur comedian as well?

"What's so funny about that?" asked Gwen. "A good man is a good man, no matter what he does for a living. That's what's wrong with you young girls out here today. Every man you meet can't be Donald Trump, you know."

"Wow, no you didn't," I said. "This coming from a woman who once told me to marry well, and repeat as often as necessary."

"Now, you know good and well I didn't tell you that, and God can strike me dead right now if I'm lying."

I hoped that God wouldn't strike her dead at that moment, because there was no way for him to get Gwen without getting me too.

Now that Gwen is older and it's time for her to get somewhere and finally start to settle down, she is starting to see the error of her ways and wants props where props are not due, or deserved.

She knows damn well she was a lousy mother, but in order

to make herself feel better, she has resorted to rewriting history and making herself out to be a saint in her own eyes.

In Gwen's new and improved version of events, she was a selfless, nurturing, dedicated mom. And not the type who packed up and left town without a word of good-bye to anyone, chasing the rainbow wherever some two-bit gig, or sapsucker she'd met in a nightclub, led her, which was usually some dead-end town where there was no pot of gold in sight.

While Gwen jabbered on a mile a minute trying to defend her mothering skills or lack thereof, I tuned her out and watched the world I used to inhabit go by.

Not much had changed on the West Side, except there seemed to be more liquor stores on every other corner, over-priced check-cashing joints, more abandoned homes, and boarded-up buildings where thriving businesses used to be.

After years of saving money from numerous side hustles, including doing hair in the kitchen, to selling her infamous gumbo for a dollar a bowl, Mama Nita finally moved out of Cabrini-Green almost ten years ago, and into her current K-town neighborhood on the west side of Chicago, which truthfully wasn't much better than the projects. "K-Town" was nick-named such because all of the streets that run through the ad-joining neighborhoods start with the letter "K"—King, Keeler, Kilpatrick, Kostner.

The area has always been infamously crime ridden, but at least Mama Nita had a tiny parcel of land that she could call her own.

And the four-bedroom bungalow-style house on Eigh-teenth and Keeler was the best-looking house on the block.

We might have been poorer than most when I was grow-ing up, but my grandmother was a stickler for cleanliness and a firm believer that whatever you had should be kept immacu-late and well maintained at all times.

As we pulled up, I was glad to see that even with her Alz-heimer's someone was making sure to maintain her standards.

It had been a year since my last visit, only that time, Donovan had come with me to visit my folks. And now, just like then, all of my immediate family was there to greet me. The group included my uncle Booney, my sister Pam, and her two daughters, Olivia and Kelly.

"There she is!" said Pam, hitting me with a flying hug, while my six- and eight-year-old nieces hugged me around the waist also. We walked inside the house.

"Girl, what's this I hear about you getting caught up in some gangster shit?" asked Uncle Booney.

"*Hel-lo!*" Gwen said, pointing to the kids as a reminder that they were present.

"My bad, my bad!" Booney said. "But did you make off with all that money like they said you did, girl?"

"Don't believe a word of it, it's all hearsay," I said, giving him a hug, and then quickly changed the subject. "Look at you, though! Looking like a ray of sunshine!"

My mother's older brother was as flashy as ever in one of his signature polyester outfits. This one was a bright yellow, bell-bottom jumpsuit with a butterfly collar, and it was putting a serious hurtin' on my eyes.

"Hey, niece, you know me. Doing what I do as only I can do it. . . . Don't let the smooth taste fool ya!"

"You sho'nuff got that right!" I said, speaking Booney-ese. I shook my head, tickled by the fact that no one had yet been able to convince him that multiple gold chains, chest hair, and butterfly collars were no longer fashionable.

The laughter died down as I looked around and noticed that the house looked and felt sad.

It was the day before Christmas Eve, and there were no Christmas lights in the windows and no nativity scene in the front yard. The only thing to give away that it was Christmastime was the sad-looking Charlie Brown pine tree propped up in front of the bay window, with not even one present underneath. It was worse than a Charlie Brown tree, because it was artificial and didn't fill the house with the wonderful scent of fresh pine, which to me was the whole point of having a tree.

It was depressing, especially in light of the fact that Mama Nita loved the holiday season and usually went all out, even on a meager budget. Clearly, what the house, and those of us who loved my grandmother, needed was her love and personal touch.

"Where's Mama Nita?" I asked, setting my bags on the floor.

"In bed," Pam said. "That medication she's on has her sleeping almost half the day."

"How is she doing?" I asked.

"The Alzheimer's is still progressing, and getting worse every day," Gwen said, with uncharacteristic concern for someone other than herself.

"Well, I'm going to go peek in and say hi," I said, causing everyone to object all at once.

"When she's sleep, it's best not to disturb her," said Pam.

"Yeah, and besides, she comes and goes so much that she probably won't even recognize you."

We all chatted and caught up with each other for a couple of hours, until later that night, Pam dropped Olivia and Kelly off with their father, then she, Uncle Booney, and I went down to the Sugar Shack to watch Gwen do her thing.

The Sugar Shack is a neighborhood blues and jazz joint over in Englewood. The club has no frills whatsoever, but it is still the place to be for live music and the best BBQ ribs in Chicago.

We walked up the long, steep staircase to the upper floor and saw that people were packed in like sardines.

Onstage, a local musician who I recognized as Lil Earl was performing a spirited version of "Sweet Home Chicago."

A voice in the crowd shouted, "Hey, everybody, Booney's in the house!"

The crowd parted like the Red Sea to make room for my

uncle, who has been well known and respected at the Sugar Shack for many years.

The Cantrell family is full of talented people who could have gone all the way and been superstars if fate and circumstances would have been kinder.

Like Gwen, Uncle Booney was also musically gifted, but unfortunately, his only claim to fame is that he was a member of the music group Earth, Wind & Fire before they made it big. He was the star and lead singer of the group until one night after the group played a gig at the old Palladium, someone slipped him a joint laced with PCP, and he had to be hospitalized for two weeks. The diagnosis: Uncle Booney was "stuck," meaning that he had lost a few of his marbles and would never quite be the same again. (Hence the fashion time warp and the choice to wear a wool coat and leather gloves in the middle of July.)

The other members of Earth, Wind & Fire made the unanimous decision to replace Uncle Booney with an equally talented lead singer named Philip Bailey, and the rest is musical history.

Ever since that fateful night, my uncle has lived under my grandmother's roof and received monthly disability checks that have to be doled out and closely monitored, or else he will end up tricking all his dough on manipulative women who know that he's generous, plus not wrapped too tight when it comes to sound judgment.

Uncle Booney led the way to a table directly in front of the stage, which a couple gladly gave up when they saw us coming.

"This place sure hasn't changed much," I said to Pam as we took a seat.

"And neither have the people," Pam said. "Girl, talk about country!" The Sugar Shack catered to an older crowd, I'd say around thirty-five and up. It was true that some of the regulars looked like they were fresh out of the backwoods, sporting finger waves and Jheri curls as if it were still 1985. It was no wonder that Uncle Booney felt so at home there.

"I'm going to go cut a rug," said Uncle Booney, his eyes following the big behind of a woman who had just walked past him. "I'll catch up with you two later."

"All right, now, cat daddy," I said, "don't hurt yourself!"

"And don't put nobody's eyes out with that bright suit!" Pam called after him, as he disappeared into the crowd.

Gwen took her own sweet time in hitting the stage, but when she did, she came out totally transformed. Her makeup was heavy but flawless, and her wig game was proper. She wore black slacks, and a black sequined top that looked like sparkling diamonds when it caught the light.

"Good evening, everybody!" Gwen said. "Before I get started, I want to say a special hello to my two daughters who are both here with me tonight—Eva and Pam . . ."

With that said, she launched into a medley of blues classics, including "Cheatin' in the Next Room" and "Let's Straighten It Out."

The crowd was loving her, and we were all in agreement that Gwen was giving it her all and was tearing the roof off the mother-sucker.

"Look at your mama; she's a star up in here!" Pam said, like a proud parent.

I was proud of Gwen, but in a way, it felt like I was watching a stranger perform up there, because really, we hardly knew each other.

Who's That Lady?

Later, in the wee hours of the morning, I woke up on Mama Nita's plastic-covered couch to the sound of breaking glass. I got up to investigate, and gravitated toward the only light that was on in the house, which was coming from the kitchen. There was food all over the counter, and my grandma had dropped a glass full of milk onto the floor, and the splatter was everywhere, including down the front of her nightgown.

"Grandma Nita, what are you doing?" I asked, grabbing some paper towels to clean up the mess on the floor.

"I'm making myself a snack, what the hell does it look like I'm doing?" she asked, sounding like her old self, but not really. There was no hint of love in her tone. She was just downright *mean*. "And what are you doing here, anyway?"

"I came to visit you for a while. Didn't Gwen tell you?"

"Gwen who?"

"Gwen, your daughter. . . ." I said, swallowing the lump in my throat. "Your youngest child? My mother?"

There was no flicker of recognition in her eyes, and Mama Nita didn't respond.

Instead, she went back to earnestly slapping together a raw bacon and peanut butter sandwich. "Well, where is LeAnn?

She's the only one that I can count on to do anything for me around here."

I didn't know how to answer that. LeAnn was my deceased aunt, and my grandmother's firstborn child who had passed away due to a car crash, years before Gwen was even born.

The story behind my aunt LeAnn's death was that Mama Nita was nineteen years old and had just learned how to drive. Car seats had yet to be invented, so when the accident happened, the baby didn't have a chance. Mama Nita was so devastated that it was her inexperience as a driver that led to LeAnn's death that she never forgave herself, and she never got behind the wheel of a car again.

"Come on, Grandma, let me help you." I tried to steer her toward a chair at the kitchen table, but she slapped my hands away.

"Will you leave me alone and get out of here?" she screamed, and then flew into a fit of rage, wildly raking everything that was on the counter onto the floor.

For the first time in my life, I was scared of her. Not only did my grandmother not recognize me, but she was volatile and many times stronger than I was.

Luckily, Gwen came into the kitchen and took control of the situation.

"Mama, calm down!" said Gwen. "What is it that has you so upset?"

"LeAnn, where have you been, girl?" Mama Nita asked Gwen. "Now, I done told you about inviting strange folks up in my house, now didn't I?"

"Yes, ma'am, you did," Gwen said, holding my grandmother close and stroking her back to calm her down. "I just had to go take care of a few things, but I'm back now. . . . Come on, let's go back to bed."

Mama Nita took hold of Gwen's hand as if she were a lost child, and let her lead her back to her bedroom.

Deck the Halls

Later that same morning was Christmas Eve. I sat at the kitchen table drinking a cup of weak instant coffee and watching the snow come down in big, fluffy clumps. If the snow kept up, it would be a white Christmas in Chicago after all. I was also trying to figure out what gifts to give everyone on my extremely low Christmas fund budget, when Gwen walked in wearing a silk floral robe and a silk sleep bonnet on her head. She was still attractive without full makeup, but she looked a bit worn out and sad.

"How did you sleep last night?" she asked, joining me at the table.

"I didn't," I said. "I couldn't stop thinking about Grandma Nita and what she's going through."

"Yeah, it's hard to watch, I'll tell you that. But, as heartbreaking as it is for us to see her deteriorate, it's even worse for her," Gwen said. "On some level, she knows what's happening to her, and she scared to death. That's why she lashes out like she did last night."

"Of all people, why did this have to happen to her? She was the most vibrant person I knew."

"That's life, baby. Sometimes all you can do is learn how to roll with the punches."

"What hurts the most is that she didn't even recognize me," I said. "Mama Nita helped raise me, and now she has no idea who I am."

"It makes you realize that life is so much shorter than you think it is, and one day we're all going to have more yesterdays than we have tomorrows."

I looked at Gwen wondering when she had grown up, and why she hadn't had all of this motherly wisdom when I needed it the most. If the sweet, levelheaded woman sitting across from me had been consistently present when I was kid, we would have a completely different relationship.

I guess the saying is true: Better late than never.

That afternoon, I braved the cold and the snow and joined the masses of last-minute Christmas shoppers at Woodfield Mall. There was a mall Santa who was popular with the kids, and the place was decorated with millions of Christmas lights and other festive decorations, but the mall was also a madhouse, times ten.

People were shoving each other and practically snatching merchandise out of each other's hands. I'm talking about no Christmas spirit being shown whatsoever.

After about half an hour, I determined that a $200 Visa gift card for the adults and $75 for each of the kids was fair given my circumstances, and called it a day.

Just as I was about to leave the mall and head to Bank of America, I felt my pay-as-you-go cell phone vibrating in my purse.

I was surprised about two things: 1) that I was able to get reception, and 2) that it was Vance. What could he possibly want?

I plugged my index finger in my ear and answered, "Hello?"

"Hey, Eva, how'ya doing? It's Vance."

"Hey, how are you?"

"I'm good," he said. "I was just calling to make sure you made it to Chicago safe and sound."

"Oh, how sweet! Yeah, I made it okay. . . ."

"That's great! I also wanted to say Merry Christmas, and to tell you that I have some meetings in Los Angeles coming up, and I thought I would make a stop in Chicago on my way," he said. "If that's all right with you."

"Yeah, it's cool," I said. "When are you coming in?"

"In a couple of weeks, but I just wanted to give you a heads-up," said Vance. "I'll be staying at the Ritz Carlton downtown, and I'll give you another call just as soon as I get in."

"Well, cool! I look forward to seeing you."

"Same here," Vance said. "And, Merry Christmas, Eva." He said it with a degree of tenderness that is usually reserved for lovers.

I didn't know why Vance was making a pit stop to see me on his way to the West Coast, but I was certainly intrigued. It had only been a day since I had last seen him, but at that moment, I realized that I kinda missed him.

Being in the midst of my family for the first holiday season since I had left home years before felt wonderful.

It wasn't exactly a Waltons' family Christmas, but it did feel like old times, and at least there was no bloodshed like the year second cousins Bridget and Marcia got into a death match over an unpaid loan.

Pam and I cooked dinner while the kids played in the living room, and my grandma sat on the couch staring blankly at the television, which was tuned to TBS and *A Christmas Story* marathon. She hadn't uttered a word all day, which was much more terrifying to me than the violent outburst she'd had on my first night home.

In the kitchen, I prepared my specialties of homemade cranberry sauce, yams topped with marshmallows, and banana pudding. Pam was now the best cook in the family because

Mama Nita was no longer able, so she took care of the turkey, ham, cornbread dressing, and all the other fixings.

Uncle Booney was off somewhere spending the day with one of his many lady friends, and Gwen had left earlier that morning for the annual Christmas Day Blues breakfast where she was performing. It was a BYOB event put on by the radio station WHPK FM and is a big deal among local blues lovers. They get a chance to dress up and go dance, eat, and get drunk from eight in the morning until one in the afternoon.

It was just as well that she wasn't there, because nobody wanted or expected her to cook anything, anyway. Gwen liked to drink wine while she cooked, which we have all learned the hard way is a big no-no for her. More often than not, all she does is end up ruining everything she touches.

For example, one year when I was about fourteen, Gwen happened to be home for the holiday and was supposed to be helping Mama Nita in the kitchen. She had been sipping on Carlo Rossi sangria for most of the day, and accidentally put two cups of salt in the sweet potato pie instead of two cups of sugar. Our aunt Anita got so sick after taking a big bite of that nasty pie that she had to be rushed to the emergency room because of her high blood pressure.

"So what's up with all that missing money, girl?" Pam asked in a whisper, as if the house were bugged.

In the middle of slicing bananas for the banana pudding, I threw my head back and sighed. "Not you, too! Look, you know me," I said. "If I had an inkling where that money was, please believe that we would all be living on our own secluded island somewhere with pink sand and turquoise water, and I would be paying my own personal team of scientists to come up with a cure for Alzheimer's."

"Now, that's true. . . ." Pam said. "But listen, I have something in the works that has the potential to make us all rich. I'm talking about dream house, and hand-over-fist money."

Pam was just as bad as Gwen was when it came to pie-in-the-sky ideas, and was always on the lookout for a big come-up. She was thirty, three years older than I was, but she had started her illustrious career as a hustler at the tender age of seven, with the usual lemonade stand and paper route. Around age thirteen, Pam got wind of a hair product called Rio Hair, which claimed to straighten even the toughest grade of hair without lye or other harsh chemicals.

Supposedly, all you had to do was comb the product through your hair, rinse, and enjoy. My sister saw Rio Hair as her ticket to riches, and saved up her allowance money she got from her dad and bought several jars. Me being an impressionable ten-year-old, I was all too eager to have long, illustrious hair like the woman on the jar, so I agreed to let Pam use the product on me.

You see where this is going, right?

Let's just say that it is very damaging to the self-esteem of a ten-year-old girl to be "ball-headed," as Jamal Junior would say.

In the years following the Rio Hair debacle, Pam's list of get-rich-quick schemes would grow to include Quixtar, phone cards, Kirby vacuum cleaners, vitamins that promised to cure all ailments, including diabetes and cancer. And the list goes on and on.

Now, I understand that you are a single mother, and have to do all that is necessary to make it and provide a good life for your kids, but if it sounds too good to be true, then it usually is.

"What do you have going on now, Pam?" I asked, trying to sound enthused, but failing.

"Sis, let me tell you!" she said, launching into a long-winded presentation about a proposed business that would operate like a personal assistant to single mothers in the Chicago area. From running errands to picking the kids up from football practice, whatever was needed Pam's proposed business would take care of it for you, for a reasonably priced annual fee.

"Members can donate their gently used children's clothes, and in exchange, buy things for their own kids at very affordable prices," Pam said, her eyes shining with excitement. "And they'll also get discounted rates from local businesses, like day care, dry cleaning, housekeeping services, you know . . . stuff like that."

"Do you have a business plan?" I asked, cautiously.

"Oh, yeah. The Small Business Administration has been helping me work on my business plan for the last month or so, and I'm almost done," said Pam. "Then the next step after that is to try to secure funding."

I thought it over for a minute or so, then put my knife down, wiped my hands on a dishtowel, and gave Pam a big hug.

I was impressed. Rather than coming up with yet another go-nowhere, boarding on illegal scam, my habitually conniving sister had come up with a very unique and practical idea that could actually net profits.

"Me likey!" I said, giving Pam a high five. "If I were a single mother, I would definitely be interested in a service like that."

"See, and you thought it was gonna be about some bull-crap, didn't you?"

"Well, it's not like that hasn't been your M.O. all these years, but I'm happy for you, sis," I said. "What are you going to name the business?"

"That is yet to be determined, but right now, I'm leaning toward Mother's Helper."

"Perfect!" I said. "Say no more, done and done!"

"Aww, thanks, Eva," Pam said, initiating another hug. "It's so good to have you home, I missed my little sis. Even though little sis is all grown up and getting into trouble on a much bigger scale."

"Girl, tell me about it! And it's not even like its some shit that I actively participated in. Contrary to what it may look like, it's all completely circumstantial."

"I know, but those are some hellified circumstances," Pam said. "The media has you looking like Queen Bee of the Ponzi scheme, and like you and Donovan sat at the kitchen table and planned all that shit out from day one."

"And that's the part I hate the most," I said. "Lord knows there's nothing I hate worse than being accused of something I didn't do."

Pam laughed. "Shoot, don't I know it!" she said. "Remember that time you wanted to fight me every day for a week because I told Grandma you broke her big, crystal candy dish, when I was really the one who had done it?"

"Oh, yeah, I remember!" I said. "I got the butt whooping of life, *and* was put on punishment for a month behind that lie, so I had to get you back some kinda way."

"Mama Nita did not play when it came to tearing stuff up around her house! I felt so bad, but my thinking at the time was 'better Eva than me!' "

I laughed at the memory, which was another reminder of how vibrant my grandmother used to be. She was very much alive, but in a way, it felt like she had already passed on.

"What do you think she would say about this whole situation with Donovan?" I asked.

"Whoo! Girl, so many things," Pam said lightheartedly, "but I think the main thing she would say to you right now is hold on tightly to your faith, and somehow, some way, this too shall pass."

I nodded. "That sounds about right."

And if I were completely honest with myself, I would have to admit that Mama Nita would also be disappointed that she had sent me off to New York with hopes of being a shining star and leader in my field, but I had inadvertently become a woman of leisure and was now embroiled in a scandal that could possibly land me in prison.

Just when everything was all done, and it was time to eat dinner, Gwen walked in the kitchen with all the grandeur of a Dream Girl. Big bouffant wig, full makeup, and a gold, sequined beaded dress that looked like it weighed about a hundred pounds. "Hey, my babies! I see ya'll have everything under control in here."

"Yes, we do," I said. "Which is more than I can say for you. Seriously, when you're drunk at two in the afternoon, where do you go from there?"

Gwen cupped my chin and sang, "You got'ta take it *higher!*" she said, putting her own spin on the old James Brown hit.

Pam shook her head and moaned, "Oh, Lord . . ."

Gwen whirled around in Pam's direction, and asked, "What are you over there 'Oh Lording' about? 'Tis the season to be jolly, right? I had two glasses of champagne, and y'all are up in here acting like I'm sloppy, falling-down drunk. And if I was, so what! I'm the mama around here!"

Pam and I raised our eyebrows and looked at each other as if to say, "Yeah, right!"

Mama of the house, indeed. As if she were the one who cooked our breakfast every morning before school and took us down to Miss Lenora's Beauty Box on Saturday mornings, if she were too tired from the previous workweek to press 'n curl our hair herself.

The true "mama of the house" was out in the living room with her mind in the grips of a vicious disease that had rendered her a shell of her former self.

While Gwen was off traipsing around the globe as if she didn't have kids, or a care in the world, my grandmother was the one making all the sacrifices and working hard to put food on the table for not only me and Pam, but for anyone who showed up on our doorstep with a long face and a sad story.

And they came often. There is at least one house in every neighborhood that people flock to the most. Ours was it.

Even though Pam, Uncle Booney, Mama Nita, and I were the primary residents, the three-bedroom garden apartment in Cabrini-Green was always crowded with neighbors, friends, and extended relatives.

People sat in the kitchen having political discussions about "the man" and the sorry state of the country. They sat in the living room and watched the *Cosby Show* and *Dynasty* on the bulky floor model TV that also doubled as a plant stand. And at all times, there were at least two people sitting on the front or back porch smoking a cigarette and/or reefer and watching the world go by.

"Looking good, looking good . . ." Gwen said, as Pam brought the eighteen-pound turkey out of the oven and set it on the stove. "What do y'all need for me to do?"

"Set the table, and rally the troops," I said, while removing the homemade cranberry sauce from the fridge, which I was pleased to see had set perfectly. Gwen went out into the living room and came back a couple of minutes later looking scared and on the verge of hysteria. "Where's Mama?" she asked.

"In the living room with Olivia and Kelly," I said.

"No, she not," Gwen said. "The kids are out there taking a nap, and I just checked the whole house, and she is nowhere to be found!"

"Well, you stay here with the girls," I said, taking off my apron. "Call all the neighbors, and go throughout the house and check all the closets."

Pam turned off all the burners on the stove, and the two of us ran into the living room where we scrambled to put on our boots and coats.

It was a very dangerous thing for a victim of Alzheimer's to wander away from home unattended, but it was even more so in extreme temperatures.

Awaiting us when we walked outside was a bone-chilling eighteen degrees that, combined with the high winds coming off Lake Michigan, forced the wind chill well below zero. To make matters worse, it was still snowing just as it had been all day, adding to the several inches that had already fallen.

There were other houses to the east and west of us, leaving north and south as the only logical directions to take off in.

"I'm going this way," Pam said, and took off running south up Kessler Avenue without taking the time to discuss a solid plan of action.

As I began to head north, I put my detective hat on and noticed that there were tracks in the snow that led straight away from Mama Nita's house and into the Hensons' yard, directly across the street. The Hensons' yard went straight through to Parker Avenue, where there are businesses and a lot more traffic.

I followed those tracks in the snow for fifteen minutes until I saw a lone figure standing at a bus stop. It was Mama Nita. We were a half block away from each other, but I recognized the gray slacks and black turtleneck sweater that I had helped her get dressed in that morning.

I don't know where she thought she was going, but she had somehow managed to remember where the nearest bus stop was, which had been her preferred mode of transportation for the more than forty years since the accident that killed LeAnn. She couldn't stand to be in a car even as a passenger, let alone behind the wheel.

As I ran to her, that infamous Chicago hawk ripped right through my bomber jacket, and frigid air stung my lungs every time I inhaled.

I was glad to see Mama Nita, but at the same time, she was a heartbreaking sight to behold.

Not only wasn't she wearing a coat, but my heart nearly stopped when I looked down and realized that she didn't have any shoes on either. Without hesitation, I pulled my UGG boots off, and luckily, she didn't fight me as I slipped them onto her feet.

I then took off my bomber jacket and put that on her as well. "Come on, Mama Nita," I said. "Let's go home."

I put my arm around her waist and headed back in the direction of home, but it was slow going. Even through her sweater, I could feel that her skin was extremely cold to the touch.

My bare feet were so cold, they burned, and felt like blocks of ice, and Mama Nita was having a hard time because there was no telling how long she had been out there.

On a good day it would have been a fairly short walk back to the house, but in those conditions, there was no way we were going to make it.

We needed help.

I stopped at a house on the corner of Twenty-fifth and Parker Avenue. The woman who opened the door said a cheery "Merry Christmas!" then screamed in horror when she fully realized the condition Mama Nita and I were in: an old woman possibly near death from the freezing cold, and a younger one with no shoes or coat, both of us so numb from the cold, we could hardly walk.

"Willie Lee and Johnny, y'all come over here and help me!" the woman yelled out, and then she and her family practically dragged my grandmother and me into the warmth of their home.

Thank God for the kindness of strangers.

Family Decisions

Hypothermia and severe frostbite kept Mama Nita hospitalized for several days.

I wasn't exposed to the harsh elements for long so I had already made a full recovery, but every day during that period of time, the entire Cantrell clan convened in my grandmother's hospital room at Jackson Park Hospital.

As a family, we were all worried, and everything was put on hold until Doctor Butler, her personal physician, announced that amputation of some of her toes would not be necessary, as they had initially thought.

There was a collective sigh of relief, however, there were also mixed reactions regarding the doctor's suggestion to put Mama Nita in a nursing home.

"Oh, hell, no!" Pam said. My sister had worked briefly as a certified nurse's aide back when she was trying out careers, and knew from firsthand experience that a great number of nursing homes were nothing more than death camps for the elderly and infirmed. The staff are usually overworked, underpaid, and just generally couldn't care less about their patients.

You can walk into any nursing home anywhere in the world and you will find that they all have that same distinctly disgusting smell. Know what that is? It's the smell of death and disease. Of hopes and dreams, and lives shriveling up and dying right before your very eyes.

Nursing homes are definitely a necessity, but it's not where I wanted my grandmother to be.

Plus, every other day on the news there is some story about nursing home abuse, violations, or misconduct. So, of course, I was in agreement with Pam.

"My grandmother is not going into anybody's nursing home, anywhere on God's green earth," I told Doctor Butler, "so—moving on, next topic of discussion!"

"Mrs. Cantrell is going to make a full recovery from her ordeal," the doctor replied, "but what you need to understand is that with this disease advancing at the rate that it is, she now requires around-the-clock skilled nursing."

"Didn't you just hear what my sister said?" Pam asked, incredulous. "In black families, Big Mama is taken care of at home until the day she dies. We don't put her away in a nursing home and forget about her."

Doctor Butler, who was not African-American, looked highly offended, not to mention frustrated.

"Eva and Pam, y'all need to calm down and hear the man out, because at this point we can't handle Mama Nita by ourselves anymore," said Gwen. "We need to try some other options."

"And throwing her away in a nursing home is not an option!" I said. "Point blank, period, end of discussion."

Regardless of the opposition, the good doctor went on to explain just what our options were in regards to caring for Mama Nita from there on out. 1) Put her in a nursing facility where her care would be paid for by insurance, Social Security, and Medicaid. 2) Contract with a home health agency for in-home care. 3) Pay for a private duty nurse out of our own pockets.

"So what it boils down to is that we really only have one

option," Pam said, "Because the second so-called option is just as bad as the first."

Again, I had to agree with my sister. Just as with nursing homes, I had heard horror stories about how some home health agencies are staffed by unreliable, unlicensed personnel with no credentials to speak of, other than the agency's eight-hour training course on how to be a home companion.

Clearly, paying for a qualified live-in nurse was really the only choice we had as a family, and for that, we were going to need some serious money.

Let's Make a Deal

Hours after that crucial family meeting, I had a sit-down with Larry Nichols from *Hue Magazine*. He was the reporter who had somehow wormed his way into Gwen's good graces and harassed me at the airport for an interview.

I hadn't wanted to speak with him at the time out of loyalty and respect for Donovan, but after thinking it over, I had come to realize that I'd been misguided. Where was Donovan's loyalty and respect for me when he was busy setting up offshore bank accounts in my name, implicating me as a willing participant in his grand diabolical scheme? Besides, Larry was offering five thousand dollars for the exclusive interview.

Technically, I was selling out, but since I planned to use every penny of that money on Mama Nita's care, it was a no-brainer for me.

I had gotten Larry's business card from Gwen, and as I dialed his number, I thought back to that moment when I was sitting in jail wondering what it was in life that I was passionate about. I'm passionate about getting my career back on track and regaining independence, but most of all I'm passionate about my family. Being back with them made me realize that there were no limits I wouldn't go to contribute to their health, welfare, and well-being.

So if some funny-looking guy with a big jughead wanted to pay me to know me, then so be it. Cut the check!

I met up with Larry at the fabulous Charlie Trotter's restaurant in Lincoln Park. One of the best restaurants in Chicago, CT's is the height of elegance and fine dining. When I walked in it almost brought a tear to my eye because I was reminded of the good old days when Donovan used to eat in places like CT's every night of the week.

I wore a cranberry Alexander McQueen sweater dress from two seasons before, and a pair of black patent leather sling back heels that I'd bought from Payless for $22.99. It was a tasteful mix of high and low fashion, of which I was sure Michelle Obama would be proud.

Larry had been waiting for me in the lounge area, and when he came over to greet me, I was instantly reminded of one of my English professors from the University of Chicago. Along with those bottle-thick Harry Potter glasses of his, he was wearing brown Hush Puppy loafers that matched his slacks, a white Polo shirt, and a tan corduroy jacket with brown patches of suede at the elbow. "Ms. Cantrell, so glad you made it." Larry said, looking and sounding relieved.

"Of course I made it." I smiled, turning on the charm, "I called you, didn't I?" My tone was sweet and friendly, because after all, he was the man with five grand in his hand, so no need to be as nasty and dismissive as I was the first time around.

At Larry's request, we were seated at a table for two in the quietest area of the restaurant. A hot two seconds after we placed our food and wine orders, Larry put a mini-cassette recorder in the middle of the table and pressed record. "So tell me a little about yourself and how you came to know Donovan Dorsey," he said, all business.

I started with the facts, which were pretty straightforward and basic. How Donovan and I met at the Maxim party, and the fairy-tale life I had shared with him up until the day he disappeared in Switzerland.

Larry listened intently and I could literally see the dollar signs in his eyes. I was giving him the story he wanted, and it was exclusive information that no other publication in the world would have except for *Hue Magazine,* which was as much a staple in the black community as Everett Hair Care products.

Larry and I talked for nearly two hours, and it became clear to me why he had chosen to meet at that particular location. Charlie Trotter's is a restaurant where you don't just go for a meal, you go for an *experience* that includes several courses, accompanied by lots and *lots* of wine.

Going into the third course, I was a regular Chatty Cathy.

"One on one, outside of this bullshit scandal that he's created, Donovan was really a great guy—I mean a good, good man!" I said. "But truthfully, the longer the two of us are apart, the more freedom I feel."

"Really? I'd like to hear more about that," Larry said in the manner of a psychologist to a patient.

If loose lips truly sink ships, then I was torpedoing Donovan's ass, giving up details of the good, the bad, and the bizarre.

Like Donovan's obsession with hand sanitizer, and his insistence that I only wear silk lingerie and pajamas. No sweats, velour, T-shirts, flannel, or flats—EVER. And sneakers were only to be worn while I was actually working out.

The man was a stickler for details most people would consider minute. For instance, the bedsheets had to be changed every other day, like clockwork, and get this, the ends of the toilet paper had to be folded into a point just as they would be at any luxury hotel.

"Sounds like a man obsessed with perfection," Larry said, still in amateur psychologist mode.

"Oh, very much so," I said, "and looking back, he looks less like a mentor who I thought was molding me into a better, more refined woman and more like a control freak."

"But you didn't feel like you were being controlled while you were in the relationship?"

"No, because it wasn't done in a domineering, Ike Turner kinda way, you know?"

"Yeah, but telling you that he preferred for you not to wear T-shirts is still a form of control, no matter how nice he was in making the request."

"Hey, no disagreements here," I said, throwing my hands up. "You said it, so it must be true."

"If you could use one word to describe Donovan Dorsey, what would it be?"

"Hmm, just *one?*"

Larry shrugged. "Or two."

I thought for a few seconds, and the words "shrewd sonofabitch" slipped out of my mouth.

"Okay." Larry laughed. "And how would you describe yourself?"

"Miss Understood."

Larry nodded as if I had his sympathy. "Well, hopefully that will change once people get a chance to read your side of the story." He raised his wineglass in a toast, and said, "To being understood. . . ."

"Hear, hear!"

The next morning, I was in line at the bank thirty seconds after they opened to cash the check Larry had given me. I hadn't done much to earn the money, except run my mouth, but I still felt a sense of accomplishment as I watched the bank teller count out all of those hundreds and fifties. Money that I in turn counted out to Beulah Hutchinson, director of the groundbreaking Healthy Mind Project.

Doctor Butler had put us in touch with Beulah, who helped us realize that we had more options than we had originally thought. For eight hundred dollars a week, Mama Nita would have in-home care from 7:30 AM to 10:00 PM, from a nurse whose specialty is dealing with Alzheimer's patients and helping to keep their brains active.

From 10:30 PM until 7:00 AM, Mama Nita participated in a

night care program, which was like a social club for Alzheimer's patients.

It was a win-win situation for all of us, but it was only a drop in the bucket. Mama Nita needed long-term care, and for that I needed long-term income.

Not for Nothing

A new year rolled in, and with it came a renewed hope that somehow, some way, I was going to get my proverbial shit together, once and for all. I was especially optimistic because it was a time when barriers were being broken left and right. Change had come to America, and anything you put your heart and mind to was possible. Not only was the incoming president African-American, but New York also had its very first African-American governor who also happened to be legally blind.

God bless David Paterson because I mean, really. What are the odds? It was stories like Paterson's and Barack Obama's that inspired me into thinking and feeling that I would not be the underdog who was always coming up short for very much longer.

This was my year. Shit! I could feel it in the air. My exuberance caused me to have a little extra pep in my step when I walked into the lounge at the Four Seasons hotel, where Vance was waiting for me at the bar just like he'd said he would be. "Vance, is that you?" I teased, noting that he was dressed casually, which made him look younger and much more relaxed. He looked good. "I was starting to think you were born in Armani!"

Was it me, or did his eyes really light up when he saw me?

"Look at you!" said Vance, kissing me on the cheek. "You've got this laid-back, stress-free aura about you now."

"It must be the Midwestern air."

"In that case, bottle it and sell it 'cause you're even more gorgeous than usual."

I shrugged off the compliment and tried not to blush. For some reason, seeing Vance again was making me feel some kinda way. Horny, to be specific. Especially since I had seen him naked in all his glory and there was a photographic, pornographic image of what he was working with seared into my brain.

However, it was useless to even entertain lustful thoughts of getting to know Vance better, because he was Donovan's lawyer— as well as mine (even though I had yet to pay him for his services).

"Happy belated New Year," I said, sitting on the bar stool next to Vance. "It's so good to see you here in my neck of the woods."

"You were kind of in a bad way the last time I saw you, so I just wanted to check in on you and make sure you're doing okay."

"Much better," I said. "My friend Tameka was right. Nothing like family to give you a whole new perspective on things."

"Would you care for a drink, ma'am?" the bartender asked, sliding a square white napkin in front of me.

It was a Monday, and barely noon, so I ordered a virgin strawberry daiquiri with extra whipped cream.

"Have you heard anything from Donovan?" Vance asked.

"Not a word," I said with a shrug. "So, how long are you going to be in town?"

"Just until tomorrow afternoon," he said, "but the real questions is, when are you coming back to New York?"

Like promises, New Year's resolutions were made to be

broken, so I had not made any for 2009. I did, however, make a huge life decision that I hadn't shared with anyone else yet.

"I'm not going back to New York," I said, letting Vance in on the secret. "I have some loose ends to tie up back there, but after that, I'm here in Chicago to stay."

Vance looked crestfallen, but what could he say? I was grown, and it was my life and my decision. "Is there anything I can do to change your mind?"

"No, my family needs me, so it's pretty much a done deal." I never thought I would hear myself say those words. All of my life, it was all about Eva and what *I* wanted and needed. I was actually looking forward to making my family the focal point instead of just myself. "But enough of all that. How do you want to spend your time here in Chicago?"

"Well, the bartender says there's some good fishing out at the Chain of Lakes."

"Fishing? This time of year?"

"Illinois is the ice fishing capital of the world," Vance said. "I'm surprised you didn't know that, Ms. Chi-City."

"Oh, I knew that, it's just that most folks I know save themselves the hassle and go get their fish battered and fried from Shark's Fish & Chicken joint."

"Ah, that's for wimps!" Vance said. "Where's the fun in that?"

"Dousing that fresh, fluffy fish with hot sauce, and eating it with some cole slaw and hush puppies—that's where!" I laughed. "And anyway, what does a city boy like you know about fishing?"

"Plenty! When I was a kid, my grandfather used to take me and my cousins up to the Catskills to fish all the time," said Vance. "It's fun and relaxing, and we're going to get some great fish out of it to share with the family."

"I don't know who's going to clean it, because I'm sure not!" I said, which was a disclaimer, and also my way of agreeing to the fifty-mile road trip out to the Chain of Lakes.

Global warming being what it is, the temperature that day was an unseasonably warm sixty degrees.

We took Vance's rental car over to Henry's Sports and Bait Shop on Canal Street and picked up fishing poles, bait, a tackle box, a portable heater, and two of those camouflage head-to-toe snowsuits with the rubber boots built in.

All this for some damn fish? I wondered when the total came out to be $347.67. If Vance had been my man, I would have put my foot down, but since he wasn't my man, and was a guest in my hometown, I felt it was my duty to oblige him in whatever he wanted to get into while he was in town. Complete foolishness or not.

The ride up to northern Michigan was as beautiful as it was scary.

There were canyons and valleys that stretched as far as the eye could see with nothing with big thickets of trees that I imagined would be beautiful come springtime.

On the other hand, it was scary because the two-lane "highway" that we were traveling on was so narrow that I suffered a panic attack each time a huge semitruck whizzed past us at a high rate of speed, headed in the opposite direction.

Following the GPS instructions, Vance took an exit that led us through a town with a population of 544, and that had a teeny-tiny cemetery where it seemed as though the families were trying to outdo one another with their extravagant flower arrangements and headstones.

Most of the homes were ranch in style, and some of the yards were even decorated with wooden wagon wheels and cheesing, black-faced lawn jockeys. I had never seen anything quite like it, and to be honest, it felt like we had somehow wandered onto the set of *The Andy Griffith Show*.

It had been many years since I had last seen a soda machine outside, but this one was outside of an auto parts store that was right next door to a two-stall carwash that only cost fifty cents. The town had a one-truck firehouse with a hand-painted sign seeking volunteers, and when we passed it for a second time, that's when I knew we were lost.

"So much for GPS devices," Vance spoke up, before I had the chance to point out the obvious. "I had heard these things weren't all that reliable out in rural areas, but this is ridiculous!"

Nightfall had come upon us quickly. The weather may have been springlike that day, but Vance had failed to take into account that it was winter and that the sun set around five in the evening. Now, I am sure it can be done, but I certainly wasn't up for fishing in the dark.

"Do you have any idea where we are?" I asked as we drove down what had to be the bumpiest back road in Illinois.

"Not a clue. . . . I was hoping you could tell me."

"Umm . . . in case you haven't noticed this isn't exactly my hood," I said with low-key sarcasm. "And it's really too bad we never even made it out to Chain of Lakes."

"Yeah, I can tell you're all torn up about it." He laughed, which caused me to join in.

"I am, actually," I said, "but at least we got a chance to take a nice ride and enjoy the countryside."

Just as I said that, a possum or some such creature darted across the road in front of us.

Vance said, "Now there's something you don't see every day in New York."

I resisted the urge to scream, because after all I had stared king rat eyeball-to-eyeball up in Harlem and lived to tell about it. Country roadkill wasn't nearly as menacing as the big-city variety.

Vance and I came across a main drag that consisted of a roadside diner, a seedy motel, a two-pump gas station, and an establishment with a flashing red sign that read JAKE'S COUNTRY & WESTERN BAR & GRILL.

Vance pulled into the bar's unpaved parking lot, which was overflowing with pickup trucks and Harley-Davidson motor-cycles.

Yee-ha!

It was clearly a redneck kind of place, but instead of running inside to get directions and continuing on our merry way, Vance found a place to park and said, "Come on, let's go grab a bite to eat."

"You're joking, right?"

"We need someone to tell us how to get back to civilization," Vance said, "and besides, I'm sure you probably have to use the restroom, so we might as well kill three birds with one stone."

Vance got out of the car and ran around to open my door for me. I didn't budge. He was right. I did have to pee, and was starving like Marvin, but I didn't like the looks of the place. I listened closely and could have sworn I heard the banjo music from *Deliverance* playing somewhere in the background.

"It's generally not a good idea to stop at hillbilly bars out in the middle of Klan country."

City slicker that he was, Vance was fearless and undeterred. "Come on, let your hair down," he said as he pulled me out of the car. "How bad could it be?"

Walking inside Jake's Country & Western Bar & Grill was like entering another world, one where only cowboys and cowgirls exist. Folks were throwing darts, shooting pool, and riding mechanical bulls, and everyone in there was dressed from head to toe in Western attire, sending out the message that it was not a game, in case you thought otherwise.

"This looks like a happening place!" Vance said, and I was surprised that he was not being facetious. While his eyes took in the dozens of couples out on the vast dance floor, country line dancing in unison to Toby Keith, my eyes were glued to the huge confederate flag hanging behind the bar.

"Let's be in and out of here with a quickness!" I said out of the corner of my mouth like a ventriloquist.

A waitress came over dressed like Annie Oakley, and I was

dead. "Y'all need a table?" she asked, chomping a wad of gum a mile a minute.

"Yes—" said Vance, but I interrupted him in a thick Southern accent.

"That'd sure be mighty fine, ma'am!"

A good percentage of the bar patrons openly stared as the waitress led Vance and me to a table for two. I guessed correctly that two black people this far back in their neck of the woods was an uncommon sight.

"Welcome to Jake's," the waitress said, whipping out a notepad and pulling a pencil from behind her ear. "What can I get y'all?"

Vance and I decided to share a pitcher of Michelob and a platter of Buffalo wings and French fries. I went to the little girls' room after we placed our order, and when I came out, I saw that several good ol' boys were heading straight for our table. These were big, tough, mean-looking guys, but Vance was no slouch himself. He stood up as they reached the table, ready for anything.

"Can I help you gentlemen with something?" Vance asked, with a mean mug on his face as well.

The spokesman for the group stepped forward, with hard eyes, and a build like a WWF wrestler. There was a long pause as he sized Vance up, and then zoned in on me. "Yeah, you can help me all right. . . . We were just wanting to know if we could trouble Ms. Houston for her autograph."

"WHO?" Vance and I asked at the same time.

"You're Whitney Houston, right?" asked another guy. "*The Bodyguard* soundtrack is one of my all-time favorites!"

While we were both beautiful, the only thing Whitney Houston and I had in common is that we were both black.

"Oh, my God, you guys, I can't believe you recognized me!" I said in a whispery voice.

It was for safety's sake that I indulged them. I smiled for

pictures and signed "auto-graphs," keeping in mind that no one knew where Vance and I were, and if we came up missing, no one would ever think to search for us in Butt-Fuck, Illinois, population 544.

After all the commotion died down, Vance and I dug into our dinner, which was greasy, but good. It was also, at the waitress's insistence, "on the house."

"You know, you really ought to be ashamed of yourself." Vance laughed, shaking his head at me. "Whitney Houston?"

"They said it, not me," I said, keeping my voice down so no one could overhear, "but look, I did everybody in here a favor. I saved our lives, *plus* gave the locals Diva, and put some sunshine into their otherwise dreary little country lives. I don't know about you, but I call that spreading the love."

"So since you're Whitney, what does that make me, Bobby Brown?"

"*Hey!*" I laughed. "Just don't get none on ya, all right?"

After we ate, Vance the party boy wasn't quite ready to leave his newfound friends, so we stayed a couple hours more, drank more beer, and rode the mechanical bull.

Kenny Chesney's hit "When the Sun Goes Down" came on, and Vance asked me to dance.

"Come on, cowboy! Let's see what'cha got!" I said, as we hit the dance floor and joined in on a line dance, which I was surprised to see that Vance did very well.

Jake's Country & Western Bar & Grill? We shut it *down*. It was after one in the morning when Vance and I left the bar, and even though we had been given directions on how to get back to Chicago, both of us had been drinking, so it would have been foolish to even try to make it back at that late hour.

Our options for lodging for the night were to either sleep in the car or rough it at the seedy motel up the street.

John, the group representative who had so menacingly approached our table earlier in the evening, turned out to be a big ol' teddy bear, who was as sweet as cotton candy. He saw our dilemma and graciously offered to escort me and Vance to his family's bed-and-breakfast a few miles up the road.

"Thank you, John, how sweet!" I said, sorry that I had completely misjudged him. He was, however, operating under the assumption that I was Whitney Houston, so I'll never know if he would have extended the offer if he had viewed me as just a regular black chick.

Whatever the case, Vance and I had a place to lay our heads for the night, and when we pulled up to the B&B, I was pleasantly surprised to find that it was a large two-story, eighteenth-century, plantation-style mansion that looked like something straight out of *Gone With the Wind*. It was stark white with black shutters, and two humongous columns framed the front porch that was about half a block long.

It felt as if we had stepped back in time, and I half expected to see Mammy come running out of the house, shouting that she needed help birthing a baby.

"Welcome, welcome, what a wonderful couple!" said John's mother, a sweet little old woman whose hair was as white as snow.

She introduced herself as Edna and showed us to our room, which was spacious enough to have its own bathroom, a fireplace, and one king-sized bed.

"Maybe we should have fessed up and told Edna that we're not a couple," Vance said in regards to there being only one bed.

"Sucks for you," I said jokingly, "but I have heard that sleeping on the floor is very beneficial for the back."

"Oh, well, cool! Then you shouldn't have any problem making yourself comfortable."

Vance and I gave each other the side eye, and then raced to the bed. He was clearly going to beat me, so I jumped on his back, which sent us both tumbling to the floor. I reached over and tagged the bed, claiming it for the night. I lay on the floor laughing, giddy from lack of sleep and too much of the suds.

Vance cried foul. "You are such a cheater!" he said. "And you made me bang my knee up pretty bad."

"Let me see," I said, scooting over to him. When I got closer, he took my face in his hands and kissed me on the mouth. With tongue. I kept my eyes open the whole time, shocked that he was being so bold, and that the kiss was so damn good. It was electrifying.

With nothing in my head except the passion of the moment, Vance and I continued to kiss as we undressed each other. Once we were both completely naked, Vance slipped on a magnum-sized condom, and then he laid me back on the bed where he entered me with both tenderness and concentrated passion.

Our bodies moved together in a slow rhythmic grind, and fit together perfectly, as if we had been made just for each other.

We made fast, passionate love, then showered together, and lay in each other's arms, talking until the sun came up.

"You know what this means, don't you?" Vance asked, lightly caressing my back with his fingertips.

"No, what?"

"You have to come back to New York. I need you, and I want you in my life."

I sighed. "Vance, don't do this to me." I had already made up my mind to move back to Chicago for the good of my family, and while I liked him a lot, one session of amazing sex was not enough to sway me. At least it shouldn't have been.

"I know you think you don't have much to come back to, but how about this: Since Sonya is about to go out for a couple of months on maternity leave, you can take her place at my law firm, and when she comes back, I'll make you my personal assistant," Vance said.

"And where would I live?"

"As far as living arrangements, you can either live with me or I'll set you up in an apartment, it's your choice."

"Whoa, slow down, kemosabe! I mean, shouldn't we ease into this?"

"It's not as if we haven't already been living together. The only thing that will be different is that we'll be romantically involved. I mean, that is what you want, isn't it?"

I looked up at Vance, touched by how much he seemed to care for me. Not only was he handsome and sexy, he was also refreshingly sweet, an excellent father, and a good person all around.

"Of course I want to be with you," I said, ignoring the twinge of guilt I felt for leaving one man, no matter what the circumstances, and moving on to his lawyer.

Technically, me becoming Vance's woman was not a moral or ethnical issue, but it was a move that I had never made before, and it would take some getting used to. Vance and Donovan may not have been the best of friends, but they did have an attorney/client business relationship, and if I didn't already have enough to overcome socially, a romantic relationship with my ex-man's lawyer would really send those wagging tongues into overdrive.

But I have never cared one iota about what anyone thought about me, or my personal business, and I wasn't about to start now.

Awakenings

"I tell ya, it does my heart good, to see young people in love!" Edna beamed, as she served Vance and me a breakfast of strong, freshly brewed coffee, corned beef hash, and biscuits and white gravy.

I wouldn't say that I was *in* love at that moment, but during the time I had lived with Vance I had come to care for both him and his daughter very deeply, and I could certainly see where our relationship had the potential to blossom into a great love affair.

Why is it that the trip back is always much shorter than the trip you took to get there? Vance and I left the bed-and-breakfast, and the small town Ms. Edna said was named Clarksville, early that morning. It took us less than an hour to get back to Chicago.

Vance pulled up in front of Mama Nita's house and wanted to come in and meet my family.

"Some other time," I smiled, thinking it was best not to scare the man off so soon.

We shared a long kiss good-bye before I got out of the car. His flight to California was later that afternoon, and after taking care of business in California, he planned to head straight to Washington, DC, for the inauguration.

"So, how soon will I see you back in New York?" Vance asked.

"Give me a couple of weeks, all right?"

"Okay, I'm going to hold you to that," Vance said, "and if you're not back by then, I am going to personally come back and get you myself—caveman style!"

He was so sweet; I wished I could eat him with a spoon. "Okay," I said, "but just don't club me over the head, and we're cool!"

I used my old key to let myself in the house, and froze in my tracks when I heard exuberant singing coming from the kitchen. "Jesus on the main line, tell him what you want . . . Jesus on the main line, tell him what you want . . . Jesus on the main line, tell him what you want . . . Call him up, and tell him what you want!"

It was Mama Nita.

I ran into the kitchen and found my grandmother at the stove cooking, while Rosalyn, her new nurse, stood by.

"Cast all of your worries and care on Him, because he cares for you!" Mama Nita preached to Rosalyn.

"Amen, Ms. Cantrell," said Rosalyn, "Amen!"

"Grandma?" I said cautiously, unable to believe my eyes, or my ears. Mama Nita turned around, and her eyes lit up when she saw me.

"Eva! Gwen told me you were in town. Girl, you better get over here and give me some sugar!" It was a miracle. I rushed over and hugged her tight, tears gushed from my eyes.

Mama Nita stepped back to get a good look at me. "I swear, you always were a dramatic little thing," she said, wiping my tears. "Why are you crying?"

"I'm just happy, that's all," I said, to which Rosalyn nodded and gave me a wink. "So what are you up to in here?"

"Me and my friend Rosalyn here are just making a little brunch. You still like smoked ham and waffles, don't you?"

She remembered!

"Yes, ma'am," I said, reaching to break off a tiny piece of ham, only to have Mama Nita playfully smack my hand away. "Not until we say grace. You know better than that," she said. "By the way, you're glowing. Did you have a big night last night?"

I cringed, totally unwilling to talk to my grandmother about the fact that I had just gotten my boots knocked. "A wise woman used to always tell me never to kiss and tell," l said.

"Glad to see that you were paying attention," Mama Nita said. "Was it that Jayson Cooper?"

My mouth hit the floor. Not only was she lucid, but she remembered minute details like Jayson Cooper, my first love.

"Why won't anybody let me live him down?" I asked, incredulous.

"Because you loved that little slew-footed boy to death! All you would talk about was 'Jayson' this and 'Jayson' that."

"Grandma, it's been over five years since I've even laid eyes on Jayson. I think it's safe to say that we can all let that go now."

"Here are the eggs, Mom," Gwen said as she walked in the kitchen with a bag of groceries.

"What did you have to do, go lay them yourself?" Mama Nita asked.

"I wasn't gone that long," Gwen said.

"Now, you know that's a bold-faced lie. You were gone for almost an hour!" Mama Nita said, then grabbed the carton of eggs and got busy scrambling them.

Gwen and I looked at each other and smiled. Mama Nita, our rock, was back to her old self. Praise God!

Doctor Butler credited the new "cocktail" of medications that he had prescribed for Mama Nita's awakening, although he warned that it would not last. "Once her brain becomes accustomed to the new medicine, the Alzheimer's will continue to progress, but hopefully not as rapidly as before."

With what felt like a time bomb ticking in the background, we all literally fought to spend one-on-one time with Mama Nita.

I washed and conditioned her hair, greased her scalp, then braided her hair in plaits.

On the days that it were warm enough, we took walks around the neighborhood, and the neighbors marveled that Mama Nita seemed to be doing okay. I slept in her bed with her every night, and told her all about Donovan and the Ponzi scheme and everything that had happened to me as a result.

"I'm gonna tell you like I told your mama when she came home pregnant with Pam at sixteen: It's not what happens to you in life, so much as how you react to what happens to you. Like those announcers used to say on TV, 'This is a test. This is only a test.' Excuse the expression, but shit happens! It's not the end of the world, though. The key is to pick yourself back up, get your independence, and stay that way. No matter how much a man has, at the end of the day it is his. Get yours, and if he is not supportive of that, then honey, he ain't the one!"

On January 20th, we made a huge pot of Mama Nita's infamous seafood gumbo and, as a family, watched as Barack H. Obama was sworn in as our nation's forty-fourth president. The mood in the house was celebratory, and the day was very emotional for all of us, as we stayed glued to the television from early that morning until early the next morning.

Visitors came and went exchanging hugs and stories of just how far black people had come.

My grandmother was sixty-seven years old, so of course a black president held a special significance for her. She was born and raised in rural Louisiana at a time when racism was not only blatant, it was a way of life.

There were so many limitations on what black people could have, and do, and be that most working-class black families, and especially those in the South, didn't see the value of keeping their kids in school when they were old enough to get out and work to help support the family.

Mama Nita was forced to drop out of school in the eighth grade, but she was still smart enough to know that education would be the saving grace of her descendants. She took me to get my first library card, and explained to me that everything I ever wanted to know was right within those walls.

It wasn't from lack of trying, but ultimately I was the first college graduate in the family, and I can still see her face on graduation day as she stood in the bleachers dancing a jig and openly praising God.

Mama Nita had been active in politics before her Alzheimer's diagnosis, and had even campaigned for Obama when he ran for a seat in the Senate.

The inauguration was a full-circle moment, and watching my grandmother be able to fully bear witness to the occasion was a gift that I will treasure for the rest of my life.

That was a good day.

A few days later, Mama Nita went silent again. It was gradual, starting with forgetfulness and the inability to put the right names to the right faces, a temperamental outburst here and there, and then complete silence.

Heartwrenching? That's not strong enough to describe my sense of loss and bewilderment.

Love and Deception

Almost two weeks after Vance left Chicago, he called me on my little pay-as-you-go cell phone one evening, and said, "They got him." I didn't know who the "they" was, but I knew he was referring to Donovan.

"How?" I asked. "When, where?"

"A few days ago, at New York-Presbyterian Hospital."

"What—I mean, why the hospital of all places?"

"Well, I don't know all the details just yet, but apparently he was visiting his grandfather who recently had a heart attack. Someone tipped off the authorities, but he gave them an alias, and even a fake ID. They arrested Donovan anyway, and it's taken them this long to positively identify him."

"Wow! So he's been in New York this whole time?"

"It's unlikely, but like I said, I don't have all the details yet," said Vance, "but I need for you to get here as soon as you can. Donovan refuses to talk to anyone until he talks to you first."

My plans to move back to Chicago had been short-lived, which was why I was so glad that I hadn't formally announced my plans to move back to town. Pam and Gwen were both extremely understanding and encouraged me to go back to New York and do whatever was necessary to put the situation behind me once and for all.

"We're not going anywhere. We'll be here just like we've always been," Gwen said when she dropped me off at the airport the next morning. I kissed everyone good-bye, and it was wheels up, back to New York City, where I went straight from JFK Airport to the Metropolitan Correctional Center in lower Manhattan where Donovan was being held.

As Donovan's attorney, Vance was there waiting for me in the lobby. He looked excited to see me, and kissed me on the lips with no hesitation. "Are you ready?" he asked.

My heart beat fast and pounded in my ears at the thought of seeing Donovan face-to-face after all the unnecessary hell he had put me through.

He had some explaining to do, but then again, so did I. "Does he know about us?" I asked.

"No. I spoke to Donovan briefly on the phone last night and it was only long enough for him to say he wanted to see you."

"Well, I would like to talk to him alone if you don't mind," I said, knowing that just seeing Vance and me sitting next to each other would tell him everything. Of course, he would have to eventually be told that Vance and I were pursuing a relationship, but first things first. I needed to know the five W's and the H of the whole situation.

I had never visited anyone in jail before, but the way they did things around there made me feel as though I were the criminal trying to break *into* the damned place.

First, I had to leave my luggage with the front lobby officer, and then show a valid photo ID. I put my purse on a conveyor belt to be searched electronically, then walked through a metal detector, which beeped when I went through it, so I was then pat searched by a pervy corrections officer who seemed to be getting off on feeling me up between my legs and across my breast. It was intrusive and demeaning, and I fully understood why Diana Ross went ballistic that time at London's Heathrow Airport. *Respectmypersonalspace.com!*

After all of that, it was determined that my underwire bra was causing the problem, and I was finally allowed entry into the lobby. Whew! I mean, really? But that was only just the beginning. I then had to fill out an application and information form, and give written consent for a background check to be performed on me, all of which had to be approved by the Bureau of Prisons before I was actually permitted to visit with Donovan. It took a couple of hours to get the go-ahead, but eventually I was escorted in a visitors' room where several inmates were visiting with their families, including teenagers and young children.

I couldn't understand that for the life of me. In my opinion, no kid should be exposed to jail in any way, shape, or form. Hell, I was traumatized just being there, so there was no telling how damaging the experience was to a child's psyche. As requested, Vance respected my wishes and waited outside in the lobby.

When the corrections officer brought Donovan in the room, I gasped so loudly that it echoed throughout the room. I barely recognized him.

"Hey, babe," he said shyly, and smiled.

Well, at least he still had those pretty white teeth.

As for the rest of him, he had lost about twenty pounds off of an already-slender frame, his hair had grown into a wild, bushy afro, and he had a full, nappy-ass beard caked with only God knows what.

And he stunk.

"I know you were on the run and everything, but didn't they have soap and water where you were?"

"Bad things go on in here, Eva," Donovan said in a hushed, paranoid voice. "And if these sick bastards think they're gonna take my manhood, they're gonna get some of the . . .

He looked like Pig-Pen and smelled like Pepe le Pew, but even on lockdown, Donovan had thought of everything. Even down to the best way to thwart a physical attack, which was sad, but it was his new reality. Not only did he plan *not* to drop the soap, he didn't even plan to use it. "Oh, believe me, it's gonna be a fight to the death, but if I lose, they're gonna get some of the foulest, shittiest, and most disgusting ass they'll ever have in their life."

"So you're gonna walk around looking like that and smelling like bullshit the whole time you're in here?"

"It sure as hell ain't pleasant, but hey, if that keeps the rapists off me, then so be it," said Donovan. "I have to do whatever it takes to survive in here."

"And how did it even come to this, Donovan? I mean, weren't you making enough money of your own?"

"It just got out of control," Donovan said, looking remorseful, "and there's really no excuse for it, but you have all these people coming at you wanting to invest a minimum of half a million dollars each. You start seeing other guys in your field and how they roll, I mean the real big billionaire tycoons, and you wanna roll like that too. But you don't have the billion dollars a year salary yet, so you slowly start spending money that is not yours in order to keep up with appearances.

"You know, it takes money to make money, and you gotta look the part to get the part, and all that. And one day you look up and you've spent more money than you intended to, and all of a sudden a client wants to cash out for more than you can give him, and that's when, slowly but surely, that house of cards begins to fall."

Even his explanation for leaving me in Switzerland was plausible—sort of. "It was wrong and so fucking selfish to take you on the run with me in the first place. I wanted to tell you so badly what was going on, but I figured the less you knew, the less it would appear that you were in cahoots with all this."

"Well, damn, couldn't you have at least left me enough money to get back home?" I asked.

"I needed for you to be angry with me," he said. "I know

you, Eva, and you're a terrible liar. If I had made things comfortable for you, and left you on good terms, you just might be sitting in a jail cell of your own right now."

At that moment, I saw a glimmer of the old Donovan.

I thought I would be angry and curse him out, but hearing how scared and vulnerable he sounded made my heart melt. I no longer wanted to rip him a new asshole like everybody else. I wanted to take care of him, and protect him.

"So where have you been?" I asked, genuinely concerned.

"Oh, here, there, and everywhere," he said wistfully. "Morocco mostly, then I made the mistake of calling Mother to check on things, and she told me about Gramps having a heart attack and all. . . . I knew they would probably catch me, but I had to come back and see him. I didn't want him to die thinking that his grandson was a coward."

"I'm sorry to hear about your grandfather. Is he going to be all right?"

Tears came to Donovan's eyes and he was silent for a couple of minutes. Just as he knew I was a terrible liar, I could tell he was willing himself not to cry.

"Yeah, they say he's going to pull through, but the stress I caused, and the shame I brought to the family name, is something—" Donovan sighed heavily, indicating that he didn't want to continue discussing the matter. "But on a lighter note," he said, "how is Flossie?"

I raised an eyebrow. The only "Flossie" either of us knew was the stuffed gray elephant that he had won for me at Coney Island years ago, and was one of the few things that Donovan's bitch of a mother hadn't tossed out or stolen for herself.

"Flossie's doing just fine. . . ." I said, playing along.

"Good, that's *real good!*" Donovan's eyes were bulging and shining. "Tell her I said hello, and that I hope to see her real soon."

Right, right . . . I nodded like I understood, even though I was confused as hell. Either he had left his mind in Morocco or it was a low-key way of trying to tell me something.

"I will definitely do that," I said, trying to put the pieces together. Donovan and I stared at each other, hoping to somehow communicate telepathically, but since neither of us were mind readers, it was useless.

Moment of Truth

Before I knew it, my time with Donovan was up, and it was Vance's turn to come in and see him.

"I have some things I need to take care of, but I'll meet you at the apartment later on," I told Vance before he went in the visitors' room.

"Okay, but what did Donovan say to you?" Vance asked, holding me back.

"Um, nothing much," I said, biting my bottom lip, which for those who knew me well was a dead giveaway that I wasn't being truthful. "He just apologized for getting me involved, and that was pretty much it—I didn't tell him about you and me, so you might want to keep that under wraps for now."

"Yeah, you're right," said Vance. "Donovan has enough to worry about, and there's no telling how he'll react to the news of us being together."

Vance gave me the spare key to his apartment, and I took off like a light to retrieve my luggage from the lobby officer. Ms. Flossie was packed away in my suitcase, and had been traveling with me from pillar to post ever since I had picked up what was left of my earthly possessions at the Funderburk.

I had no clue what a stuffed animal had to do with any of this, but I was damn curious to find out.

Returning to Vance's apartment after being away for more than a month felt like coming home, but at the same time, it felt kind of weird knowing that I would be sharing the master bedroom with him.

The thought of it made me smile, even though I did not look forward to the inevitable conversation that I would have with his baby's mama.

Candace was already a loose cannon, and there was no telling how far this new turn of events might set her crazy ass back.

I took Flossie the elephant out of my luggage and looked her over carefully. She had a red bow on her head and wore a red-and-white polka-dot dress with ruffled panties underneath. Nothing out of the ordinary about that. . . .

I turned Flossie over and lifted her dress, where I noticed for the first time that a zipper ran down the middle of her back.

My heart started pounding so hard, I could feel it in my ears. I took a deep breath to calm myself down, and peeked inside. Tucked in the middle of a bunch of foamy stuffing was a folded note with a small key taped to it.

Dear Eva,

The fact that you are even reading this letter means that all the wrong I have been doing in the dark has come to the light.

The time we spent together were the best years of my life, but unfortunately, my actions have caused this to be the point where we must part. I hope that the money I have set aside for you will ensure that you have a wonderful future.

The key unlocks a safe deposit box at the UBS Bank in the Cayman Islands, which holds $10 million dollars' worth of T-bills, jewelry, and cash. I have made special arrangements with the bank officer, and all that is required for you to gain access to the safe deposit box is the box number, 1605, and

*the password, "Flossie." Once you get to this box, you will
find that there are other keys that belong to other safe deposit
boxes throughout the world.*

*You can pull this off, Eva, as long as you play it smart,
and play it safe. Tell no one about these accounts. Trust no one!
Go get the money, have a good life, and forget about me.*

*I apologize for any hurt that I have undoubtedly caused
you.*

Please forgive me.

Love always,
D

P.S. Check Flossie inside out . . . 250K.

I ripped out the rest of the stuffing and found dozens of
humongous rolls of hundred dollar bills hidden inside the cav-
ity.

Two hundred fifty thousand dollars in cash, plus hidden
treasure boxes around the world containing millions of dollars.
Hallelujah!

I felt like Dorothy in *The Wizard of Oz,* and that I'd had it
all along. Lord, if only I had known about this sooner, things
would have been different!

With all that money, I could pay off all of Mama Nita's
overdue medical bills as well as pay up her participation in the
Healthy Mind Project for the rest of her life.

The cards had been re-dealt, and I was now holding a winning hand that I fully intended to play the hell out of.

"Honey, I'm home!" Vance called out from the living
room. I jumped at the sound of his voice and scrambled to stuff
Flossie, the money, and everything else back into my suitcase.
By the time Vance walked into the room, I was as breathless and
jittery as a crackhead, but at least I had hidden the evidence.

"Hey, sweetheart!" I said, nervously wiping sweat from my
brow.

"What's up, Eva," he asked, a bit suspicious. "Did I scare you?"

"*No!* It's just that seeing Donovan today wrecked my nerves a little bit, you know?"

"Yeah, it was unsettling to see the physical condition he was in,"Vance said, "and frankly, I'm worried about Donovan's mental health as well. I'm going to have someone evaluate him soon to see what's going on. If there is a problem, maybe we could use that in his defense."

"That makes two of us," I said. "I think being locked up is literally driving him insane. So will he be able to get out of there pending trial?"

"It depends on how much the judge sets his bond for. Considering that all of that money is still out there unaccounted for, and Donovan has absconded before in order to avoid jail time, I'm certain that they are going to set the bond pretty high," Vance said. "I keep hearing varying figures from ten million all the way up to fifty million, which is ridiculous! Ten we can do, but if his bond turns out to be anything more than twenty million, he's just going to have to sit in jail until trial."

My head was spinning from all the legalese. Enoughalready. com!

"Whew, it's been a long day," I said, wrapping my arms around Vance's waist. "Kiss?"

Vance bent down and kissed me on the mouth, and play-fully bit my lower lip. "Hmm, you taste good," he said. "So, what do you want to do to commemorate our first evening of cohabitation?"

"Hump." I laughed. "*Not* talk about Donovan Dorsey, how about that?"

"Done! And how about we include dinner and a Knicks game at the Garden?"

"I knew there was a reason why I like you so much," I teased. "Yeah, how 'bout it?"

The Knicks lost to the Bulls 111 to 119. Afterwards, Vance and I had dinner at The Palm Restaurant near our apartment where they have the best Shrimp Bruno and double-cut New York Strips, and then we went home and made fast, passionate love.

The sex was phenomenal, but I could not get Donovan's face out of my head. Not the one that I'd seen earlier down at the jailhouse, but the face of the man that I loved dearly prior to the scandal.

While I still cared for Donovan, I was not *in love* with him. How could I be with all that had transpired, added to the fact that he was facing a long prison sentence?

Still, I felt guilty about my budding relationship with Vance— like I was a low-down, out-and-out cheater. I felt sorry for what Donovan had gotten himself into, but damn it, I deserved some happiness, didn't I?

Dirty Money

After only a couple of days of working at Vance's law firm, I was performing Sonya's job duties just as well as she had.

"You have reached the law office of Vance Murphy, Attorney at Law, how may I direct your call? One moment please . . . Mr. Johnson, line five . . . Mr. Murphy, line two . . . Ms. Greer, line seven . . . Hello, you have reached the law office of Vance Murphy, Attorney at Law, how may I direct your call? One moment please . . ."

My days were spent handling a barrage of incoming calls, making appointments, light filing, greeting visitors, and occasionally making love in the boss's office.

It was easy work, but it was also boring as hell and made me long that much more to get back into publishing and my first love of writing.

Ronald Nash, the Manhattan D.A., came in to see Vance one afternoon, and as you can imagine, it was difficult for me to maintain my civility. Especially after he had treated me so harshly that day in his office when he was questioning me about Donovan's whereabouts.

Donovan's idea to keep me completely in the dark until well after the fact had been genius, because if I knew before what I knew at that moment, I would have definitely cracked under pressure.

I was just dying to singsong to Mr. Nash, *I know something you don't know . . . onion-head bastard!*

But I maintained my professionalism and showed the onion-headed bastard to Vance's office, where they had a long, closed-door meeting.

The following week, Donovan plead not guilty to a laundry lists of criminal charges, and the federal judge presiding over Donovan's case set his bond at an unprecedented forty million dollars. Donovan was clearly guilty as sin, but Vance's strategy was to make the district attorney's office prove their case on a victim-by-victim basis.

"We're going to force all the alleged victims to produce paperwork, receipts, etcetera, because there is a good chance that not everyone will be able to come up with proof, which will weaken the prosecution's case and possibly reduce the sentence that Donovan will ultimately be given."

At that rate, the trial had the potential to last for years. Of course, that didn't sit well with me. Hundreds of lives had been ruined, including mine, and I wanted nothing more than to get out from under the shadow of this whole ordeal—once and for all.

Adding fuel to the circuslike atmosphere was the revelation that Mama Dorsey was sitting on thirty-three million dollars even though the only income she had earned in the last several years was from meager sales of her 2001 nonfiction book *From Queens to Wall Street: Raising Successful Children in Today's Society.*

Yes, Mama Dorsey, and please tell us how you were able to do that, especially in light of your child's current set of circumstances.

Also, according to Vance, Annette refused to pony up any money toward Donovan's bond, which is the reason she had given me for liquidating his assets in the first place. Annette's reasoning was that Donovan will be headed to prison anyway, whether she forked over that much cash or not, which was true, but still. What a ruthless bitch. Annette Dorsey was truly about saving her own ass, even at the expense of her own child, who was the reason she had been able to live so well in the first place.

Full Circle

"I'll tell you one thing: whoever says money can't buy happiness is not shopping at the right stores!"

That's how I used to feel about money, but since I've been on this rags-to-riches roller coaster, I have definitely changed my mind. Money doesn't buy happiness per se, but what it does do is give you freedom, peace of mind, and more control over your life and circumstances.

I knew that I could do a lot of good with the money that Donovan had stashed away, but the problem was, it wasn't my money

It was a couple of weeks after my discovery of all that loot, and while I had kept my mouth shut all that time, I was bursting at the seams and needed some advice on how to proceed.

I called my two most trusted advisors, Tameka and Kyle, to meet me for lunch and a powwow at Cornelia Street Cafe in the West Village.

"Hypothetically speaking, what would you do if you had access to millions of dollars," I asked. "Would you keep it, or turn it in?"

Kyle and Tameka sat across the table from me, looking at me as if I were growing a second head right in front of their eyes.

"Well . . ." Tameka said slowly, giving it some serious thought, "I would break off everyone I love with a high six figures, and definitely pay off all my debts and financial obligations."

Hint, hint . . .

"And is that before or after they cart your ass off to jail?" Kyle asked. "Because make no mistake about it, you will be watched, and you will be caught." Kyle looked me directly in my eyes when he said that, and his point was taken as well.

"Hypothetically speaking, of course," I said.

"Oh, but of course!" said Tameka.

"No doubt, no doubt," Kyle said, "but please elaborate on this situation with Mr. Murphy."

"Yeah!" Tameka said. "Where the hell did that come from?"

"Hey, like Pebbles and Babyface told you way back in the day, 'Love Makes Things Happen,' " I said, hitting my glass of iced tea against each of theirs. Neither of them drank to that. Haters!

"Yes, but is it really love, or is it just daddy hunger rearing its ugly head again?"

"There you go with that bullshit again," I snapped. "Look, the fact that I prefer older men doesn't have anything to do with my father not being around, all right? Over and out!"

"Ooh . . . careful now, she gon' cut you!" Tameka said to Kyle under her breath.

"Okay, sweetheart, don't go taking your extreme bitch disorder out on me," Kyle said. "If you love it, I *live* for it!"

"Okay, good," I said, "so we're in agreement, right?"

"Mmm-hmm . . ." said Kyle, exchanging the side-eye with Tameka.

"You know, I can't stand it when people think they know more about my business than I do," I said. "Vance is my new man, and that's that. No couple starts a relationship being head over heels in love right off the bat. You build, and work up to that.

"And as far as my so-called daddy hunger, everyone is entitled to their preferences, and when it comes to men, mine just so happen to be men who are mature, stable, and already are what they want to be when they grow up."

"Now that is something I'll toast to!" Tameka said, hitting her glass against mine. "But back to your original question, what would you do? Keep it, or turn it over?"

"If I were in that situation," I said, "it would be hard as hell, but I would do the right thing and turn the money over."

"Yay!" Kyle applauded me. " 'Cause it sure wouldn't be cute if I had to come see my Boo-Boo up in the big house. I mean, hypothetically speaking, of course!"

I wondered what Tameka and Kyle would say if they knew that the oversized hobo bag I was carrying was bulging because it contained three plastic Pathmark bags filled with a quarter of a million dollars. Considering that I could get mugged, it probably wasn't the smartest thing to do, but seeing as how I had no other alternative, it was the safest.

Before we parted ways outside of the cafe, I slipped an envelope into Tameka's tote bag, which contained twenty thousand dollars. I wasn't as smooth about it as I wanted to be, so it did not go unnoticed.

"Eva, what is this?" Tameka asked, and then peeked inside the envelope. "Say word!"

"Word!"

Tameka grinned and gave me an appreciative hug. "Wait, this isn't part of what you were talking about earlier, is it?"

"Well, yes and no," I said, "but trust me, it's all good. And if I do go down because of it, then it was well worth it just to see that smile on your face."

How I Got Over

So, there it was. I had made the decision to turn over the safe deposit key, and Donovan's note over to the authorities. Well, the note minus the part about the $250K in cash. I took a pair of scissors and snipped that little bit of information right on off the bottom of the letter.

Why?

Because, well, this was not some feel-good episode of *Good Times*. This was real life—my life. And besides, that two hundred and fifty thousand dollars wasn't just going toward my benefit. It was for my grandmother's well-being, for Tameka and her kids, as well as for Belle, who had lost every penny of her late husband's insurance policy to Donovan's scheme. Of course, I didn't have enough cash to replace all that she had lost, but I thought that Belle would be thrilled to have some money back in her hands, even if it was just a measly two hundred thousand in comparison to the one million that had been stolen from her.

"Welcome to Belle's, how can I help you?" Belle beamed from behind the counter, her usual radiant self.

The place was packed, something that I had never seen out of all the times I had been in there and passed by.

"Hello, Belle," I said, "how are you today?"

"I'm doing just fine," she said, while staring at me and try-ing to remember where she knew me from. "Oh, hey, baby!" she said after a few seconds. "Eva, right?"

"Yes, ma'am . . ."

"Oh, yeah! I couldn't place you at first 'cause you look so much happier—almost like a brand-new person. You must have gotten that thing worked out that had you so upset."

"Not completely, but things are much better than they were the last time I saw you."

"Praise God! I was praying for you, so it just goes to show that God answers prayer."

"And I thank you for that, because Lord knows I needed all the prayer I could get!" I said. "I see you have a pretty nice crowd today."

"And that's just another reason to praise God," Belle said. "I finally took my son Steve's advice, and added a couple more items to the menu, and business has picked up ever since."

Belle handed me a to-go menu, which now included chicken and turkey panini and a soup of the day.

"Corn chowder? Yum! I'm gonna have to get some of that to go," I said. "But since it's close to Mardi Gras, maybe you should consider adding gumbo to the menu, just for that week leading up to Fat Tuesday."

"Chile, what'chu know about Mardi Gras and Fat Tues-day?"

"Everything there is to know," I said. "My family is from Chicago, by way of Shreveport, so I've been celebrating Mardi Gras and making gumbo since I was ye' high."

"Oh, yeah? Well, my people are from down South too, but instead of gumbo, King Cake is my specialty," Belle said. "Chile, you know something? That's a good idea. You think I should do a whole Mardi Gras menu and theme this year?"

"Sure, why not? I'm sure your customers would really ap-preciate it since people love to celebrate, no matter what the occasion is," I said, "and you definitely can't get a good bowl of gumbo anywhere within a twenty-mile radius of here."

"You're sure right about that. . . ." said Belle. "Only thing is, my gumbo is not the best. Do you have a good recipe?"

"Oh, yeah! I have a recipe that's been in my family for I don't know how many generations, and it's all up here," I said, tapping my temple.

Belle's eyes lit up. "Ooh, this is exciting!" she said. "I'll tell you what: you whip up a pot of that gumbo when you get a chance, bring it by, and we'll take it from there, okay?"

"Good deal! Now can I get a turkey panini on rye and a bowl of that corn chowder to go, please?"

"Coming right up!"

I had stopped by Belle's to give her one of the Pathmark bags filled with two hundred thousand dollars, but after talking to her, I realized there was no way I could give her all that money without a lengthy explanation. She didn't know that I was Donovan's ex-girlfriend and I wanted to keep it that way.

A gift-wrapped box via messenger would be best.

Before I left, I gave Belle a hug and the number to my pay-as-you-go cell phone.

At that moment I realized that I could have bought myself a new and improved, superdeluxe and superexpensive cell phone with some of the money I had hustled up, not to mention all the cash that I had found in Flossie, but I was so consumed in making sure that everyone else was taken care of that splurging on things for myself hadn't even crossed my mind.

Considering how spoiled and self-centered I was just a few months before, that was real growth, and I have say, it felt real good.

Smoke & Mirrors

I decided to break the news to Vance in the same indirect manner that I had told Tameka and Kyle.

Later that evening we were in our bedroom getting undressed after a dinner party, when I started the conversation off with hypothetically . . .

"Forget all the 'hypothetical' stuff. Talk to me straight, Eva, what's up?"

I showed Vance Donovan's note, and after he finished reading it, he chuckled. "I figured as much. Ever since I've known the dude, Donovan always had a trick or two up his sleeve."

"So what should I do?"

"Absolutely nothing! Do you know how damaging this information would be to Donovan's case? At this point, it would be the equivalent of handing his head over on a silver platter."

"Okay, fine," I said, "I won't tell the feds about the accounts and hidden money until *after* Donavan has been tried and sentenced."

"No, you won't tell them about it *ever!*" Vance shouted, his eyes bulging. "I'm Donovan's lawyer, so you let me handle this aspect of things, okay? As a matter of fact, where's the key to the safe deposit box?" Vance had had several drinks during the evening, but I didn't think he'd had enough to alter his personality so drastically.

"*Oh!* I wondered when we would have our first fight, and what it would be about, and here it is," I said. "First of all, talking to me like that is a no-no, bruh! Let's just get that straight right now, and as for the key, it's in a safe place." And that was right on my key ring, in my hobo bag, along with twenty-five thousand dollars, which was all that was left of the money.

"Look, this is serious business. Do you know how it would look for you if you turned that letter over? I mean, let's be real here. You're not exactly in the clear yet yourself, Eva."

"I know you're the legal expert here, but to me, that letter says it all."

Vance ripped Donovan's letter to shreds and threw the pieces up in the air like confetti. "What proof do you have to take to the feds now?" Vance asked, looking more and more sinister by the minute. I was determined not to show it, but he was scaring the hell out of me.

"Look, why don't you just go take a shower, lay down for the night, and we'll talk about this in the morn—" I said calmly.

"Listen to me real carefully," Vance said quietly, grabbing me roughly by the arm, "you and I need to get on the same page on this, all right? Now, Donovan spelled it all out in his letter. All we have to do is lay low until all of the hoopla dies down, then we're set for life."

I yanked my arm away from him. "Oh, no, I'm not down with that," I said. "True, that type of dough would change anyone's life, but I don't want to have to look over my shoulder for the rest of my life."

Vance gave me a hard, disappointed look, as if I were an incorrigible child who was getting on his last fucking nerve.

"Okay, how about this," he said, pulling at the hairs in his goatee. "Since you're all about the Benjamins, I will give you one hundred thousand dollars to give me that key and forget what you know."

That disturbed my spirit and drove home the fact that I didn't really know this man at all.

The last couple of months flashed before my eyes, starting with the day I returned from Switzerland, and walked into Vance's office. Standing there in that moment with him begging me for the key that would essentially unlock a whole new life for him, it was as if the pieces to a huge puzzle suddenly arranged themselves and formed a complete, vivid picture.

"The only reason you took me in and stuck by me was because you figured that somehow, some way, I would eventually lead you to the money," I said. "Hell, even coming to Chicago was just your way of keeping me close and luring me back here to New York."

Vance clapped slowly, and sarcastically. "Finally!" He put my face between his hands and kissed me. "You're starting to use that head of yours for more than just a hat rack," he said, "although I have to tell you that I initially thought that you knew more than you actually did."

"Fine," I said, "since that's all you wanted from the very beginning, give me the money and I'll give you the key."

"Aww, why that sad face, Eva?" he pouted, mimicking me. "Look, I care for you, I really do, but this is New York City, baby. Nobody does anything for free unless there is something in it for them somewhere down the line."

"Oh, I know the mentality quite well: 'If I can't use you in some way, then I have no use for you.' I had forgotten that for a moment, but fuck it, let's do this."

While Vance went into the closet where he kept a small safe, I removed the post office box key from my key ring.

I dropped the key in the palm of Vance's hand. He placed the stacks in my hand, but quickly snatched them back.

"C'mon, hand over the money, Vance. The sooner I can get out of here, the better."

"You know, you really don't have to go," Vance said. "I really would like for us to share in this newfound fortune together."

"Naw, I'm good. Can I have the money, please?"

"No, I don't think so," he said with mock sadness.

I'd had enough. Cool, and calm, I whipped a can of pepper spray out of my pocket and blasted Vance dead in the eyes.

He freaked out and started clawing at his eyes, and screaming like a little girl. "Ah, you bitch! It burns. . . . Aaah!"

For good measure, I went into a martial arts stance and hit him with a rapid combination of kicks, punches, and well-placed karate chops that I had learned in a self-defense class.

I was both surprised and relieved when Vance dropped to the ground, out cold.

The Pursuit of Happiness

Which brings us to today.

A year after the real Vance Murphy revealed himself, I am back in Chicago where I couldn't be happier. It is one of the best moves I've ever made, actually, because I am back working in print media, and back to doing what I love.

Larry Nichols became editor-in-chief of *Hue Magazine* and hired me on the spot as a features writer when I went in and inquired about a job. And believe me, Larry hadn't made the decision because we'd had dinner together once and he thought I was cute, but because I had walked in there armed to the teeth with excellent writing samples and a portfolio that even Rupert Murdoch himself couldn't front on.

Today, I had one of those days at the office that proves as long as you're doing what you love, you'll never work a day in your life.

I'd had an interview with none other than the legendary homegirl herself, Ms. Chaka Khan. I was nervous at first because of her notorious aversion to journalists and the media in general, but I spent half of the day with her and found her to be a sweetheart who was very approachable, honest, and *funny* as all get-out.

"Great job! You put her at ease, and got her to really open

up," Larry said after reading a rough draft of the interview. "Ms. Khan rarely does interviews, so this edition with her on the cover is gonna be a home run!"

I left work feeling like I could fly.

Spending quality time with a music icon had been wonderful and inspiring, but news had come from New York earlier that day that I couldn't wait to share with the rest of the family.

It had been a couple of months since I'd last been to the Big Apple, and at the time it was for Kyle's commitment ceremony to Alvin, a wonderful guy who came and swept Kyle off his feet after he got rid of Irwin's lying, cheating ass. Due in part to my testimony to a federal grand jury, Vance Murphy lost his license to practice law in the state of New York due to misconduct and ethics violations.

The last I'd heard through the grapevine was that Vance had relocated to the Atlanta area where he was working for peanuts as a paralegal and trying to get a law license in the state of Georgia.

Since Vance was abruptly removed from Donovan's case, Donovan's new team of attorneys suggested he do the opposite of what Vance had suggested and to go ahead and plead guilty in exchange for reduced jail time. Donovan is now serving a thirty-year sentence at Butner Federal Prison in Durham, North Carolina, which I hear is the equivalent of "Camp Cupcake" where Martha Stewart served her sentence for stock fraud.

Shortly after her son's conviction, Annette Dorsey's 6,800-square-foot mansion is Scarsdale was unceremoniously auctioned off by the IRS for $3.2 million, the minimum bid, and in addition, Mama Dorsey was made to pay back the $22.5 million dollars that she hastily, and prosecutors say unlawfully, liquidated from Donovan's estate.

I pulled my BMW into the driveway of the new Cantrell family home, which was a spacious five-bedroom on the north side of town.

"Well it's about time!" Gwen said when I walked through the door. "Girl, we've been waiting for almost an hour to hear this big news."

It was a Friday night, and I had called Gwen earlier in the day to tell her to gather the family together for a big announcement.

Besides Gwen, my nieces, Pam, Uncle Booney, and a few extended relatives were also there waiting with baited breath.

Unfortunately, we were still on the Alzheimer's roller coaster, so Mama Nita was there in body, but her mind wasn't with us on that particular day, as it wasn't on most days. She'd had a few more "awakenings" since the first one, where she was lucid and coherent and almost back to her old self. Those days were very few and very far between, but if the smile on her face was any indication, then at least what little she could comprehend made her happy.

"Sorry I'm a little late, but you know how traffic is on the Loop this time of day," I said.

"Yeah, yeah, okay, so what's the news?" Pam asked, simultaneously working on her BlackBerry. She has her hands full with Mother's Helpers these days, which took off and was much bigger and more successful than even she had anticipated.

After just thirteen months in operation, the business has earned $743,000, and Pam is already making plans to franchise the business into major cities across the country.

"All right, so I got a phone call and a few faxes from Belle today, and the distribution deal with Victory Foods finally came through," I said, "and Mama Nita's Authentic Creole Gumbo will be available in the frozen section of over fifteen thousand grocery stores nationwide!"

Uncle Booney shouted, "We're in the money! We're in the money!" and started doing the typewriter dance made famous by MC Hammer.

"Wait a minute." Gwen was shaking visibly. "When is all this happening?"

"Well, from what I've gathered so far, it's going down within the next six months," I said, "and Belle is going to meet me at the plant in Buffalo to sign the contracts next week."

Everybody started screaming and jumping for joy, like we had all just hit the Mega Millions jackpot. Specialty food distribution deals are hard to come by, and had the potential to earn millions upon millions of dollars per year.

Victory Foods was *major* in the industry, and I had Belle to thank for helping to bring the Cantrell family recipe to their attention.

Belle had screamed as if she had hit the lottery as well, when a messenger delivered that gift-wrapped box with a white bow on it.

Me, Belle, Steve, and a handful of Belle's regular, loyal customers had all gathered at the bakery-slash-sandwich shop one evening after closing time for the big gumbo tasting.

"This, my dear, is definitely going on the menu," Belle told me after just one spoonful.

Everyone else had adamantly nodded their heads in agreement, and then the messenger had knocked on the door. He peered in the window, holding up the package, and I thought that if only he knew what was inside maybe it would have been his life that would be changed instead of Belle's.

Steve had unlocked the door and signed for the package that he in turn handed to his mother.

The look of surprise and sheer joy on Belle's face when she opened the box was priceless. "Thank you, Jesus! Hallelujah!" Belle had shouted so fervently that for a minute I thought she was going to start speaking in tongues.

"What is it, Mom?" Steve had asked, rushing to hold his mother up, who looked on the verge of collapsing. Steve's eyes got big, and he stared in disbelief at the contents of the three plastic Pathmark bags inside the box.

I had hung back along with the other customers so as not

to invade Belle and Steve's moment, but Steve pulled out the letter I had written and read it aloud.

> *Dear Mrs. Clarkson,*
>
> *Please accept my apologies for your financial loss that oc-curred at the hands of Donovan Dorsey. Also, please don't have any qualms or reservations about accepting this money, which altogether is two hundred thousand dollars. Do not view this as charity, this is YOUR money! And my only regret is that it could not have been eight hundred thousand dollars more.*
>
> *Stay blessed, and thank you for not letting such a devas-tating turn of events dampen your beautiful spirit.*

We all said how great it was, and that no one was more de-serving than Belle to have recouped some of her money.

"Who would do something like this?" Steve had asked in-credulously, his mouth still agape.

"Whoever it is, God bless 'em!" Belle said, pulling me into a hug.

Later that night, when we were cleaning up and it was just Belle and me in the kitchen, she had turned to me and said, "Thank you."

"No problem, it was my pleasure," I had said. "I'm just glad that everyone seemed to really enjoy the gumbo."

"Well, thank you for that too, but I'm talking about the money," she'd whispered. "I never miss an episode of *Most Wanted Fugitives* . . . it's my favorite program."

Belle had winked at me, and we smiled at each other, shar-ing the understanding that she had known for quite some time that I was once Donovan's girlfriend, yet she hadn't shunned or judged me, but instead welcomed me into her life with open arms.

The doorbell rang, and I opened the door for my sweetie, Jayson.

"Hey, babe, what did I miss?" he asked, bending down to kiss me.

It was the Jayson Cooper that had been my first love and first everything.

I had taken Mama Nita to an appointment with Doctor Butler, and went down to the hospital cafeteria while she was getting her brain scan.

After paying for a cup of coffee and a slice of lemon meringue pie, I'd looked for a place to sit and had seen Jayson with his head buried in the sports section of the *Chicago Tribune.*

"Paging Doctor Cooper," I said, taking a seat across the table from him.

Jayson had smiled with his eyes when he saw me, and laid the newspaper aside. "Eva Cantrell, *wow,*" he said, "what a sight for sore eyes."

For the first couple of minutes, Jayson and I had just looked at each other as if neither of us could believe what we were seeing.

Jayson and I had been the hood version of Romeo and Juliet. While other teenaged couples spent time hanging out and engaging in fun but nonproductive activities, the two of us studied together and quizzed each other on various subjects, because both of us knew that education was the only way we would ever get out of the projects.

Once we'd gotten over the initial shock of seeing each other so unexpectedly, Jayson and I got to talking and he told me he had just graduated from medical school and was now practicing pediatrics right there at Jackson Park Hospital.

Jayson was single with no kids, and was a Doctor McHottie if there ever was one, with smooth dark skin, a low-Caesar fade, and a body that I could tell was buff up underneath that doctor's coat. The two of us had reconnected that day, and easily fell back into our relationship as if we had never spent any time apart.

"See, didn't I tell you? I knew you two would eventually find your way back to each other," Kyle had told me when I'd mentioned it at his commitment ceremony to Alvin.

While I was in New York, I checked the post office box that I had renewed the rental on for another year, and surprise, surprise! There was a three thousand dollar reimbursement check from Swiss Air.

Gee, thanks! I think there is something fundamentally wrong with an airline losing a hundred thousand dollars' worth of brand-new goods, but only being obligated to pay a maximum of three thousand. It was nothing short of highway robbery, but whether I had gotten the luggage back or more money, I didn't plan to keep any of it. Still striving to keep my karma slate clean, I cashed the Swiss Air check and donated every penny of it to Girls Educational & Mentoring Services, or GEMS, a wonderful organization that strives to keep young women from being sexually exploited. Tameka worked with GEMS, which was a cause near and dear to her heart, and if the check from Swiss Air had been thirty thousand, I still would have donated every bit of it to them.

Tameka ended up getting a four million dollar divorce settlement from her ex-husband Jamal, plus monthly alimony and child support totaling forty-five thousand dollars a month, which serves Jamal's trifling ass right. Tameka and I celebrated her divorce by taking her sons to Disneyland for a week. We then journeyed from Florida to Bermuda, where Kyle met up with us for five days of relaxation and fun in the sun.

The only thing I miss about living in New York is not being able to hook up with Kyle and Tameka on a whim. To do lunch, go shopping, or just hang out and talk over a glass of wine. However, we visit each other back and forth often enough so that I don't miss them too terribly.

There is nothing quite like chilling with folks you love, and one thing I know for sure is that all the money in the world can't buy true friendship.

Just the other day, Tameka e-mailed a poem she'd had written especially for me by poetess extraordinaire, Sharmina T. Ellis.

EVA'S JOURNEY

She was a fashionista, used to bright lights and big-city living.
Her once thoughtless spirit caused her to take for granted all that she
had been given.
Now she is in the midst of darkness, and surrounded by lies and
deceit. Eva is feeling helpless and abandoned,
wondering how to get back on her feet.
In a state of panic, nomadic and confused, she seeks to find common
ground, in a place where she couldn't lose.
Eva makes her way home, to the place where she felt three feet tall.
Only to find herself still amidst users, abusers, divas, dons, pseudo
friends, flaws and all.
Which road should she travel, who can she trust? Hesitant to share
her mind, body and soul, into isolation she would thrust.
Silence is golden, for peace of mind Eva had found. While on
Sabbatical she spoke with God, who provided her with Rebuilding
blocks to a life in His Image; nothing could be better or
more profound.
Confidently, and considerably, she speaks her story without doubt
or hesitation.
The life that she now leads is of His creation.
She now understands what it means to gain lessons from her trials
and tribulations.
How to do things on her own, and live a purpose-filled life regardless
of reputation.
She has a strong, and generous heart
and her Light Shines the Brightest, her inner beauty and glow truly
sets her apart. Her search over the river and through the woods has
granted her a new Start.
Eva has risen and is now set on a new lane of existence.

*Has gained strength, knowledge, and wisdom, she remains steadfast,
and unshaken by things that once caused resistance.
She has sampled both the sweet and savory fruits of life, battled
adversity, and overcome heartache and strife.
Through humiliation, fire, and ice, the things she knows to be true,
the Beginning and the End is all determined by the GOD
in You.*

Mama Nita's Authentic Creole Gumbo

INGREDIENTS

4 large chicken breasts, cut into chunks
1 package of large chicken drumsticks, about 10
1 cup vegetable oil, plus ¼ cup
2 pounds of smoked spicy sausage, sliced into disks
2 cups flour
3 one-pound bags of cut frozen okra, defrosted
2 quarts of chicken stock
2 tablespoons of seasoning salt
2 tablespoons of OLD BAY Seasoning
2 tablespoons of black pepper
2 tablespoons of Accent
¼ cup of garlic powder
2 tablespoons of cayenne pepper
1 tablespoon of dried basil
1 tablespoon of dried thyme
1 tablespoon of sugar
1 tablespoon of onion powder
1 teaspoon of paprika
1 teaspoon of crushed red pepper flakes
4 bay leaves
5 celery ribs, chopped
3 large green bell peppers, chopped
3 large yellow onions, chopped
5 cloves of garlic, minced
1 16-ounce can of diced tomatoes
1 14-ounce can of crushed tomatoes
1 small can of tomato sauce

3 tablespoons of tomato paste
1 dozen medium-sized crabs, or 1½ dozen small crabs, cleaned but still in the shell
¼ cup of parsley, minced
3 pounds uncooked medium-sized shrimp, peeled and deveined
White rice (Follow manufacturer instructions)
1 cup of green onions, chopped
½ quart of water

DIRECTIONS

Preheat oven to 400 degrees Fahrenheit.

Lightly coat the chicken with the ¼ cup of vegetable oil, then roast for 25 minutes. Let the chicken cool, then remove the skin and bones. Set aside.

Cook the sausage in a large stockpot, over medium-high heat, until browned and the fat is rendered, about 7 minutes. (It is very important that the sausage you use be both spicy and smoked. This is what will help give the gumbo that authentic taste.) Remove the sausage with a slotted spoon, place on a paper towel–lined plate, and set aside.

TO MAKE THE ROUX

Pour ¾ cup of the vegetable oil into a skillet so that the bottom is covered, and heat over medium to medium-high heat. Add the flour a little at a time until it's all blended. Add the rest of the oil as needed. Stir constantly until it's browned to a dark fudge consistency. Be very careful not to burn or scorch the roux. It will be necessary to adjust and lower the temperature as necessary so that the roux does not burn. You will know that you are on the right track when the roux changes from a light tan shade to a dark chocolate color. This takes about 45 minutes.

In another skillet, heat 4 tablespoons of oil and fry the okra over medium heat.

TO MAKE THE GUMBO

After the roux cools to room temperature, transfer the roux into a large stockpot and slowly add the water and chicken stock while stirring continuously to make sure that it blends evenly. Add all of the seasonings, and all of the raw vegetables except for the parsley.

Next, add the sausage, chicken, okra, tomatoes, tomato sauce, tomato paste, and crab meat.

Simmer over low to medium heat for three and a half hours, covered. Stir frequently with a long-handled spoon, and be sure to taste periodically to check the seasonings, and adjust as necessary.

Add the shrimp, sugar, and parsley during the last 20 minutes of cooking. Remove bay leaves.

Serve over white rice, and garnish with chopped green onions, if desired.

TURNING YOUR FAMILY RECIPE
INTO A FORTUNE

1. Start with the three P's: patience, passion, and perseverance.

2. Before investing a single dime marketing your Aunt Lucille's strawberry pound cake, do your homework first, and thoroughly research the specialty food industry. As with any business, the Small Business Administration is the best place to start. They have a wealth of information available, and offer free seminars and workshops.

3. No matter what your specialty food product is, be it salad dressing or peanut butter cookies, you have to perfect the ratios so that they can be produced on a large scale. In this regard, it may be necessary to partner with a chemist to convert your recipe to a commercial formula that can be mass produced without negatively affecting the finished product.

4. Find a rental kitchen large enough and properly certified to test and perfect your recipe.

5. What influences shoppers to purchase a gourmet product is the packaging. You have fantastic product, right? Fantastic products deserve high-quality, eye-catching packaging. Spend a considerable amount of time developing and designing your packaging and labels. It could make all the difference between success and failure.

6. The Farmers' Market is a cheap way to get started selling your product to the general public. They offer affordable retail space, but it will be up to you to come up with creative ways to make your space more inviting.

7. Once you have perfected your presentation, start knocking on the doors of small independent grocery stores, specialty gourmet shops, and national supermarket chains. Ask the owners/managers to stock your product, and for the opportunity to give free samplings of your product to their customers.

8. Contact specialty food distributors and arrange a meeting to present your product.

9. Breaking in is tough, but not impossible. If you can come up with a creative product that the big companies like Kraft and ConAgra have yet to touch, then you will be better able to find your space on grocery store shelves. Don't expect blinding success right out of the gate. Small daily growth will sustain your business over the long term.

(*Sources:* The Food and Drug Administration: www.fda.gov; The National Association for the Specialty Food Trade: www. specialtyfood.com)

ALL ABOUT EVA

DEIDRE BERRY

ABOUT THIS GUIDE

The following questions are intended
to enhance your group's reading
of this book.

DISCUSSION QUESTIONS

1. Can money buy happiness?

2. Do you agree with Eva's belief that most women harbor the fantasy of being taken care of?

3. If presented with the chance to be well taken care of, would you abandon your career, goals, and dreams to be at the beck and call of your man?

4. If your significant other were involved in a lucrative but illegal financial scam, would you turn a blind eye? Leave him? Or turn him in to the proper authorities?

5. Financially speaking, do you think it is better to have had and lost than to never have had at all?

6. When you are the only minority in a situation, do you ever feel the need to "represent" for your race or gender?

7. Would you keep an elderly relative at home with family at all costs?

8. Is it ever okay to keep dirty money, even if you plan to use it for a good cause?

9. If given only one choice, would you rather be poor and happy or rich and unhappy?

If you enjoyed *All About Eva,* don't miss Deidre Berry's debut novel

The Next Best Thing

Available now wherever books are sold.

Turn the page for an excerpt from *The Next Best Thing.* . . .

Prologue

The Bride Is Coming!
The Bride Is Coming!

Finally. After three years of shacking up, Roland and I were jumping the broom—and *baby* we were doing it in style!

The invitations were beautiful. Burgundy suede covers opened to reveal embossed roses and elegant fourteen-karat gold calligraphy. Each one of our three hundred guests received these invites via Federal Express along with a gift basket packed with François Payard praline truffles, a magnum of Laurent-Perrier Rose Champagne, and Cuban stogies from Le Comptoir du Cigar.

Pure Opulence. That was the theme, and "my day, my way" had been my mantra from the minute Roland whispered, *Marry me* in my ear, then collapsed on his side of the bed in a sweaty heap. Two minutes later, he was snoring.

And that was it.

No ring, no loving words of endearment, and nowhere near the romantic marriage proposal that I had been fantasizing about since I was eleven years old.

Afterward, I pulled the bedsheets up to my chest, shocked,

elated, and just a skosh disappointed that Roland had asked for my hand in marriage in such a half-ass manner.

Men were supposed to plan these things out, weren't they? I mean, seriously—come *onnn*! I can't one day tell my grand-babies that Paw-Paw proposed while he was banging Grandma.

If we could rewind the tape and do it all over again, Roland would have gotten down on both knees and proposed to me on Christmas night in front of my entire family. Of course I would have said *yes!* and the Christmas party would have instantly turned into this big, emotional affair with everyone hugging and crying, happy that Roland was finally going to make an honest woman of me.

Barring that scenario, a hot air balloon ride in the country-side would have been memorable; and atop the Eiffel Tower would have been most impressive. Hell, now that I think about it, the very least Roland could have done was the old ring-in-the-dessert trick.

But, half-ass as it was, it *was* a marriage proposal.

I sprang into action the next morning, giving myself a one-year deadline to plan the wedding of the century.

And to think. This long, crazy journey to the altar began four years ago when the two of us met at a wedding. Courtney Adams, my old roommate from Kansas University, was marry-ing Aaron Graves, a fraternity brother of Roland's.

Ironically, I hadn't even wanted to go to that wedding.

Not because I disliked Courtney so much, but because I was going through the breakup blues, and just was not feeling very sociable that day.

The source of my doldrums was Joseph.

A wonderful man with whom I had spent eleven wonder-ful months, only to find out that this fool had umpteen kids by umpteen different women.

Ooh! The breakup was nasty.

It almost got to the point where I had to put a restraining

order out on his black ass, because the brother just refused to accept that I was breaking off the relationship.

This is about me and you, Joseph had said with tears in his eyes. *What do my kids have to do with us?*

Hello! Who in their right mind would unnecessarily invite all of that baby mama drama into their life? I'm sure as hell not the one. I don't care how good the sex is.

Besides, if Joseph and I had gotten married his financial obligations would have become my financial obligations, and I just can't see myself handing over my entire paycheck for someone else's child support payments.

Don't get me wrong, Tori loves the kids.

However, when those kids number close to double digits, baby, that's where I have to draw the line. Hasta la vista, baby. See ya next lifetime.

So, there I was at my old college roommate's wedding, single, and cynical as hell.

Roland may have been tall, dark, and Tyrese Gibson–fine, but as he confidently strolled over and introduced himself, I was certain he was just another well-dressed loser who would promise everything, expect everything, and give absolutely nothing in return.

But Roland proved me wrong.

Right off the bat, he struck me as being warm and sincere. By the end of the night, he had won me over enough for me to give him my phone number; and we proceeded to fall for each other fast and hard.

After just a few months of dating, I was already marveling at my good fortune in landing such an outstanding catch. This man was the ultimate romantic. He cooked for me (okay, so the meals weren't always that great but the point is, he tried), wrote me poetry (he's no Langston Hughes, but the effort was sweet), and handled his business in the bedroom like no man before him ever had (well, except for Vincent, but that's a whole 'nother story).

As far as I was concerned, I had finally found the one.

In spite of my mother's adamant warnings about giving the milk away for free, I allowed Roland to move into my two-bedroom condo on the Plaza, and all was blissfully right with the world.

Fast-forward four years and here we were, about to become man and wife, with a wedding tab of $202,536.24, and counting. My friend, Simone, jokingly compared the out-of-control budget to one of those telethon tote boards with the numbers rising rapidly by the second, but seeing as how I had an image and a reputation to maintain, I didn't give a damn about the cost. Being a senior event coordinator with over a decade in the business, I'm known for throwing ridiculously extravagant soirees, so naturally, it was expected that my own nuptials be over-the-top *fabu-lous*. It was a lot of work, but it was truly a labor of love, and in the end, the stage that I had so painstakingly set, conveyed over-the-top opulence that had to be seen in order to be believed.

Tori's Big, Beautiful, Fantasy Wedding

ORDER OF EVENTS

The Ceremony

Built in 1873, Mount Zion is the oldest African-American church in the Kansas City area. The massive gothic-style structure boasts a bell tower and magnificent stained-glass windows.

Inside the church, the heavenly scent of seven thousand gardenias fills the sanctuary, which is the size of a football field. Uniformed ush-

ers seat our guests, while an eighteen-piece orchestra plays an assortment of contemporary and classical music.

The wedding party enters to "Ava Maria."

Seven groomsmen escort seven bridesmaids down the aisle. My
cousin Cookie is among them, as well as my best girlfriends Simone,
Nadia, and Yvette. My bridal court ranges from sizes zero to eighteen,
but they are all equally stunning in strapless, burgundy gowns with
matching chiffon scarves.

The orchestra segues from "Ava Maria" to the "Wedding March."
The chapel doors open and here it is: the big moment I have spent the
last year orchestrating, and my whole life waiting for.

Entering on the arm of my father, I am a life-size version of Grand
Entrance Barbie in a silk, halter-style Badgley Mischka gown with a
hand-beaded bodice, crystal-beaded seventeen-foot train, and satin Manolo
Blahnik high-heel sandals. My bridal jewelry includes a gorgeous double strand of Mikimoto pearls and matching pearl earrings encircled
with diamonds. I smile at my guests through a nine-foot-long tulle veil,
held in place by an antique diamond tiara. Even my bridal bouquet is
spectacular, with four-dozen full-bloom red roses interwoven with
Swarovski crystals.

Looking up ahead, I see that Roland has tears in his eyes as he
waits for me at the altar under an enormous canopy of red roses and
sweet-pea blossoms. My man looks so handsome and dapper in his
Giorgio Armani Black Label tuxedo that I am already thinking about
the honeymoon.

Reverend L. C. Thompson, the man who christened me at birth,
leads us all in prayer before Roland and I light a unity candle and exchange traditional vows.

The Wedding Reception

To quote Shug Avery from The Color Purple, "I's married now!" A
Maybach limousine whisks my husband and me to the Roseville
Country Club Mansion where we are greeted by our guests, and so

many photographers that it looks like an army of paparazzi. (There's no such thing as too many wedding pictures.)

The reception kicks off with cocktails and hors d'oeuvres out on the veranda, overlooking the rose garden and a twelve-mile-long lake.

After an hour of mingling and picture taking, two trumpets sound to signal the beginning of a sumptuous sit-down dinner.

Inside the eight-thousand square foot ballroom, there are so many fresh flowers that it resembles a botanical wonderland. And adding to the elegance are gold and crystal chandeliers that, all together, are worth millions.

In addition to the head table, there are forty round tables that seat eight, each one dressed in gold silk cloths with burgundy overlays, lit by gold four-wick candles, and topped with centerpieces made of lush red orchids and pink peonies in cut-crystal vases.

At each individual place setting, there are gold Tiffany charger plates adorned with gold-rimmed bone china, matching crystal goblets, linen napkins embroidered with our initials, and elegant printed menus that offer:

PISTACHIO SALAD

KOBE FLATIRON STEAK

WITH GREEN PEPPERCORN SAUCE

CHILEAN SEA BASS

ROASTED WHITE ASPARAGUS

LOBSTER MASHED POTATOES

SPICY SAUTÉED SCALLOPS

PASSION FRUIT CRÈME BRÛLÉE

CHOCOLATE FONDUE FOUNTAIN

ROTHSCHILD BORDEAUX 1997

CHASSAGNE-MONTRACHET CHARDONNAY 2002

VEUVE CLICQUOT CHAMPAGNE

Next to each place card is a snow globe containing a black Cinderella holding hands with her prince. The keepsakes are engraved with the words: ROLAND AND TORI—HAPPILY-EVER-AFTER.

So cute!

Immediately following dinner, the reception is moved into a sepa-rate ballroom where we have a round of champagne toasts, and then cut the seven-tier Grand Marnier chocolate truffle cake with buttercream icing that is adorned with fresh orchids and red rose blossoms made of sugar.

Roland and I dance our first dance as husband and wife while Ms. Patti LaBelle serenades us with her version of "The Best Is Yet to Come," followed by "You Are My Friend." (Yes, I got Ms. Patti! It cost a queen's ransom, but hey, Mademoiselle LaBelle is worth every penny.)

Once Ms. Labelle wraps up, the DJ takes over, and we party hearty all night long to a mix of everything from Earth Wind & Fire to 50 Cent.

Hours into the festivities, Yvette takes center stage to sing Natalie Cole's classic "Inseparable." I made sure to schedule her performance waaay late into the evening with the hopes that everybody would be too tipsy to notice that the girl can't hold a decent note to save her life. She had begged me to let her sing at some point during the wedding ceremony, which was a definite no-no; but since Yvette is my oldest and dearest friend, whom I love like a sister, I compromised and agreed that she could "sing" one song at the reception.

After partaking in Louis XIII cognac and vanilla-flavored cigars hand-rolled on the spot, we all gather outside for the grand finale, a huge twenty-minute fireworks display. The second that's over, Roland swoops me up into his arms and we head off for a blissful month-long stay at a five-star luxury resort in Aruba.

Sounds like the start of a beautiful life together, right? Well, that was the way I envisioned my wedding day from start to finish. Unfortunately, though, things did not work out as planned. Not even close.

Those beautiful wedding invitations that I loved so much were quickly replaced with announcements that read:

*Mr. and Mrs. Cedric Carter announce that the nuptials
of their daughter Tori Lorraine
to Mr. Roland E. Davis
have been canceled and will not take place.
All gifts will be returned. We are sorry for the
inconvenience, and ask that the privacy of this matter
please be respected. Thank you for your support.*